OFF EDGE

ADDISON BRAE

Black Rose Writing | Texas

ISBN: 978-1-68513-486-0
LIBRARY OF CONGRESS CONTROL NUMBER: 2024936215
PUBLISHED BY BLACK ROSE WRITING
www.blackrosewriting.com

Printed in the United States of America
Suggested Retail Price (SRP) $21.95

Off Edge is printed in Garamond Premier Pro
Cover design by Harrell Creative https://harrellcreative.com/

*As a planet-friendly publisher, Black Rose Writing does its best to eliminate unnecessary waste to reduce paper usage and energy costs, while never compromising the reading experience. As a result, the final word count vs. page count may not meet common expectations.

Praise for
Off Edge

"Much like the world of figure skating itself, *Off Edge* immediately immerses the reader in action and drama. The protagonist's story is one of self-discovery and empowerment, including a candid look at the struggles and mistakes that must be endured along the journey. For young adult readers, the topics are on point – we all yearn to discover who we really are, understand where we fit, and obtain knowledge of self. As an adopted Olympic figure skater myself, I can candidly say that this book hit home. Enjoy! It's a spicy story."
–Aaron Parchem, U.S. Olympian and Former Pairs Skater

"Filled with secrets, suspense, and a dash of romance, *Off Edge* will have you rooting for Docia as she struggles to choreograph a life of her own choosing—on and off the ice. Addison Brae has landed a winner!"
–Dorian Cirrone, award-winning author of *The First Last Day*

"…a powerful and mature young heroine in Docia, who learns she cannot just stand up, but can leap and spin above all others – for herself and those most important to her. *Off Edge* is perched on the highest podium of great YA reads."
–J. Ivanel Johnson, award-winning author & former high school teacher/coach

"*Off Edge* is an easy-to-read YA, a captivating page turner. I thoroughly enjoyed watching Docia bloom, and highly recommend this uplifting and motivating tale."
–Maya Tyler, author of *The Magicals Series*

"*Off Edge* is an emotionally engaging coming-of-age story about a young athlete who must learn to stand up and fight for what's right after a devastating challenge. Brae's skating descriptions are so vivid I felt like I was out on the ice with Docia. And I don't even skate!"
–Sharon Skinner, award-winning author and certified Book Coach

This book is dedicated to my dad,
whose dream inspired Docia's courageous story.

Deepest gratitude to Tina, my critique partner who motivated me to keep writing and my dear friends Hope, for making sure my figure skating facts are accurate, and Docia, for graciously allowing me to use her beautiful name. I'm thankful each day for John, who designed the amazing cover, creates the fun extras that go along with a novel, and is my daily creative inspiration.

OFF EDGE

CHAPTER ONE

The next twenty-four hours will define the rest of my life—whether I'm a winner or a nobody. The familiar feel of my lucky gold pendant as I step onto Olympic ice centers me. The arena explodes with applause, just like I imagined during practice here yesterday. Spectators wave a color palette of flags from around the world. Television cameras and photographers line each end of the rink.

I skate around the edge, then stop in the center of the five rings painted in the ice. As irritating as the sequins are on my shoulder, I do not adjust the strap.

At the sound of the first notes of my music, everything Lena taught me flows through my feet, my fingers. I nail the triple-triple jump combination. The quad Lutz entry is wobbly after the ridiculous footwork Dad insisted on. A hand down on the ice saves it. Then the triple Axel. Just footwork and a spin left in the two minutes and forty seconds. I'm running on pure adrenaline and muscle memory, a marionette on Dad's strings.

The crowd clapping between the taps of my blades against the ice during my footwork cheers me to the finish line. The back scratch spin is so fast it may never end. I jam in my toe pick and stop absolutely centered in my final pose. Every required element was as perfect as I could make it—almost good enough to please Dad.

Except the music still plays.

It doesn't matter.

The judges will count off since I finished before the music stopped and for the hand down, but I didn't fall and landed the triple Axel. The crowd surges to their feet as I bow to each side of the arena. Cameras flash like fireworks. I circle the ice and wave to the crowd while dodging stuffed animals fans toss across the rink. American flags flutter throughout the crowd and my reflection in giant TV camera lenses follow me off the ice. They both remind me of the huge responsibility it is to represent America at the Olympics.

I slide on skate guards that protect my blades and step up into the kiss-and-cry area where Lena waits and wave to the crowd. "Good girl, Docia," she says as I sit on the bench next to her. Lena's chubby cheeks and warm smile have greeted me in kiss-and-cry areas after every competition, and she still pinches my cheeks like she has since I was little.

"Do you remember when I finished before the music in my first competition?" I whisper to Lena out of lip-reading sight. "At least I didn't cry into your fur coat this time."

She nods. "It is nothing. Very good performance."

While we watch the digital board at our feet and wait for the judges to tally the final short program scores, I take a drink from a water bottle and wiggle my nose with my finger for the television camera in front of me. The wiggle is my secret hello to Lily, my best friend at home. For Diego too, but I don't know if he's watching after Dad treated him so badly.

A roar rises from the crowd. I point to the 71.4 score on the electronic board in front of us and grin. "Look Lena. Fourth place!"

I jump to my feet and wave to the fans. Camera flashes fire again.

Lena slips one arm of my Team USA jacket on me, then the other as we step out of the kiss-and-cry area among reporters, coaches, and skaters. An ESPN television camera focuses on me and a reporter approaches with a microphone. "Would you like to tell America how you feel, Docia?"

Since Dad hasn't surfaced through the crowd, Lena nods approval.

"One more program," the reporter says, "and you could be on the medal stand. How does it feel to be America's youngest medal contender?" The reporter positions the microphone in front of me.

Dad stops next to the rink behind the camera operator, folds his arms, and scowls. Mom is beside him. I clench my fists, refocus on the reporter, and hope the words I'm supposed to say come out right. "It was a solid short program. I'm only halfway there and up against some incredibly talented competitors. Representing the United States at the Olympics is *enormous*. The chance of a lifetime. It felt good. I may only be fifteen, but I'm prepared. Tomorrow, I'm determined to perform my absolute best free skate."

"Thank you, Docia. We're all behind you," the reporter says then turns back to the camera. "Docia Sikorsky. America's surprise medal hopeful."

•   •   •

Mom greets me down the hallway near the athletes' lounge with a giant smile and an even bigger hug.

"I did it!"

"You did, and I'm so proud of you, sweetie. You looked beautiful out there."

Dad's embrace isn't so warm. "Nice job, Docia. I've told you a million times not to rush your elements. You know better."

I stiffen and pull away. "But I'm in fourth place," I whisper out of the media's view.

Mom rubs Dad's elbow. "Relax, Jerry. The judges have to be fair. Docia, sweetheart, your free skate will prove you're the real winner. Fourth? At the Olympics?" She squeals and hugs me again.

"Your arms were all over the place on your footwork into the Lutz. What do we pay Lena for?" He shakes his head. "I'll have to talk to your choreographer. We should be in first place now."

This is the confident version of Mom I like best, and the Dad I've gotten used to. "No, Dad. I'll talk to the choreo—"

"Nope, that's my department."

"Dad, I wasn't finished. My next programs will be the ones I want to do. Choreography and music I like." The sequins that irritated my shoulder before I skated now feel like tiny knife blades slicing into my skin. "And no more of these glammed-up sparkly little-girl dresses."

"Not open for discussion." He fiddles with something that jingles in his pocket, like my career is no more important than a few stray coins. "And that's no way to speak to me."

He turns away to see who the reporters are interviewing now. Shut down. Again.

Next time, I won't ask first.

Over Mom's shoulder, I see my teammate Stacy Gaston, her coach and her parents approach us. She does not look happy. My heartbeat revs since I never know what to expect from her. Sixth place is savable. Well, if she skates perfectly tomorrow, and if the rest of us don't. With only a triple-double, how does she expect to medal?

She prances up, arms open for a big hug. "Congratulations, Docia. Enjoy your fourth place...." She leans in close, "...until everyone finds out...." She skims past me and her voice fades into the noise of the crowd.

What? She just tried to make me feel like the poor adopted kid from West Texas I am. I ball my fists up inside my jacket pockets and control my breathing. If there weren't so many cameras, I'd run after her. Dad must not have noticed Stacy's comment, since his eyes are glued on the reporter interviewing the Japanese girl who's in the lead. If he had heard Stacy's threat, the other coaches, competitors, and reporters around us would have too. I maintain a smile so Dad can't see my clenched teeth. She's taking whatever issue she has with me way too far.

Dad turns and looks me square in the face. "There are less than twenty-four hours until your free skate. Is there anything I haven't done yet to make sure you're prepared?"

I glance down the concrete hallway where Stacy disappears into the skaters' lounge. "If I'm not ready now," I say and punch Dad in the arm, "twenty-four hours ain't gonna make a lick o' difference." I exaggerate the Texas twang he and Mom have tried so hard to fix.

"Docia." Dad's growl knocks the humor out of the moment. As usual, my stomach tightens from the anxiety he triggers.

Mom puts her hands on my shoulders with a Mona Lisa smile and whispers, "You will do great tomorrow. Watch your language, though. You've seen reporters follow you. Remember, you're a celebrity now."

"Celebrity? Seriously?" I roll my eyes. "What would really get me ready is to see some of Moscow after practice tomorrow morning."

Mom looks at Dad. "We could take in a few sights after breakfast—"

"Not a good idea." Dad shakes his head.

"Come on Dad. I feel great." And like an eight-year-old kid. "I can rest all afternoon."

"Do I have to remind you why you're here? We are not here for vacation or some piddly regional competition." His folded arms and stern eyes cancel out Mom's smile. "You know how I've taught you to stick with your routine."

"Do you expect me to stare out my window all day? I'll be a nervous wreck. Not what I had in mind for my first Olympic experience." I drill my gaze into him instead of my feet, like I usually do while he lectures. "Lena said I need to do things to take my mind off competing."

"This is not the time or place to argue," Dad says.

I used to get my way with Dad with my pout. Do I still have my touch?

"Please please please, Dad. We haven't seen anything here yet. Not the Kremlin or Red Square. I learned so much about Russian history last fall and it would be so cool to discover more about Lena's heritage. You know what else? Dancing across the stage at the Bolshoi would make me feel like a prima ballerina. Get me in the right frame of mind for tomorrow night." I caress the Russian Orthodox cross pendant Lena gave me. "I'll go back to the Village and get tons of sleep tonight. Promise."

"Okay, okay, I hear you." Dad gives me the sideways nod he does when he tries to figure out how to make my idea his own. His expression softens. "We'll see how practice goes and how you feel in the morning. No hanging out in the lobby or Café when you get back to the Village tonight."

I haven't lost my touch.

"You asked what I need. Getting out is exactly what will prepare me for tomorrow night."

And help me avoid Stacy.

"Hear me?" Dad reaches for my skate bag and wags his finger again while I wrap myself up to face the Moscow chill. He will not push away the thrill of this event. "Let's get you back to the Village, then straight to bed. Don't stay up talking to that roommate of yours all night."

"Her name's Lucy."

Dad ignores my answer as we get into the cab for the now-familiar trek between the arena and Athletes' Village. Then he turns around from the front seat. I take a deep breath and glance at Mom next to me to fight off the dread.

Please, not another pep-lecture. I'd rather watch the city lights and bundled-up people on the sidewalks. If he starts, I'll try the trick Lucy says works for her mom:

Tell him he's repeating himself. Again, she says. *That should shut him up.*

"I have some good news for you, Peanut," he says.

I'm too old to be his obedient Peanut.

"Oh yeah?"

A little silence would be the best news.

"I talked to the gal at your agency today. She says you've clinched the next cereal box if you're the top U.S. medalist—bronze, silver, or gold. I'd say that's a sure thing. Then, *Teen Vogue* is interested in your story because of 'your swagger,' so they say. Those are the highlights. I've got more interested in you too. We'll see if you have time for the little opportunities."

"Isn't it all fantastic?" Mom reaches over and squeezes my knee with a grin like I've just won my first beauty pageant. "*Everyone* will know who you are."

"She's right. That's just the beginning." Dad turns and talks to the windshield like we're not here. "That *Sports LIVE!* reporter who was at the airport before we left—Jane, Jenn, Jessica, whatever her name is—wants to do a 'Rise to Fame' feature on you as soon as we get home. That means another cover."

"Her name's Joy, Dad." I sink further into the car seat.

My fame is more important to him than I am.

I'll never get used to my face on magazine covers. Wondering what the articles will say is even weirder. Reporters always dig up some skeleton, true or not. What if they talk to Stacy and she spills whatever's bugging her?

"So, what do you think?" Dad looks back from the front seat again. "It's your destiny to be a legend."

"It's cool, I guess." His pressure pushes me deeper into the seat. "The media coverage is embarrassing. You know, all your business out in front of the world."

"The price of fame, Docia," Dad says.

Mom's eyes stay fixed on Dad, but he doesn't say a word until we reach the sculpture of the five Olympic rings outside the Village where the athletes stay.

"Sleep tight, honey." Mom hugs me and whispers in my ear, "Can't wait for tomorrow."

When the cab stops, Dad gets out and opens my door.

"I know I still have to skate well tomorrow. Against the world's best skaters. I have to medal." I kiss him on the cheek. "I'll check in after practice. Our little Moscow tour will help me focus."

"Remember," Dad shakes his finger. "No promises about the sightseeing."

Yeah, yeah, no promises. We'll see about that.

•   •   •

Inside the lodge, the crackle of the roaring blaze beckons me to the middle of the lounge instead of the cold stairway to my room. My stretched-out gloved fingers begin to thaw in front of the flames. Clusters of athletes huddle together in their tight little groups. The fire keeps me from feeling lost in the room of strangers.

I pull my phone from my pocket to update my followers. *Thanks for the positive vibes. Felt great out there tonite! Wish y'all were here!*

No matter what, I've worked my butt off to get here and will make the most of it.

I look out again to the room full of competitors and freeze on Stacy. She steps around the giant hearth with her nose in the air, red ponytail bouncing.

Should I confront her about her stupid game?

She stops in front of me with a smug expression. "Honestly, I thought you'd withdraw." She inspects her shiny orange fingernails rather than my face. "Are you strong enough to make it through tomorrow night? You know, your injury last year, not being able to finish Nationals and all."

What a cheap shot. If I let it go, she'll know her little game to psych me out didn't work. "Never felt better, Stacy. Thanks for your concern."

Only Stacy and my dad can suck the joy out of my mood. "Nice spins in your program tonight."

"Thanks. Tomorrow will be better for sure." She twists her finger through her ponytail. "Not many people get to skip such a major competition and still come to the Olympics. It won't matter how you skate once everyone finds out who you *really* are."

"What's that supposed to mean?"

"You'll find out. Manufactured. Totally. Luck doesn't last forever."

Stacy swings around and strolls toward the elevator in the lobby. That's all my so-called teammate says. I shove my phone into my pocket and stare down her back.

I turn back to the warm flames. *Manufactured. Who you really are?* What was that? I reach into my memory for clues. When we were still friends, Stacy always thought she was better than me, even though I've placed ahead of her these last two years. She's got to be mad because reporters selected me as the frontrunner instead of her. That's it. She is trying to psych me out.

CHAPTER TWO

To finish practice, Lena has me repeat tonight's long program back-to-back to spend my remaining energy. I step off the ice, grab a towel from my bag, and blot the moisture from my face. My phone lights up with a text from Dad.

Talked to Lena. Says good practice. Pick u up from rink at 10.

Even nailed the free skate on the second go-round, I text back. At least I'll finally get to see more of Moscow than the buildings between the Village and the rinks. Stacy can say about anything for the rest of today, and I won't care.

After changing clothes, I stop in the lobby to wait for Dad and try to imagine what tonight will be like. Does everyone feel lonely and nervous when they're so far from home? There are so many strangers from all over the world who all want to win. Friends and supporters at home can fill in even though it's through social media.

Feel great after practice. Taking in a few Moscow sites, then resting up for tonight. Wish you were here! XOXO

Dad walks through the heavy glass doors, arms outstretched. "Good morning, Peanut. How's my Olympic champion?"

I grab my bag to avoid his embrace and try to ignore his controlling expectations.

"Ready to get my mind off skating." I gaze through the lobby's giant paned windows. "Where's the cab?"

Dad points at a shiny black limousine. Mom waves through the open window.

"A limo?" What is he thinking?

"Absolutely. I don't want people to see my Olympic star around Moscow in a dirty, cramped cab."

I shake my head and follow him to the flashy car. "We can't afford a limo." All I need is for a reporter to see me being driven around like some spoiled starlet.

"Sure, we can. Or we will, after tonight."

The driver holds the door open for me, as I am, apparently, my family's new breadwinner. No pressure. I slide onto the seat beside Mom and Dad sits facing us.

"So, here's the plan," Dad says. "We'll drive by a few sights, then have lunch."

"Drive by?" When Mom doesn't react, I lean forward in the seat. "Why see them at all if we don't get out of the car?"

"Nope. Quick car tour, then daytime curfew for you. I don't want you chilled and tired out. Driver, Red Square."

"But what about—"

"No discussion, Docia. Haven't I always done what's best for you?" He stares at me for a second and then looks through the window at the buildings we pass. He can think he's made his point. I refuse to fight with him on competition day.

Mom shrugs and mouths the word "sorry." I disappear into the corner of the plush leather seat like a disappointed kid who has to experience Disneyland through a car window.

The driver takes us by a few famous museums I've never heard of. Why see beautiful museum buildings when we can't see the treasures inside? When we stop near the famed Kremlin at Moscow's city center, the driver glances back in the rearview mirror with sympathetic eyes. Now my disappointment is even more real. Even through the cold glass, knowing Lenin's grave is just outside the tall red-brick wall surrounding the white fortress sends a chill crawling up my spine. His mausoleum is beautiful but creepy after the stories my teacher told of how Lenin stripped away freedoms from the Soviet people.

The austere palaces and cathedrals of the Kremlin sit on one side of Red Square's vast grayness. Giant pyramid shapes jut out from the stone wall that surrounds it creating a harsher silhouette. The Kremlin's gold towers reach for the sky as if they're trying to escape captivity. I think I understand what captivity must feel like. I wish I could see more.

The driver rolls by the infamous site as Dad drones on about every historical fact.

"I know, Dad. We studied Lenin in history."

He raises his eyebrows and leans forward. "I'm sure those teachers in public schools don't know everything I told you. Remember, I spent a good bit of time in Moscow when I worked for NASA."

I wave my hand toward the window. "The building is right in front of us, and we can't even get out of the car to see the tsars' thrones? The murals?" I turn my head and speak into the window. "Useless."

I wish I were old enough to travel without my parents. Lena would give me a better tour than this.

Dad ignores me and rattles on. A couple of tourist groups huddle together as their tour guide points across to Saint Basil's Cathedral. One is a group in red Canadian Olympic team jackets with white maple leaves. They get to reach out and touch the city. Why can't I? I grab the cross hanging from my neck and think of Lena's stories about services here when she was young. My thoughts block out Dad's ramblings. I follow the Canadian group's gaze across to Saint Basil's colorful domes that resemble playful puffs of smoke dusted in snow and suck in a breath at their beauty. Muted tones from the tolling tower bells travel through the thick car glass.

"We've seen enough here." Dad grins at me. "I've saved the best for last. Driver, our final site."

If fame means I must follow Dad's orders and watch the world go by from inside a limo, I'll pass.

We round the corner, and the Bolshoi Theatre comes into view atop a hill. My breath goes shallow. Now I know how much I'm missing as a hostage in the car. Scaffolding obscures the theatre's tall columns, but the building's beauty still shines through. The car almost rolls to a stop. Without a thought, I reach for the handle, throw open the door, and run.

Another door opens and Mom shouts to Dad, "Let her go." I pump my legs as fast as I can through the snow toward the theatre and between the columns.

Where I can breathe again.

I tug on one of the massive theatre doors. It doesn't open. The next door is locked too. *Dang,* Diego mentioned the restoration that would close the building. The memory of Diego giving me his painting of the Bolshoi on my birthday two years ago melts away the winter chill. He was so proud of his work. "Until you get to see it for real when you're in Moscow for the Olympics," he'd said. At the time, I laughed at the thought.

Eight massive white columns line the front of the structure like soldiers in *The Nutcracker.* The world's best dancers have performed Tchaikovsky's ballets here. Diego saw me skate a couple of my programs to Tchaikovsky pieces, one of the few music choices Dad and I agreed on. Since I can't get to the stage, I strike a ballet pose and take a quick selfie that Diego will like. Well, he would have.

A heavy hand grips my shoulder. I don't turn around.

"Let's go," Dad says.

I take a final look at the theatre and follow him back to the car. As I'm told.

We stop for lunch at a little place overlooking the Patriarch's Ponds area of downtown. Dad orders for me, and I'm left to chew bland chicken and a pile of gluey pasta as I stare out the window. A couple of swans float together on a small part of the pond that isn't frozen.

Dad squeezes my hand. "They're just like you, Docia, our beautiful swan."

One stretches its wings and skitters a few feet to land. I'm nothing like a swan. Swans are free to fly.

"Can we go now?" I want to be alone.

"Yes," Dad says. "Let's get you back to the Village so you can rest. I knew this outing would wear you out."

The limo feels much smaller. I wrap my arms around myself, close my eyes, and try to relax. Diego's Bolshoi auditorium painting redraws itself in my mind. Like precious jewels, the stacked rows of gold seats neatly line the walls from floor to ceiling. Colorfully dressed onlookers fill each seat with angel-like figures on the ceiling that watch over them. I see myself on the ornate stage like the dancers he painted. Delicate. Powerful. Like a prima ballerina.

Like I hope to be on the ice tonight.

•   •   •

Back in my room, I try to rest but my mind won't stay still. The oversized vase of purple and pink tulips from my skating club reminds me of my real friends back home. Rachel, Hope, Sabrina, Jane, Chris, Tina—almost every member signed the card. Even the coaches. In the middle, Stacy had started her name with a sprawling red *S*. The sight of her signature makes one of Dad's recent pep-lectures race laps through my head. "Docia, always know your enemies."

Enemies? I try to be nice to people. To everyone. I can see his finger wagging. I never thought I had real enemies. Not my competitors. Not even Stacy.

It's five o'clock, one hour until the first group warms up for tonight's free skate. The event that will determine if I stand on the podium for the medal ceremony. The event that will determine Dad's destiny for me.

I wrap my hair in a tight bun and add a touch of mascara, the only makeup Dad allows me to wear. The mirror catches the glittery sequined sections at the top of my new skating dress. The red, orange, purple, and yellow create an abstract pattern that resembles a stained-glass window framed by long black sleeves. Dad chose the costume because it reminds him of the church he went to as a kid. More like a Vegas casino to me. Of course, it was expensive. The dress is beautiful, but next time, I'll choose my own. One that's more me. Elegant. Simple. Sophisticated. I smooth the dress at the waist where it fades into the black chiffon skirt that I tuck into my pants. Just a few more hours.

I sit on the side of the bed, wrap my bad ankle, and take inventory of the items piled by the door. My purple roller bag holds freshly polished skates with new laces. Backup music. Security badge. Everything I need is packed. I'm the last skater in the final group. Again.

It will be a long night.

In my head, I hear the first notes of my music. My hands move in harmony with my body as I step through each movement and finger position in place. Every muscle knows what to do. When to set up and complete each of the six triple jumps and one quad.

Relaxed. Soft. Powerful.

My breath quickens when I visualize the set-up for my quad Lutz-double toe combination. Lead with the hip, up and around, then check the landing with my hip to stop the rotation. Big smile.

Toe pick, vault up, three revolutions, then check. I imagine the row of judges peering at me over their glasses to make sure I didn't under-rotate the Axel and scrutinizing my footwork. Lena's voice rings in my head, "Don't rush! Smile!" The same reminders since I was three years old. The pretend crowd claps along. Their energy pushes me through the jumps that give me bonus points in the last half. I finish the program with my favorite spin, and everything goes quiet until there is a soft knock at my door.

"Little Docia," Lena calls.

I run to the small hallway and throw open the door. Her face is barely visible through her thick fur coat and hat.

"Time to go," she says. "How do you feel?"

"Good, I think." Everyone's expectations and the pressure of representing my country close in on me. "Now that I'm here, the Olympics and this giant media show are so huge."

"It is the same as other competitions, Docia, just a little bigger."

Lena holds my hands. Her fuzzy gloves calm me and soft blue eyes help push the doubt clouds away.

"I have a job to do. I owe it to fans, my country, and myself to skate my best—and you, too." I wrap my arms around Lena. "Thank you for always standing by me. I'm ready." *And I really am.*

When we slip into the car, the wonderful aroma of her kitchen reaches me through my thick scarf and radiates her home's warmth through me. "Lena, you didn't." She nods and I throw my arms around her. "I love your pelmeni! The best dumplings on the planet."

Lena hands me a fork. "Eat, eat!" The sweet onion and salty pork scent rises from the Styrofoam container.

"Okay, a bite." I pop a dumpling into my mouth, and it melts on my tongue. "Oh Lena, these are delicious."

Dad would have a fit if he were here. I grab another.

"I used to make pelmeni for Anna before the big competitions." Lena dabs a bit of sauce from my lip. "I make it only for my most special students."

"Thank you, Lena. I wouldn't be here without you—or your pelmeni."

•   •   •

With my skating dress hidden underneath my USA team warm-up suit, I pull my bag down one of the long hallways of the Megasport Arena. The bag's wheels whir in rhythm and echo off the hard concrete.

We stop at the security area where cameras focus on us, and uniformed agents poke around inside my bag. As we approach the athletes' lounge where Mom waits, a reporter finds me with her camera. Crap, I can't hide. I wave. Lena smiles, but my stomach twists. Dad is talking to the same reporter. He's probably saying something that will embarrass me.

"I'm so proud of you, Docia." Mom wraps her arms around me. "You've worked so hard to get here." She flutters her eyelids to hold back tears and straightens my necklace. "My daughter, the Olympic star."

"Oh Mom, stop."

"Your mom's right, I taught you to be a star." Dad clasps my shoulder. "You wrapped your ankle like I showed you, right?" He squeezes tighter.

I nod but stiffen. "I'll do my best."

I swallow the rest of the words I'd like to say. *I have to focus on skating, not you.*

Lena stands behind him with a stern look. "Time to get ready."

Dad kisses me on the cheek. "I'll be the one yelling loudest. Those judges better do their jobs. You're destined to be an Olympic champion."

I hope the crowd drowns him out.

My parents disappear down a brightly lit tunnel, Dad a few feet ahead of Mom like always.

Lena gently pinches my chin. "Will wait for you in the athletes' lounge."

I pull my phone from my jacket pocket, tuck in my earbuds, and select my favorite playlist. As I jog my warm-up mile down the arena's emptiest tunnel, the hip-hop beat draws me into the zone. My zone. The place where I'm most focused. This is where the ice, music, and crowd drive me to skate my best. Where I see perfectly executed elements and nothing else.

The place where no one can control me.

I find an empty corner to stretch then jog to the athletes' lounge where I settle on one of the orange vinyl sofas just as the official appears.

"Next group warms up in fifteen minutes!"

This is it. Feel good. Ready. Wish me luck! I post.

Well wishes immediately stream in.

*You rock, Docia! Your triple Axel kicks a**! Simply amazing* ☺

Knowing so many people care gives me a boost.

Lena hands me my skates. While lacing up, I glance to the next row of seats. What's that god-awful Pepto-pink skating dress peeking out from underneath Stacy's USA jacket? A redhead like her should never wear that kind of pink.

She looks at me. I smile and say, "Good luck!" Stacy turns her head away. "Figures," I mutter. I Velcro my tights underneath the shiny white skates as the coordinator calls the final group to the ice. A journalist's words run through my head: "In this sport, it doesn't matter if you're happy or unhappy. You just deliver the goods."

I pace among the competitors near the edge of the rink. I've competed against these girls for years. Some are friends. Some aren't. Only one of us can win the gold. One hesitation, one missed edge, and no gold. The familiar steady hum of the Zamboni's engine purrs the same as it smooths the rough ice surface whether the ice is at home in Texas or here in Moscow.

I bounce up and down to keep my injured ankle loose and shake away the jitters while we wait. When the monitor calls the final group of six, I take off my skate guards and follow one of my competitors onto the ice straight into left and right crossovers to warm up. The ice feels good—hard and fast like during practice. I tick off each jump. Waltz jump then Axel then double toe loop then triple loop. The loop entry is off, and I slide down on my hip like I've done hundreds of times. Concentrate. I set up and do another triple loop, this time landing solid on my back outside edge. Textbook! Tension escapes with the air I exhale.

Power builds in my legs, one foot over the other for my quad-double. I glance behind me to make sure none of the other five skaters are in my path for the blind entry into the Lutz. I steady my arms to not recreate the out-of-control entry in my short program. The blade edge cuts into the ice, toe pick in, and takeoff. Four strong, swift revolutions. I start to check the landing but a blinding flash of bright pink speeds past and pushes me off balance. I land on the wrong edge and reach my hand out toward the ice to keep from falling.

Stacy turns and sneers. I skip the double toe loop and glide by Lena for support. She pulls her hand away from her mouth and nods. My heart races. *What is Stacy's problem?* I skate to the other end of the ice and take deep breaths to relax and try another Lutz. The monitor calls our warmup is over. *Thanks, Stacy. Now it's too late to try again.*

Lena hands over my skate guards and jacket and I look up into the stands while I slip the guards on my blades. Mom waves down at us but Dad's scowl stings like I've been ambushed by a swarm of yellow jackets.

Lena drapes her arm around me and leads me away from rink side. We stop behind the black curtain inside one of the hallways, her hands on my shoulders. "Concentrate, and everything else will come naturally. Do not worry. My little Docia can do the quad-double."

I yank my gloves off and select a classic rock playlist to push Stacy and Dad out of my thoughts. I step just inside the emptiest of the cold gray corridors where I can still see what's going on. With thirty grueling minutes to wait, I lean against the painted brick wall and slide down to the floor. The music drowns out the other arena noise. Behind my closed eyes, all I see is Lena's soft smile and sorrowful eyes.

"Stacy Gaston," the announcer's voice rumbles over my music and jolts me out of the zone. I've heard competition announcers say her name dozens of times. Now hearing her name tastes as bitter as Toxic Waste candy. I stretch to stay in my zone and visualize myself flying through the quad-double and landing like a feather.

After her performance, Stacy leaves the ice and paces. The scoreboard says Stacy is currently in second place, better than after her short program but likely off the medal stand. She watches the next skater then walks then watches another skater. I laugh when the television shows that a camera caught her gnawing on her fingernails with a big chip of orange polish stuck to her lip for the world to see.

Then the monitor waves me over. I'm next.

My body tingles as I make my way to the wooden boards that create the wall surrounding the rink. The official calls my name and I remove my guards and hand them to Lena. I step onto the ice, close my eyes, and fill my lungs with air to help me focus. Lena holds my hands over her heart like she always does before I skate.

"I'll do those jumping passes my way. Not Dad's. Just the way I practiced."

"Good idea. Skate like I know you can, my little Docia."

I reach for my pendant after her final instructions, then skate over the patterns the last five skaters made in the ice. The row of judges peers at me over their computers. Gaping camera lenses line both ends of the rink to capture every mistake for the world to see. *I hope they can't see me shake.*

"Representing the United States of America, Docia Sikorsky." The announcer's voice booms over the speakers in Russian and then in English.

Each stroke around the rink picks up the energy I felt in yesterday's short program. It flows up through my feet to my lungs and covers my skin with a blanket of confidence as I skate to the center of the ice. Cameras flash around the stands like twinkling stars scattered across the night sky. The roar from the crowd engulfs me. I stop in my opening pose at the top of the five Olympic rings.

My Olympic rings.

CHAPTER THREE

The crowd goes silent. I'm so deep in my zone a bomb could go off and I wouldn't know. All I hear is my breath and tapping heart until the music's soft melody fills the arena. While I've heard *Hedwig's Theme* hundreds of times, the gentle wind chimes still carry the magic Harry Potter must have felt.

The swirling strings lift me up—quad Lutz, then double toe loop. Applause rise. *Concentrate.* I smile like Lena taught when I land like a feather. Then the double Axel. My way.

I command the ice as I complete each connecting step, spin, and jump with the music's slow march rhythm. Cool air brushes my skin as I glide in a giant s-shape through my spiral.

"*Smile,*" Lena's voice says in my head.

I connect with the faces in the stands and enjoy the few restful moments. *Half over.*

The music builds to recharge my energy. Another jump combination then the triple Axel I've worked so hard to master. The crowd grows louder. *They like my new choreography.* As the music swells, another rush of adrenaline pushes me to tap and swoosh through every step and turn in my footwork sequence. *Almost finished.* My split jump series and catch-foot layback spin pull the crowd in as always.

I race to the center of the ice to set up for the final spin combination that starts with a flying camel. I bring my signature back scratch spin to a sudden stop with a tap that cracks the ice and freeze in my pose on the final note, still emotionally spinning.

Four minutes are already over? A clean skate? Am I delusional?

The crowd is on its feet waving American flags all around the arena. I pump my fist in the air and break into what must be the most obnoxious cereal box smile as I try to catch my breath.

A crew of little skaters in fur-trimmed skirts chases stuffed animals the crowd throws onto the ice as I bow to each side of the rink. During my victory lap, I pick up a fuzzy white polar bear and wave it at the standing onlookers.

After stepping off the ice, I fall like a rag doll into Lena's arms. Her eyes twinkle. "Beautiful little Docia. Just beautiful," she whispers into my ear and strokes my cheek with her rough hand. We step up into the kiss-and-cry area and I search the stands for Dad.

I don't breathe until I see his reaction. What grief will I catch from him this time? What wasn't perfect?

He's...? Smiling! My shoulders relax and I turn my attention back to Lena, the crowd, and the cameras.

"I've never seen so many stuffed animals in my life!"

Lena hugs me again. I glance from the camera to the scoreboard to Lena and back to the camera. If only I could hug each fan who cheered me along. Instead, we sit and wait with the rest of the world while the judges finalize the scores.

Lena squeezes my hand tighter. I follow her eyes to the scoreboard where my technical elements mark appears, then the program elements. Then the total long program points—160.74. Time stands still while it sinks in.

It's the highest long program score and my all-time best.

The total score lights up before I make sense of the math in my head. At 236.02, it's three points more than I needed to take the lead.

My jaw drops open. "Is it true? Did I really—?" I watch a tear trickle down Lena's cheek.

"I knew you could do it just like my Anechka." She squeezes me tight. "Enjoy your moment little Docia."

The Olympic champion.

The crowd thunders and I forget to breathe. All the anticipation. Preparation.

"Up, up up," Lena says patting me on the back. "Your fans."

I stand, wave both hands at the crowd, and jump up and down on my skate guards. A group of fans above me chants, "Docia! Docia! Docia!" More stuffed animals land at our feet. It must be true. The cameras focus on me. It's like I'm flying!

We step down into the rink-side chaos. Dad hugs me, "Olympic champion, just like I taught you. I knew you'd push the Japanese and Chinese girls to silver and bronze. The Russian girl and Stacy are off the medal stand altogether. We will talk about the choreography you changed later."

Even his words don't bother me.

Mom furiously waves behind the row of cameras. She mouths, "I love you," and kisses the tip of her finger then makes an x shape across her heart. *Our special signal.*

Workers in matching blazers roll out the carpet and stair-stepped platform to the center of the ice where the winners will stand.

An official leads the three winners over to the boards. *One of them is me.* "You walk out together and take your places," the official says. We nod like we do when we take in our coaches' instructions. "We announce the bronze and then the silver medal winners. The Olympic official will put your medal around your neck and give you flowers. Your countries' flags will be above you."

I listen, but my eyes and mind wander out to the crowd.

"Then, Docia, we announce the gold medal winner." The official speaking my name grabs me back. "The American national anthem will play. Then photos." His eyes grow larger and a smile spreads across his face. "Are you ready?"

We all nod.

"Let's go then." He leads us across the long burgundy carpet toward the center of the ice. Even though I've been in lots of medal ceremonies, this is the Olympics. I feel small. Walking across the carpeted path rather than skating takes forever.

I stop at the center platform with thousands of eyes focused on us. One of the officials holds his arm out to help me up the tallest step. Remembering to breathe while taking in the full experience is a struggle. The rumble in the arena is so loud it almost seems silent. Lena beams with her hands crossed over her heart at rink side.

The booming voice announces the bronze and silver winners. After each name, the throb of the crowd grows louder. Flags wave. Camera flashes blink around the stands. When he announces my name, a cold breeze surrounds me, and I reach over to rub the goosebumps off my arms. I lean forward to allow the official to put the heavy gold medal around my neck. He hands me a giant flower arrangement and I don't feel the weight at all.

The cold, round disk is so big it fills my hand. When I hear the whoosh of the massive American flag unroll from the ceiling and the *Star-Spangled Banner*, the tears start. I've come so far over the last year. It's been hard, but I've achieved so much.

After we step off the ice, photographers and cameras are everywhere. Joy Reznik catches me for a quick interview. "How do you feel now?"

"Tired. Pretty awesome. I've smiled so much my face hurts."

Joy laughs. "Hold those thoughts for the profile story. Nice new moves you added."

"You liked it?" My confidence swells even more.

"Beautiful. I'll see you right after you get back to Houston."

Behind Joy, Stacy is already in her coat. She pulls her skate bag like she's leaving. Our eyes meet for a millisecond before she turns back like she hoped I didn't notice. Sixth place. The almost girl again.

ESPN catches me for another interview. Dad stands with Mom off camera within earshot so afterward he can tell me what I should've said. During the interview, a couple of official-looking men in dark suits start talking to the head judge. The judge's hands are on his hips, and he does not appear happy. A man in a thick brown coat waves his arms around and points to me. Stacy, her coach, and her father are nearby. I try to keep a smile while I talk to the reporter, but the judge's stern face is like a magnet pulling the excitement out of the moment.

"I'm so grateful to my coach, Lena. The amazing fans that are always behind me." I ignore Dad's judging eyes and try to not look back at the heated discussion. "And my parents' constant support. I wouldn't be here without them."

Lena walks over to join the dramatic conversation. Perspiration drips down my back underneath my dress. People notice the loud Russian voices and flailing arms. The judge stands stoic. By now, Dad has stopped watching me. His eyes are glued on them. My mind races everywhere except on the interview and the camera focused on my face.

"Docia?" the reporter says.

"I'm sorry, what was your question?"

Dad stands up straight and scowls when Lena looks over at him.

Ignore them, Docia! I scream at myself. Out of the corner of my eye, I see Lena approach Dad and say something. Then Dad's here next to me, his hand grips my arm.

"I'm so sorry, but Docia is needed elsewhere," Dad says to the reporter and points toward the athletes' lounge. He reaches his arm around my shoulders and leads me away.

"What's going on Dad?"

"It's nothing to worry about."

I stop and face him while he tries to push me along. "Nothing to worry about? Why were those people pointing at me?"

He squeezes my shoulders super tight forcing me to continue alongside him. "Docia, do as I say, and don't ask questions. First, give me your medal."

I keep walking. "I'm a big girl. I can take care of my own medal."

Dad steps up his pace. "It has nothing to do with that, Docia," he says and holds out his hand.

"Then why?" I refuse to reach for the medal. His eyes bore into me. Every hammering heartbeat hurts.

"I said, do not ask questions. Keep walking. Give me your medal. Now."

I take my medal off and hand it to him leaving only the circular red impression on my palm.

We pass the athletes' lounge. "Isn't this where I'm supposed to be?"

I slow down, but Dad doesn't. "No Docia. We have to leave."

"Why?" This time I stop and pull him to a halt. "What's going on? Why are you acting so weird?" I hear footsteps behind us and turn to see Mom and Lena.

"Here's Docia's passport," he says to Lena. "Docia, get your things out of the athletes' lounge and go straight to the airport. I'll call ahead so tickets are ready at the airline counter." He squeezes my hand and his stern look drills into my eyes. "I have to take care of this, and you shouldn't be here. Your mother and I will meet you at the airport. Do as Lena says, no matter what. Do you understand?"

Dad glares at Lena without waiting for my reaction. "Get her out of here."

My heart pounds in my throat. "But Dad—"

He walks down the hall toward the rink, the ribbon from my gold medal floating in the breeze behind him.

CHAPTER FOUR

The muffled announcer's voice sounds over the arena's speakers in Russian and then in English. "Attention. The final results are under reevaluation pending an investigation of the eligibility of one athlete."

I look at Mom and Lena. My heart races faster. "Is this about me? Why would I not be eligible?"

"Go quickly. Get your things," Lena says. "Go, go, go!"

I wave at Mom as we slip out a back door into a taxi.

Lena rattles something off about the airport in Russian to the driver.

"Tell me what's going on. I will not get out of this car without an explanation."

Lena answers with a worried look, one I hadn't seen since I woke from my pain medicine daze in the hospital after my accident last year. She faces me and holds my hands.

"Docia, your mama and papa, they are not actually mama and papa."

"That's no headline. My birth parents are in some West Texas map dot."

"No, Docia, real mama and papa never in Texas."

"What?"

Lena pauses and looks past me out the window to the black sky and then back at me. "You were born here in Europe."

"That's crazy. I was born in Texas."

She squeezes my hand tighter. "Docia, your mama is Russian. You are Russian like me."

I look down and realize I'm still wearing my skates. *We're headed to the airport. In my skates. Without my medal. Now Lena says I'm Russian.*

I slide my hands out of Lena's grip. "I have to take my skates off." My fingers shake as I yank the bright white strings away from the metal hooks by feel since tears cloud my vision. Why didn't Mom and Dad tell me a long time ago?

Lena hands me my sneakers and pulls my chin over so I'm looking into her eyes. "No matter what, Mama and Papa love you."

I blink away the moisture so I can see to tie my sneakers. Then I stare out the window and wish away this conversation—and the last thirty minutes. Moscow's lights fly by like illuminated brush strokes. "You are Russian" fills my senses. I think back to my first practice session at the Olympic arena. I knew my life was about to change in a big way. Now my gold medal is getting further and further away.

We get out of the taxi at the airport and I can't stop shivering.

Lena drapes her arm around my shoulders. "You okay?"

I can't speak so I nod and follow her inside where we wait in line to pick up the tickets Dad arranged for us. Same airport routine—skates out of the bag and in a separate bin on the security conveyor belt.

On the other side of security, I stop.

Lena turns. "Come, come."

A sense of confidence creeps through me. "I don't want to leave. There's too much here. The closing ceremony. Exhibition show. There's so much I still don't know. I'm supposed to celebrate with my friends tonight. I'll take a taxi back."

"No, Docia. Must hurry." Lena grabs hold of my arm and drags me through the airport.

It feels like the people and brightly lit newsstands and restaurants whiz past while I stand still. Do the people hurrying to their destinations know my skating dress hides under my USA team warm-ups? Do they know I'm a new Olympic medalist? Have they heard about this crazy scandal?

I glance back expecting to see my parents racing to catch up. They're nowhere in sight. My eyes stop on a magazine display full of covers with my face and a headline splashed across in Russian. Lena leads me to the empty gate.

"Please wait!" Lena waves and leads me straight to the closing door.

"Today's your lucky day," the agent says as she pulls the door open. "You made it with about three seconds to spare."

Lucky is the last word I would use.

The door closes behind us and we walk down the jet's narrow aisle. Every eye not fixated on their phone is on me until we reach our seats.

"Lena, we can't leave them. Dad said they would meet us here." I peer through the window through the darkness to see if Mom and Dad are by the gate.

Then we take off. For somewhere. Without them. Without my medal.

I stare out the window and think about Dad's face in the arena. I'm used to his determined look—the one I've seen my whole life when he tells me I'm the best. This time his face screamed fear. His words, "Do as Lena says, no matter what." Warmth spreads across my face and my heart races.

"Here, please take this." In Lena's hand is an oblong white pill.

"Why? That's one of Mom's sleeping pills."

"Your papa says it will help you rest on the long flight."

Maybe I'll wake up and this nightmare will be over. She hands me a bottle of water and I pop the pill in my mouth as I'm told. Instead of listening to the flight attendant's safety talk, I take a deep breath to ask Lena a question. "Wh..." is all that comes out. There are so many I don't know where to start. Where are Mom and Dad? Who would try to have me disqualified? And why? Why didn't someone tell me before? Who are my real parents?

"Why did we leave so fast?" is the question that comes out.

Lena's voice is calm and soft. "Docia, do not worry. Not important now."

"It's important to me."

Lena gently pats my knee. "Lay your head back little Docia. Sleep. You had a long day."

None of her usual tricks to calm me work this time. "I have to know, Lena. Of all people, you're the one I trust most. You're like another mother to me. Please tell me what's going on."

"I already said more than I should have." Lena stares at her lap. "Your papa asked me not to tell you anything."

"Lena, you have to." If my pleading face doesn't work, nothing will.

She takes a deep breath and glues her eyes to the gray table folded up against the seat in front of her.

"Yes, you need to know. Your papa should tell you. We had to leave because Papa was afraid Russian authorities would keep you there."

"In Moscow? Why?"

"It is very complicated. Your papa will have to tell you the details. Russian officials claim your papa did not follow the right process. They say your adoption was not legal."

"Not legal? They've been my parents for as long as I can remember. The only parents I know. Who would've kept me in Russia?"

"The man in the brown coat was a Russian government official." Her look tells me she's serious. "He is a bad man. They didn't care about the adoption before. They only want you now since you are a winner."

"But why would they take my medal? What difference does it make to them who my birth parents are?"

"They claim they found your Russian birth record. It has a different birth date, which makes you fourteen. Russian officials do not like to lose."

"That's crazy. Everyone knows competitors have to be fifteen to compete in the Olympics. I've been fifteen since November." The airplane's cabin closes in. "Who are they to question when and where I was born?"

Could that strange man claim me like a piece of property? I wish I could claw my way out of this seat. This plane. "So, who's telling the truth?"

"You do not understand what the U.S.S.R. could do. The International Skating Union along with the United States Figure Skating Association will follow what they say." Lena brushes her hand across my cheek. "But you are more important than any medal."

She has always said the U.S.S.R. still exists like when she lived there, and those organizations rule the skating world. One does what the other does.

Together they are powerful enough to take away my ability to compete in any competition that matters. *I'll be stuck as a beginning coach at some shopping mall rink.* I shrink against the window and wrap my arms around my knees fighting my heavy eyelids. My strength ebbs away draining my mind and my body into numbness.

Until I get bumped around. "What?" I groan. "Still sleeping..."

"Just landed in Houston, Docia. Time to wake up."

A hand on my shoulder gently shakes me.

"Houston? But I have to skate tonight. Have to be in Moscow."

"Little Docia. You already skated in Moscow. You won. Now we are home."

My eyes open to Lena's soft smile. I stretch my legs in the small space and reach to my waist for the cold, hard disk. Nothing's there except for the memory of my gold medal ribbon floating in the air behind Dad.

CHAPTER FIVE

"We're already home? Are Mom and Dad on their way?" I turn on my phone and screens of messages from friends and fans float by. Questions in need of answers I don't have. A text message from Mom.

Will be there soon. Hopefully tomorrow.

"We will go home and rest and wait for Mama and Papa to arrive."

Through my sleeping pill haze, I follow Lena through the Houston airport and obey every command like I'm a kid again. We get into the taxi and follow the familiar route past the glistening brick fountain and drive through the iron gate into the housing subdivision. When we round the corner, I see the place I've called home for as long as I can remember. Someone has put a "Welcome Home Docia!" sign in the front yard, but it has gone limp. It doesn't feel like home anymore.

I feel nothing.

I follow Lena through the front door like a duckling trailing its mother. The house is familiar but now feels empty. My eyelids get heavier as I make my way to the living room sofa.

I want to sleep. Until my life is normal again.

Falling on the sofa is the last thing I remember until Mom's sing-songy voice wakes me.

"Hi, sweetie. I'm home." She gently pats me on my leg. "I'm so happy Lena was able to stay here with you."

I pull myself up and yawn, unbury myself from the heavy blanket Lena must have put on top of me and forget for a moment my world has been turned upside down. "Hey. You're back." Suitcases line the hallway near the front door. "And you got my stuff from the Village."

"I did. Lucy sends her love. She had already packed your things for you. What a sweet roommate. I got home a few minutes ago. Sorry we didn't make your flight."

"That's okay. I slept the whole way. Where's Dad?"

"Well, honey, he didn't get to come back with me."

"Why not? Is he coming home today?" Lena doesn't look up from her newspaper.

"No, sweetie, I think it will be a few days."

I shake my head awake. "Why?"

"He's trying to straighten this mess out. Nothing to worry about. He'll be home before you know it." She smiles, but as she stands, I catch her worried glance at Lena. "Oh, I ran into Joy Resnik, that nice reporter. She will be here this afternoon to start your profile story. She adores you. Who wouldn't? I'll get you some lunch. You must both be famished."

This time my eyes meet Lena's and I sink back underneath the warm blanket. "So soon? I just got home."

"What do you mean?" Mom shouts from the kitchen. "You've been home more than a day."

It's Monday already? The sleeping pill knocked me into oblivion for twenty-four hours.

Mom's heels tap on the hardwood floors. "Get cleaned up while I make your lunch. Joy will be here in about an hour."

"Can't we postpone?" I know she hears me because the clanking dishes pause.

"No," she yells above the noise. "Lucky for you the other two interviews your dad set up are canceled."

I drag myself and my suitcase up the stairs to my room. Lena must have brought my skates up already. The giant teddy bear Dad gave me after my first medal still sits in his spot next to my desk, but the photos from family vacations and all the competition medal ceremonies that sit on the shelves above it seem off. I shove the one of me in my fake parents' arms on the day they brought me home in my dresser drawer. Even the snapshots of Lily and me and the strip Diego and I took at the Texas State Fair photo booth are out of place. The goofy faces that usually make me happy don't have their same magic.

I stand in the warm shower and let the water wash the memories of Moscow away. I want the blankness to swirl down the drain too. No amount of water, soap, or scrubbing can make the emptiness leave.

At the sink, my face looks back at me through the fogged mirror where I wipe away the steam. *Yep, it's still mine, but I still don't know where I came from.* "What will I say to a reporter?" A blank stare answers back.

I trudge down the stairs in a bulky sweatshirt and leggings with my wet hair pulled into a ponytail, aware of what Mom will say, "Don't you have something cute to wear?" I beat her to it. "Yes, Mom, this is the cutest thing I feel like putting on today."

She pauses her sandwich prep and looks over the bar. "It's okay. She knows you've had a tough week. I'm sure she'll understand. At least there are no photos today. Oh, and Lena says goodbye. She was so exhausted she went home. She expects you back at the rink Wednesday."

I lean forward on the bar stool as close to her as I can. "Mom, what's going on? Lena told me about my real parents. It's time to come clean. All of it."

"So thoughtful of Lena to pick up some groceries for us." She slices off pieces of roasted chicken like a machine.

"Mom!"

"I know you have questions, sweetie." She continues to make neat piles on two slices of bread on top of cheese, tomato slices, and lettuce. "We'll have this conversation when your dad gets home. He can explain why the skating union suspended you from competitions."

"Great, let's add suspension to the list." I slam my palms on the bar. "No Mom. We need to talk now. I need to know who my parents are. Also, what Dad's up to in Moscow and if I'll ever be able to compete again. No, it can't wait until Dad's home."

"Well, Docia, you're a little wound up. Your dad's trying to straighten out your birth records so you can compete again." She hands me the tall sandwich. "The Russian adoption authorities say he didn't follow the correct procedures when we adopted you. You're suspended because of the age discrepancy."

"Unbelievable." Her words sink in but still don't understand. *Why me? Why now?* Life without skating would be even worse than never speaking to Lily again.

"Your dad says the adoption procedure and the age questions are both misunderstandings, just like your suspension. Your father handled the adoption through his contacts in Russia while he was with NASA. He gave me an attorney to call."

"An attorney? How could you and Dad let this happen?" I push the sandwich away untouched.

"I wish I could tell you more." She takes a bite and chews fast like the hamster I used to have. "I talked to the lawyer this morning. He assures me he'll clear up the misunderstandings so your dad can come home soon."

"How will we pay for a lawyer? There's no chance I'll still have those endorsements after all this mess—especially if I'm *suspended*!"

"I'll get a full-time job. It's nothing for you to worry—" The doorbell interrupts.

I screech the bar stool across the floor. "I can't talk to a reporter now. I have no idea what to say."

"Calm down, sweetie." Mom pats my cheek on her way to the door. "You won the Olympic gold medal. Your journey to the medal stand is quite an experience to tell."

"Mom!" I can't believe she invited an almost stranger into our house to hear my story when I don't know it. The Russian birth certificate may say I'm only fourteen, but now I feel like the only grown-up in this family.

Mom waves me over. "Docia honey, let's set you two up in the living room."

Then my training kicks in. Just like Dad taught me. "Hello, Ms. Resnik. It's so nice to see you again."

"You too, Docia. Thank you for talking to me so soon. Deadlines, you know."

I reach out to shake her hand. "I understand. How was your flight?" I want to ask why anyone still cares about my story. My fifteen minutes of fame. Literally.

Joy pulls a notepad and digital recorder from her purse as she settles into a chair. "It was fine, and you can call me Joy. Do you mind if I record our conversation? I want to make sure not to miss anything."

I glance at Mom before answering and she nods. "No problem," I say. I squeeze into the corner of a chair facing Joy where I can see out the window.

Joy hesitates while she studies my face, her pen poised and ready for something quotable. "How did you *feel* when they took your gold medal away?"

Her question stings more than I thought it would. *How does she think I felt? It sucked to lose the gold, especially because of something dumb my parents did.*

Mom nods encouragement from the doorway over Joy's shoulder. I look back at Joy and force the sweetest smile. "Disappointed." Deep underneath my rehearsed soft expression, I aim fireballs at her mouth. What a stupid question. "Winning an Olympic medal? It was such a huge dream. Something I worked hard for. Honestly, it hasn't completely sunk in yet— earning the medal and losing it." I pause. "But then again, if anyone had said I'd almost kill myself when I dove into a lake last summer and still win the Olympic gold, I would've called them nuts."

Joy puts her pen down and tilts her head. "Exactly why we want to tell your story. It can inspire others. I know you've been through a great deal over the past year—physically, emotionally, and now the age scandal."

That's an understatement.

The gray sky outside the living room window brings back memories of the aluminum ceiling and walls at the rink where I've spent at least half of my life. The bright lights. Its vast emptiness and the crowds around it. "As long as I can remember, Dad has told me the ice would always be mine. Two nights ago, in Moscow, it was."

I was unbeatable.

"What's happened since you returned to Houston?"

I take a deep breath to put off my answer and curl my knees under the bulky sweatshirt. Maybe she'll forget I'm here. I stare out the window pondering where to begin and hope she doesn't bring up my real parents. The slow drip of raindrops sliding down my huddled-up reflection starts to extinguish my anger. *I know she just wants the story.*

"Truthfully, not much but sleep until Mom got home this morning." The crumpled blanket and pillows on the family room sofa are proof.

"What will you do for the rest of the week?"

"Rest. I was so exhausted from rehab after the accident. Then the training schedule leading up to the Olympics was grueling. I need the downtime."

"When will you get back on the ice?"

"I don't know." My face softens as two squirrels chase each other up a tree. "I want to savor the Moscow experience. Being there for the Games. Staying in the Olympic Village. Meeting all the athletes. It was all so unbelievable."

"Lena says two more days off, right Docia?" Mom answers for me and walks by to pat my leg as a reminder of the instructions. "Then it's time to train for Worlds."

What fantasy does Mom live in?

"Can you get past this awful experience? I mean, do you *want* to compete anymore?"

My smile fades and fingernails dig into my palms. *If she'll just stop asking questions I don't know how to answer.* "Skating's all I know. I'll be lost without it..." My voice trails off while her pen scratches across the notepad. I turn my head toward the window so she doesn't see tears fill my eyes and hug my knees again. *Do not cry. Do not cry. Do not cry.*

"It doesn't seem fair for you to be suspended. You had nothing to do with what happened."

Silence fills the room, but I'm not ready to say anything. *What can I say?*

"Do you remember the first time you skated?"

My glance pauses on the scar on my wrist where I hit the stump at the lake last year, a daily reminder of how hard I worked to prepare for the Olympics. A clear memory paints itself in my mind and pushes away the more recent disturbing ones. "I do, Ms. Resnik. Parts of the experience, at least. I haven't thought about it in forever."

"Seriously, you can call me Joy." She glances at her recorder while she continues to write.

"Okay, Joy. My aunt took me skating at the mall for my third birthday. I fell all the time. It was part of the fun. I'd laugh and get back up soaking wet and zoom past everyone, so she tells me."

"So, you were a natural from the start?"

"She was," Mom nods from the chair next to me.

"My parents say I always loved it." I rest my cheek on my knee and watch Joy straighten the scarf over her lavender sweater and look around the room. "I bugged my parents until they finally signed me up for lessons. I've lived to skate ever since, and competing is the best part."

Joy walks over to the long wall almost completely wallpapered in competition photos. "Look at you in the sparkly pink skating dress. You're like a tiny cupcake. Didn't it make you nervous to be out on the ice all by yourself?"

"Funny, but it didn't. I remember that competition so vividly. It was my first..." I close my eyes and the sights and sounds in the photograph come alive. "The rink seemed enormous. When I stepped onto the ice, it didn't matter. Lena had created a machine that made all the moves she had drilled into me for weeks. I smiled, raised my chin, and put my arms out to each side like she taught me. The audience's applause helped me push my little legs to the center faster. It felt like home."

I hand the recorder to Joy and point to a man in the photo standing rink side with his arms raised. "My dad yelled, 'Docia, the ice is yours!' *Somewhere Over the Rainbow*, blasted through the speakers, and I came alive. I still remember that program. The waltz jump, bunny hops, spiral, and even the spin were almost perfect."

Joy looks from the photo to me.

"It felt like electricity rushed through me. I hurried through the program so much I finished with about ten seconds of music left. Holding my final pose until the music stopped seemed like hours. I was so mortified I didn't hear the applause. Instead, I skated into Lena's arms, buried my face in her fuzzy coat and bawled my eyes out thinking I had messed up my chances to medal. Lena squeezed me so tight and I can still hear her whisper, 'You were be-yu-ti-ful my leetle Docia.' I'll never forget it."

As I talk, my legs turn to jelly and I reach for the sofa back to steady my footing.

Joy leans forward. "Are you okay? Let's sit down."

"Docia, you are exhausted." Mom heads toward the kitchen. "I'll get us some water. Maybe we should wrap this up."

"I'm fine." And I've been too busy sleeping to eat since that horrible pasta and chicken meal Saturday before the long program that night.

Joy sits on the front of her chair and checks her recorder. "What else do you remember?"

"Well, I know Dad said, 'You will be the best skater in the world, Peanut!' He drilled those words into me from that day on. After my first competition, he pushed me through the rest. Local and regional competitions. Then sectionals."

"Has he helped you accomplish what you've achieved?"

"In a strange way, yeah. He always told me I'm the best. I had some natural ability but never had to work as hard as some of my competitors, so I believed him. Well, until I won Nationals. Lena shifted into heavy training mode. She made me practice like crazy to build strength and stamina. Oh, and all the ballet. I could never be fast enough or graceful enough for her. She would always say, 'You must vork very hard to vin Worlds...and maybe Olympics my leetle Docia.'"

Joy walks along the living room walls. "How many medals and trophies do you have?"

"I don't know. I counted every one of them—63—until I was about 10, then gave up. When I made it to the senior level, my life changed. U.S. Nationals last year were amazing. Even though it had been a lifelong dream, I never imagined I'd actually win—especially when I was only fourteen."

"It turns out there were others who thought you didn't deserve to win," Joy says.

"I know. I don't understand why anyone would have it out for me. I've worked hard to do what I love."

We both look up at the sound of Mom's footsteps. "Here's some water and lemonade. Docia, I think the cheese and crackers might help since you didn't eat your sandwich." She sets the tray in front of us. "I hope you don't mind if I still sit in."

"Uhm, we're doing just—"

So much for telling Joy more of the story today.

Joy looks down at my foot and I realize it's tapping the table like it does when I get annoyed.

"I'll be quieter than your father when it's time to take out the trash. I promise." She winks. My foot shakes faster. "You need to wrap this session up soon so you can catch up on your rest and schoolwork."

"Mom, I don't feel like studying."

"Excuse us." Mom turns to Joy and does her whisper thing, "My daughter seems to be having a moment."

I sigh. I'll never understand why she whispers when she wants to emphasize something. "I'm not ready to go back to school yet." Mom puts her index finger under my chin to raise my stare up from my shaking foot to her face. *Do not treat me like a kid.*

"We already talked about this, Docia. Your father insists you keep up your studies so you don't get further behind while you train for Worlds."

It's hard to avoid her eyes when they're so close I can smell her tangerine lipstick.

"Yeah, Dad's made such smart decisions for me so far." I push her hand away and slip over the side of the chair to escape. Joy gives me a tiny smile while Mom's head is turned.

"Docia, do not walk away from me," Mom says.

I roll my eyes as I shuffle toward the kitchen.

"Our daughter is such a great student—straight A's—and we never have to hound her about her studies," she tells Joy.

When I reach the refrigerator, I turn back toward the living room and say under my breath. "Fine, I won't study then." The pile of schoolbooks on the dining table taunts me as I head to my room.

CHAPTER SIX

Mom slips on her sling-back pump with one hand and tucks in her blouse with the other. "I have a job interview," she whispers. "I made you some lunch. I'm sure you're starved after so much studying. You look smarter already."

"Thanks, Mom." I hope she goes back to work so she'll be too busy to take care of Dad.

"Are you finished with today's lessons?"

"Almost." Books are spread around me on the kitchen table. She doesn't need to know I'm still staring at the same first paragraph. "I'll email my homework to Mr. Fuentes later."

"You finished all three subjects so fast? He must be very proud of your progress," she says as she puts on her earrings.

"Yeah, thrilled."

She looks at me funny but doesn't respond. "Your lunch is on the bar when you're ready." She kisses me on the forehead. "Wish me luck. I hope I get this job. We could use the money."

"You'll do great, Mom."

But I'm another story. What will I do all day if I can't skate?

I stare at the pile of books for the answer. Lily survived life after skating. She has more fun now. I grab my phone and text her.

Come by after practice?

B there @ 4. Can't wait to see you! Lily answers.

I still miss her at the rink every day.

Perched on a kitchen barstool, I stare at *Sense and Sensibility* page one and take a bite of the turkey sandwich Mom made. After half of it and a chapter, the book is as dry as the sandwich. I stuff the sandwich down the disposal and imagine the book going with it. What would I do today if my life hadn't fallen apart? I would be on my whirlwind media tour, having my skin pampered and makeup touched up, skating in New York's Rockefeller Plaza, and wearing fabulous clothes for photo shoots. Schoolwork shouldn't be on the schedule. Not right after the Olympic gold.

A headline in Mom's copy of the *Houston Chronicle* at the end of the bar catches my eye. *Local Olympian Stuck in Eligibility Holding Pattern.*

It's a he-said, she-said between Russian adoption departments, Olympic officials and parents. Until something surfaces to prove when Docia Sikorsky was born, she can't reclaim her Olympic gold or compete at all.

Well, that about sums up my future in two sentences.

Endorsements are canceled or on hold. "My daughter needs to get back on the ice," her father Jerry Sikorsky said in an email from Moscow where he is working to resolve the issue. "Docia is old enough. It doesn't matter where she was born. She's legally my daughter and was born to skate."

The newspaper falls back to the bar. Great. Now everyone knows companies dumped me. On top of losing sponsorships, Dad talks like I'm a possession.

The doorbell startles me out of my hell.

"Docia!" As I open the door, Lily's embrace almost knocks me over. "I'm so glad you're back!"

"I missed you!" She stirs up the first bit of home since I returned.

"I can't believe my best friend is an Olympic champion!"

"Whatever." I walk back to the kitchen and Lily follows.

"What do you mean 'whatever'?"

"I'm not a champion anymore."

"You are, and I won't listen to any negative talk." She's still wearing her practice cheerleader uniform and walks with the perky bounce she picked up when she stopped skating. "Why are you still in your pajamas?" She breezes by me to the kitchen.

"I *was* doing homework until I got sidetracked by the newspaper. There's a front-page story about me and everything I'll never be."

"Ignore it," Lily says. "You've got more important stuff to do."

"Like what?"

"You have to get ready for Worlds, Einstein!"

"There's this little detail you forgot. I'm disqualified. Suspended. Definitely no Worlds."

"I said no more negative talk."

Lily never dwells on a problem. She moves on like she did when she had to quit skating and expects everyone to do the same.

"I stared at my chemistry book for over an hour. Isn't that enough?"

"Get dressed, girl! I'm used to the Docia who's up and out of here by five o'clock in the morning. Come to the basketball game with me."

Before the Olympics, I wouldn't have thought twice. Now, with the questions. The stares.

"I don't think so."

Not that I expect Lily to understand until she hears the rest of the story.

"You hungry?"

"How about a glass of your mom's peach tea? You'll never believe what happened at practice."

I recall the last drama at cheer practice. Amy Gandy got mad because she wanted to be at the top of the pyramid, so she dropped the girl she was holding. "Who did Amy let go of this time?"

"Well, it's not Amy this time." Lily pours a glass of tea while the ice cubes make crackle sounds then takes a dainty sip. "You remember Jennifer's going out with Cameron, right? She found out Stacy went out with him before Moscow. Jennifer was not happy. It was intense."

I shudder at the sound of Stacy's name again. How did she have time to go out before Moscow?

"Stacy's turned into such a little sh—," I can't say it, even to Lily. "...something else. She makes an art out of hurting people. And Cameron? Lethal. They deserve each other."

"I know, right?" Lily gasps and slaps her hand to her mouth. "I'm so sorry. What she did to you is so much worse than a fight over some guy." She bats a sincere apology with her long eyelashes.

"Don't worry about it. I'll survive." I tell myself that, at least.

"Are you skating in the morning?"

I look at the floor and shake my head. It will only be a matter of time before Lena pushes me out on the rink again. She'll hold my chin and say, "No matter what, must keep skating."

"Why?"

"Not ready."

"Come to the game then. Should be a good one."

"No thanks, not ready to face a game either. Besides, you'll be cheering. Who would I sit with?"

Lily swivels back and forth on the bar stool and sips her tea. "I'll bet Diego will be there."

The tingle deep in my stomach comes back. Of all the whispers, his would hurt the most.

"I can't see him yet."

"I've never heard you say no so much."

"I can't face Diego after the way my dad treated him. He hates me now." I hug my knees under my sweatshirt.

"Docia, he's crazy about you." She wipes a tear away before it drips off my chin.

"You know Dad still blames him for my accident. It was awful. You didn't see the look on Diego's face after Dad lit into him at Nationals." I stare out the window while the whole scene comes back. In the warm-up before the free skate, I had just landed my quad-double I had worked on for so long. The rink started spinning. Then I hit the ice. The next thing I remember, I was in the medical room with a bunch of strangers over me. I blacked out. I couldn't believe the doctor wouldn't let me do my free skate.

"I can still hear Dad screaming at Diego in the medical room doorway, 'Are you happy now? You've ruined her career. Her life. She never wants to see you again!' I can't imagine how Diego must have felt."

"Why didn't you talk to your dad then? Or Diego?"

"I don't know. Maybe because the room was spinning."

"Doesn't your dad know Diego had nothing to do with you going to the lake that day?"

"And Diego tried to stop me from diving off the pier. I told Dad a million times, but he refused to accept the truth."

"Diego knows you don't blame him." Lily strokes my arm. "Nothing else matters."

"He traveled halfway across the country to watch me at Nationals and Dad treated him like crap. Diego looked so hurt."

"What happened at Nationals didn't matter. They gave you a bye to the Olympics since you won Nationals the year before. My best friend, the Olympian. You won!" Lily squeezes my hand.

"Yeah, until I didn't. Here I sit. No medal. Now I have a reporter who wants to tell my bizarre story. Not the happy one about the amazing career ahead of me."

"Docia, you're strong and famous. You *will* get through this."

Lily could, but I'm not so sure about me.

"Tell me all the juicy details. Is everything I hear about athletes who hook up at the Olympic Village true?"

"Yeah, pretty much. It was really awesome being there, but not much fun with my parents around." I fill her in on the cute Canadian snowboarder and Lucy and the packed rink and reporters and my two minutes at the Bolshoi.

"You made my day, Lily. Thanks for cheering me up."

"That's one thing I can do. Speaking of cheering, I need to get changed for the game. Are you sure I can't talk you into coming?"

"No thanks. That reporter will be here for another interview soon. Tell Jennifer something for me?"

"Sure, what?"

"Tell her to let Stacy have it next time. She needs to learn to stop taking things that don't belong to her."

Lily laughs and walks to the front door. "That would be a sight to see."

I close the door behind her and then face the empty house. When have I ever had so much time on my hands? I have no idea what to do next.

CHAPTER SEVEN

Dad said I should always know my enemies. Until we arrived in Moscow, I thought I didn't have enemies. Now I sit across the kitchen table from Joy again, about to have to talk about those enemies I thought I didn't have. I'm not sure I'm ready to face the answer if she asks me about what happened in Moscow. I can't even face that Lena wants me to start training on Wednesday. At least Mom doesn't know about this interview.

"Let's start when you won Nationals last year and set off on the Olympic path."

My mind is stuck in the Olympic Village when Stacy and her entourage ambushed me. My eyes fixate on the vegetable-shaped salt and pepper shakers always neatly arranged on the end of the kitchen table. Stacy's smirky voice replays. "It won't matter how you skate once everyone finds out who you really are."

Joy stops the recorder. "Docia, are you okay?"

"Sorry, just distracted." I hope she doesn't see the disgust my face must show.

"What's on your mind? It can be off the record."

"Seriously, it's nothing." I want to take a drink of orange juice, but my arm won't move. Everything that's happened weighs down my shoulders, my arms, my legs, my head. My mind tells my mouth to talk but no words come out.

Then Joy does her tilty-head thing and turns the recorder back on. "What was your favorite Moscow sight?"

A safe question.

"Well, aside from the rink, definitely the Bolshoi Theatre. All those dancers who have performed there.... I wish we could've gone to a ballet, but it was closed for renovation. The Kremlin creeped me out because of what's happened there."

"Yes, I know what you mean. I felt the same thing. Some of my family immigrated to America from Russia because of those very events." Joy pauses and gazes out the window. "I remember my grandmother taking me to the Bolshoi when I was little. Maybe you will dance there someday." Joy picks up her notepad again. "It's great you had enough downtime for you and your parents to enjoy the city."

If she only knew the half of it. I left out the part about how I bolted out of the car to get away from Dad.

"Your dad seems to be your biggest fan. What advice did he give you before the Olympics?"

"Which time?" I laugh and recall Dad's talks from as long as I can remember. "I woke up super early and stared out the window our first morning in Moscow before I moved over to the Olympic Village. Jet lag, I guess. My dad sat with me. The first thing he said was, 'Docia, you are a champion.' He droned on about the good decisions he had made for me, how everything he did was for my own good to prepare me for my destiny. At the time, I thought he was right."

"Your destiny to win the Olympics?"

I nod. If only time could roll back to the day before my world fell apart.

Joy leans forward in her chair. "Were you ready? Did you feel like you could beat all those girls?"

I shrug. "I guess. Dad said I was."

Wow, Dad's not here now to think for me for the first time ever.

Joy nods. "Tell me about your practice sessions."

"My first practice ice at the Olympic rink..." My voice trails. Chills travel up my spine. I never dreamed one simple practice session would set off such a crazy series of events.

"Docia, are you okay? You're shivering."

"Yeah. At the time I didn't worry about it, but something weird happened. Stacy Gaston had practice ice before me. I was putting on my skates...." I picture the motions of pulling each boot on like I had done thousands of times. "She congratulated me. Then what she said next was strange. 'Enjoy it, until everyone finds out.'"

"Did you have any idea what she meant?"

"Not a clue. If I had confronted her, I would have been more prepared when I lost my medal. I never mentioned what she said to Lena, but I asked Dad about it. He said, 'Docia, you know Stacy is your enemy. She only wants to beat you mentally. Don't let her get to you.'"

Dad would explode if he knew what I just told her.

"Did she?"

"A little, I guess. My practice was great until she showed back up. I had so much energy since I was off the ice for the last couple of days. Lena kept telling me, 'Slow down leetle Docia. Save your energy.'"

Joy glances down at my shaking foot. I wrap my hand around it to make it stop. "It was almost like she sucked the entire rink's energy away just with her presence. I could hardly land a clean jump. Afterward, I tried to ignore her. The Olympics are too big."

"They certainly are. Tell me about Stacy," Joy says.

"Stacy and I have skated together since we were kids." Her name still tastes bitter. "She, Lily, and I used to hang out together."

"Lily?"

"Lily's been my best friend almost forever. We met in our very first skating class. Learned every jump and spin together. Suffered through edges and field moves. Shared gardening pads and ice packs to protect our boney butts from the brutal falls while we learned our doubles and triples. Then her parents divorced a few years ago and she had to quit. Lily, Stacy, and I, along with our families, used to all travel to Regionals together."

"When was this?" Joy asks.

"Four years ago. Along with the Regional competition, we were all scheduled to do our Novice test. Lily and I passed, but Stacy didn't. Then she didn't place in the competition.

"She didn't speak to us the rest of the trip. Neither did her parents."

"What did you do?"

"What could I do? I was upset. Dad told me what Stacy did or thought didn't matter." I pause and think back over her comments in Moscow. "I guess he was wrong."

CHAPTER EIGHT

No matter what Stacy said to me at the Olympic rink, the Village, or anywhere, she couldn't stop my ache to get out on the ice. I had to win.

While I wait for Joy's next question, my mind travels back to the first afternoon I went to the Olympic rink. I'd skated at rinks in many countries, but this time was different. I close my eyes and see the amazing structure; the place that would change my life.

"The practice sessions I watched were pretty spectacular," I open my eyes at the sound of Joy's voice. "Your dad's talks must've helped you focus."

"I pulled it together. There was so much buzz that I was a favorite to medal. Reporters from all over the world wanted interviews. It was crazy. Then my agent called Dad about the flood of endorsement offers if I medaled. He said we'd be set for life."

"Those are big expectations. How did you handle the extra pressure?"

"Competition nerves usually don't get to me—" and I hadn't realized what it meant to be the family's breadwinner until now.

Joy interrupts. "But this was the Olympics. Your first. No nerves at all?"

"Well, a little. I think it made me focus more. The enormity didn't sink in until the day I performed my long program."

I walk from the table to the kitchen. For the first time since I've been back, my body craves to speed across the ice. My mind simply wants me to stand still. "Orange juice?"

"Some water would be great. Thanks."

"I'm sure you saw me finish ahead of my music." I laugh and shake my head. "At least I didn't cry like when I was little."

"Yes, I saw. I also remember the look on your dad's face when you finished early."

Great. Reporters even noticed.

"Dad always overreacts. He told me the judges cheated me...'" My voice drifts off as I fill a glass of water.

"This must be difficult for you to talk about."

I take a deep breath, think about what Joy said. "Yeah, it is. It's almost like some other skater won the Olympics and I just watched."

Joy sits silently and gives me her tilted head look again. This time her face is soft with an understanding smile, like she sincerely cares.

"How did you feel?" Joy asks.

"I felt great. Ready. I had worked on some different choreography that I love. Being the last skater in the final group was brutal."

"The wait must've been excruciating," Joy adds. "Did you watch your competitors?"

"A little. I snuck a look at Stacy's program and a couple of others but mostly just listened to my music to stay in my zone. Then the announcer called my name. You know the rest."

"It was the best performance I'd ever seen you skate. Your smile after you landed the quad-double was good enough for a cereal box."

My eyes drop to the floor. Thanks for the reminder of the endorsements not to be.

Joy gasps. "I'm sorry. That was insensitive. I know everything will be back to how it's supposed to be once all this mess is over."

"I always practice smiling after my quad-double, but the huge audience, the TV and news cameras. I didn't want to deal with Dad if I missed the jump."

Joy shakes her head. "Your dad certainly seems to care a lot for you."

"I don't know if I'd call it care." Until now, I thought all of Dad's decisions were to help me. My knees go weak, and the windowsill catches me before I slide to the floor. I hope Joy doesn't notice and ask why. "I had never seen so many stuffed polar bears in my life. The few minutes in the kiss-and-cry area seemed like an eternity, then they announced I had won. I had won at the Olympics. I saw a tear on Lena's cheek. She said, 'I knew you could do it.' All the anticipation. All the preparation. My dream for so long. It hardly seemed real."

"How did you feel at that moment?"

"Pretty awesome. I smiled so much my face hurt."

"Don't stop there."

"You know what happened next, the medal ceremony."

Joy nods. "Of course."

"It all happened so fast. Dad joined us by the rink. 'You're an Olympic champion, Docia, like I taught you.' He seemed so proud."

I wonder what Dad thinks about me now.

"Medal ceremonies weren't new to me, but this was the Olympics." Still leaning on the windowsill, I turn to look at the blue sky that seems as vast as the most amazing moment in my life. "The crowd got louder after the announcer said each name. When he announced mine, I felt chilled and warm at the same time." I look down at my empty palm and think about the cold, round disk filling my hand.

"I had imagined the moment so many times and promised myself I wouldn't cry. By the time the first three notes of the *Star-Spangled Banner* played, I did. The enormous flag reminded me how hard the last year had been. How out of reach the Olympic medal stand had been."

Joy lets out a sigh. "So exciting. I was curious what you thought at that moment on that top medal stand."

"Afterwards, a reporter interviewed me when the little crowd gathered around the head judge. Stacy and her dad were there too. They all kept looking at me."

Joy's happy expression fades. "Please continue. I had to file my story, so I only saw the news replays."

"I had no way to know how major the moment was."

Joy watched intently. "What did you think was happening?"

"I had no idea." But I'll never forget those words, 'Give me your medal.'

"Docia, are you okay?"

When I look up, Joy's staring at my white knuckles. "Saying all of this out loud is bizarre." I stretch out my tight fists and try to let go of the tension. "They wouldn't tell me anything, so I took the medal off and handed it to Dad."

As I talk, I grab a fistful of sweatshirt and rest my hand on my stomach the way I remember gripping my gold medal on the podium. My heart pounds in my throat like it did in that awful moment when Dad took it away. The frustration, anger, and fear had left me so confused I didn't know what to do. What to think.

"I grabbed my stuff then Lena and I slipped out a back door."

Joy scoots to the front edge of her chair. "To the airport?"

"Yes. Like a couple of fugitives. When we got into the taxi, Lena told me about my birth parents. My real ones. That I'm Russian."

"So, it's true. You were born in Russia. I didn't want to write it until you confirmed."

I nod. "That's what Lena told me."

"How do you feel about the news?" Joy slides to the edge of her seat again.

"I don't know yet. It's like Lena meant someone else." I gaze out the window and wonder what Dad's up to. "I wish Mom and Dad had told me sooner."

Reliving each experience and emotion drains every bit of my strength so I slide into a chair, rest my head on my hands, and let the table hold me up.

Joy gently squeezes my arm. "Do you want to take a break?"

I hear Joy's words, but they don't register in my brain. For a moment, I think I'm still beside the cab at the Moscow airport. Joy's gentle touch feels like the soft fur of Lena's coat when she tried to warm me up.

"Docia, you're shivering again."

I try to speak but no words come out, so I nod. Now I've told the story, my head feels completely void of thought. With the strength gone from my arms and legs, it's like floating in nothingness, not sure of where I'm going. I hear talking next to me but don't comprehend the words until Joy touches my arm again and brings me back.

I'm not sure how much time passes until I gather the strength to speak. "After so much drama, my long program seems so insignificant."

"It certainly was very significant." Joy's soft voice calms me. "You landed a quad-double and a triple Axel, and you're only fifteen."

"The scandal cancels all of that." I still see the look on Lena's face when she told me I'm Russian. "If it hadn't been for Stacy, her coach, and their reporter friend, none of this would have happened."

CHAPTER NINE

I lock the door behind Joy and put one foot slowly in front of the other until I reach the sofa. That's the last thing I remember.

"Docia, sweetie, time for dinner."

Is it Mom's voice?

"Did you do lots of homework?"

"I don't feel good. I'll make up for it tomorrow."

"You don't sound well. Do you have a fever?" She reaches over the back of the sofa and lays her hand across my forehead. "You feel a little warm, and you're shivering. You've been so down the last few days, maybe you are sick. How about I make some chicken soup? With a warm dinner and a good night's sleep, you'll be back to normal."

I close my eyes and huddle up under the blanket. Yeah, what's normal?

"It's a good thing you're such a fast learner. You'll be caught up in no time."

"Joy came by for another interview, and Lily visited after school."

"You had a busy day. No wonder you're exhausted. Your father would prefer I be here when you and Joy meet." She straightens my blanket. "By the way, I didn't get the job."

"I'm sorry, Mom." She has bigger worries than me talking with Joy alone.

"Times are a little tough, I guess. I hope the next interview has a better outcome. We have to pay the lawyer at the end of this month. He made some progress with your dad's situation. At least I have the part-time job."

I pull the blanket tighter. At least we have that.

• • •

I feel something on my shoulder and reach up to brush it off. Then I hear a voice.

"Docia, it's morning. You were so dead to the world you wouldn't wake up. I let you sleep on the sofa again."

I curl up tighter, refusing to open my eyes. Maybe the essays and calculus problems are making me sick.

"You didn't eat a thing last night. How about some breakfast? Oh, and Lena called. I told her you'd be back at the rink as soon as you're better."

"I'm not hungry." And the thought of skating makes me nauseous.

"Let's see if you have a fever."

I feel a tickle in my ear and try to push it away. "Mom, stop."

"Hmmm, your temperature is normal. How do you feel?"

"I don't know."

I'm a lifeless rock.

Mom puts her hand on my forehead. "You can sleep a little longer and hold off skating for a couple of days. I'll call you from work in a little while. You need to study before your interviews in New York later this week."

• • •

I spring up on the sofa and suck in a lungful of air. *What was that noise?* It happens again. My phone is right next to where I slept. "MOM" splashes across the screen.

"Mom, you scared me to death," I say into the phone.

"I know. I turned the volume on and up to make sure you wouldn't sleep through it."

"I'm awake. *Real* awake."

"Docia, tell me you're up. For real. I put *Sense and Sensibility* and your laptop on the coffee table next to you."

"Mom, I'm up. I'll study."

"And eat, sweetie. You need nourishment. Chicken soup's in the fridge."

"Okay. See you when you get home." I turn the volume off so it won't send me through the ceiling, fall back on the cushion, and close my eyes again. Another day of nothing to do and too much time to do it.

I reach for the Jane Austen novel. A few chapters in, Mr. Fuentes' essay assignment makes sense. I turn on the laptop and put a few thoughts down for the essay.

The socioeconomic environment in Sense and Sensibility *sucked for girls. If those sisters just had a talent, they'd have an income without the need to depend on their dad or wimpy brother.*

Halfway into the five-hundred-word essay, the screen flickers. I frantically hit save. My heart leaps up to my throat when the screen goes dark. Crap! Mom didn't charge the battery? Please let auto-save work! My heart races until my phone vibrating startles me. I look down to see Joy's name on my phone. "Hello?"

"Hi Docia. We didn't schedule an interview this afternoon, but I wondered if you might be available. I'm in the neighborhood and could come by in about ten minutes."

"Umm, yeah, I guess that would be okay. Can we go somewhere else though? Maybe the coffee shop down the road?"

The further away from responsibility I can get, the better.

"Sure. I'll meet you there. Thanks, Docia."

I let out an enormous breath.

CHAPTER TEN

I sip a Chai tea latte from the corner table and glance at the clock on the coffee shop wall. Joy sits across from me. I expect Mom to check in at any second. She'll be pissed I'm with Joy again. Without her. Not studying. My stomach lurches as her name and a text message pop up on my phone.

You awake?

Maybe this wasn't such a good idea. I text back, *Studying. Promise.*

"Sorry, you were saying?" My eyes are drawn to the cross around Joy's neck. "It's lovely."

"What?" Joy answers.

"Your necklace. Are you Eastern Orthodox?"

She touches the pendant. "I am. Well, my parents are Russian Orthodox. My grandmother gave me this when I turned sixteen."

"May I?" Joy nods as I reach for the pendant.

"It's beautiful. Lena gave me a similar cross." I slip the necklace from under my sweater. "It's the one I wear when I compete, but I haven't taken it off since the Olympics. She says it will always protect me."

It has done little so far.

"Yes, I've noticed it." Joy smiles back. "My babushka told me she would be with me as long as I have it on. It's comforting, especially when you're under the microscope."

I'm not sure if Joy means any particular microscope, but I'm still not ready to admit Stacy has come anywhere near sabotaging me. Then Lily walks through the door, a perfect excuse to ignore Joy's comment. "Oh, there's my friend, Lily. The one I told you about." Lily waves. "Do you mind if she joins us?"

"Sure. I'd love to meet her," Joy says.

Lily leans over to hug me. "Oh my god, Docia, you actually left the house!"

I roll my eyes. "You make me sound like some weird recluse. I'm not that bad yet. Lily, this is Joy Resnik, the reporter I mentioned."

Joy reaches her hand out. "Please join us. Docia's told me about you and your friend, Stacy."

"Our *former* friend, Stacy?" Lily's face twists as she pulls up a chair. "I'm sure Docia's told you about that too."

I nod. "Our trip to Regionals when she stopped speaking to us."

Lily's eyes grow big. "Do you remember Sectionals the year before? Stacy's skating dress ripped down the back in the middle of her performance."

"How could I forget? She totally fell apart. Couldn't finish her program," We both giggle. "Oh, sorry, Joy. Please don't quote me. I don't mean to laugh at her."

Joy grins. "You're safe."

"Do you remember the look on her face when she left the ice?" Lily covers her snicker. "You'd think she had done her program naked."

"She cried like such a baby. I mean, grow up. It's not like anyone saw anything." My smile fades. "It was kind of sad how she crumbled. We've all had a broken lace or costume problem at one time or another. Wonder what else was going on."

Lily sips her coffee. "She's officially dating Cameron now. They totally deserve each other."

"Who's Cameron?" Joy asks.

My eyes lock with Lily's. "Cameron goes to our school. He's bad news," Lily says. "He's partially to blame for Docia's accident. Did you tell her about it?"

"Not yet." I see Joy's curious expression. "I guess now's as good a time as any."

"May I record this part?" My heart revs as Joy reaches for her purse.

I gulp and nod at the familiar recorder beep. If I tell Joy the truth, Dad will be angry to no end. I'll only tell the truth. "After I won Nationals last year, I trained less. Actually, had time for a bit of a life. That's when I hung out with Cameron."

"I was hanging out with a friend of his," Lily adds. "Cameron had a thing for Docia. The day we got out of school for spring break, a bunch of us went to his parents' house on Lake Conroe."

The conversation at our lockers that day is vivid. "He mentioned taking me out there when it got warm. Whenever Cameron wanted the lake house keys, his parents handed them over."

Lily nods. "Cameron's brother got a keg and vodka for trashcan punch. People got pretty messed up."

An involuntary chuckle comes out. "My dad believes Cameron's perfect. 'He's from a successful family,' he always said. 'That boy will go places.' Maybe on paper." I flip the cardboard coaster over. "It was the first warm spring day so I didn't think twice about blowing off my afternoon practice ice. I don't know why I wanted to drink when I was around him."

"I do," Lily interrupts. "He teased you constantly. 'Perfect little skater girl never has fun.' Jerk."

"I already had a couple of cups of punch." The details flow like the story is about someone else. "Then I drank another cupful while we watched Diego and a few other guys do cannonballs off the pier. What was I thinking?"

"You weren't," Lily says.

"Then Cameron whispered to me, 'Do some fancy dive like your jumps. Unless you're too goody-goody.' That smile and challenge would've made me do just about anything. I emptied my cup and walked to the edge of the pier like it was nothing."

Lily nods. "You yelled, 'My turn!' You were totally into it."

"Diego grabbed my arm. 'Docia, it's too dangerous with these water levels.' I can still hear him warn me. I didn't care. My dad says I can do anything."

"I wanted to stop you too, but there were too many people in the way," Lily says. "No hesitation. Not that you ever do."

"I wanted to get some speed before I went in. I remember thinking; *I did front flips at the pool last summer so there's no reason I can't do one now.*"

Lily reaches across the table and squeezes my hand like she'll never let go. I wish she'd done the same that day at the lake. "But you hadn't just had god knows how much vodka in your tiny body."

She's right, but hearing Lily say what actually happened instead of Dad's scrubbed version seems so harsh. I must tell the truth—even though the world will know I'm not perfect.

"I ran down the pier. Then whoosh! I squared out and went in. Arms first. The cold when I hit the water was such a rush. Straight in with hardly a ripple."

Lily's eyes grow. "I watched you turn in the air at the highest part of the dive and felt weird—even though I've seen your blades leave the ice for jumps hundreds of times."

"When I went into the water, something was off. I couldn't stop. Couldn't see a thing. I sunk like the lake had no bottom. I knew it did. That's the last thing I remember."

Joy gasps and she slaps her hands over her mouth. "This wasn't how the news reported this."

"I know, thanks to Dad."

Again.

Lily's concerned eyes blink faster like she's reliving the moment with me. "Luckily you were still conscious—at least enough to get to the surface," Lily adds, "or we would've never found you in the murky lake water."

Joy's shaking head reminds me of Dad's looks of disapproval for weeks after the accident. "Was it stumps?" she asks. "You're lucky you weren't permanently injured—or worse."

Lily nods. "Pretty sure. I mowed through at least eight people to get to you. Someone pulled you out of the water." Lily pauses and looks over at Joy. "Just as I got to her, one of the guys tried to stand her up. She stood for a few seconds. She had no idea there was blood everywhere—on her head, her arm and hand, her knee." Lily covers her face before continuing. "Docia, you looked at me with the goofiest grin, and I'll never forget what you said, 'Lily, what did you think? Am I a champion or what?' Like you were in slow motion, you sat down on the grass and slumped over into a ball."

This time, I stare back at Lily wide-eyed. "I don't remember any of this." My stomach tosses. "Dad never let me hear the true story."

"Diego ran over, stretched you out, and put his jacket over you. Then he called 911. He was so calm. I held your hand and rambled on about something—anything to keep you awake. All Cameron did was run around dumping the booze. I thought the paramedics would never get there. Docia, I was so scared."

Lily's eyes fill with tears. Wow, she really cares about me. How stupid I've been.

"You rode in the ambulance with me, didn't you?"

Lily nods. "And Diego rode in the front with the driver. On the way, I called your dad from your phone. Your dad was livid. 'Who did this to her?' Then he screamed, 'It was that lowlife skateboarder Diego, wasn't it?' I told him no, but he didn't believe me. I didn't know what else to say—like he would've listened."

Joy continues to prop on the edge of the chair. "Did her dad ever ask if Docia was okay?"

Lily shakes her head. "Not until he got to the hospital."

Nice to know he was so concerned about me.

Lily reaches over and grabs my hand like she knows what's on my mind. "He screamed at everyone like some lunatic. 'What's wrong with her?' 'She's got to get back on the ice immediately.' 'I only want the best doctors in Houston working on my daughter!' Then he saw Diego in the waiting area. Came unglued and yelled like a maniac, 'Boy, get out of this hospital. You're not wanted here.'"

I gulp. "My dad said that?"

Lily nods, both hands gripping her cup. "Diego got up and left without a word."

Joy shakes her head. "Did Cameron come to the hospital?"

I already knew the answer. My eyes stop on the scar on my wrist. It will remind me of that day forever. The day I should have known better.

"No." Lily looks from the cup to my face.

Joy's recorder beeps off. That day in the hospital was when my life changed. Why didn't I realize it before now? It was the day Dad completely took over.

"I missed the whole summer of training. No more school every day. Or parties. Or hanging out with friends. Dad controlled my every move."

CHAPTER ELEVEN

From Lily's front seat, I think about dozens of better ways that horrible day at the lake could've turned out.

"You're quiet," Lily says.

"Out of words." I lean against the window and stare at the crumpled takeout bag on the floor. "I've never heard what happened after the accident. Going to the hospital. Cameron not showing up. My dad and Diego." I slump lower in the seat. "I was so focused on my recovery I never asked."

"All history, Docia."

"Don't be so sure." Trees fly by as the blocks pass. "Where are we headed? My house isn't this way."

"I know," Lily answers. "Just a quick detour before I take you home. It's time for a taste of normal life again."

"Oh yeah, where?"

"You'll see." Lily smiles.

This road is familiar. Traveled it millions of times. Then the neon Ice & Sports Center sign comes into view. "Nope, not the rink."

"For a minute." Lily turns into the parking lot. "It's only the afternoon public skate. Now that you're finally out of the house, it'll be fun to hang out." She reaches over and brushes my hair out of my face.

"Lily—" Two little girls bound out of an SUV with their skate bags toward the entrance. "That's okay, I'll wait in the car."

"Come on. You *have* to come in. For me? I want to introduce you to my friend who works here now. He's great."

I squirm in the seat at the thought of seeing the ice again. *That* ice. Where I've spent half of my life. "Why didn't you mention your new guy?"

And of all places, why does he have to work at the rink?

"You know about him now," Lily answers through the car just before she slams the door closed. "Come on! We won't stay long. Promise."

We cross the parking lot. I'm just a visitor here—no lesson, no competition to prepare for, no pre-dawn freestyle session. My arm is light without my skate bag. Inside the front door, three little girls look at me and then at each other. One of them points, and another runs over, giggling. Her eyes are huge.

"You're the skater from here that's on TV; Docia from the Olympics."

One of the others follows. "Can I have your autograph?"

My stomach clinches. Why did they have to recognize me?

"Umm, sure." Lily hands me a pen from her purse and grabs a skating lesson schedule from the counter. "What's your name?"

"Stephanie," the girl answers. I write her name on the paper and my usual message, "Always jump your highest! Docia Sikorsky," with my signature figure eight underneath.

"They idolize you!" Lily whispers. By then, a small crowd has gathered. Little hands reach out with paper and skates.

Voices come from every direction, "What was it like to be at the Olympics?" "How did you learn to skate so good?"

Chills travel down my back. They don't care I ended up a loser!

A mother approaches and takes her daughter's hand. "You don't want her autograph, Kimmie. She's a fake," the mom says.

The woman never looks at me, but the bright smile on the tiny blonde girl's face fades and she continues to stare back at me as her mother leads her away. She looks like I ripped her little heart out. I know how that feels.

"Ma'am, she's no fake!" Lily yells after the woman. "She's your national champion and the Olympic gold medalist."

I can always count on Lily.

The noise from the rink is so loud the other girls don't notice.

I force a happy face and sign more autographs, pretending like nothing happened until the crowd thins out.

"Let's watch the skaters." Lily grabs my hand and pulls me to the bleachers. My stomach twists tighter. "Those little girls are in awe of you." Lily reaches her arm around my shoulders and squeezes gently as we sit. "Don't pay attention to what that woman said. What a witch. She's jealous her daughter won't accomplish half of what you have."

People skate around the rink in an orderly oval. The order my life used to have. Lena leads a group of kids in matching green tee-shirts onto the ice, the foster kids who skate here every week. A tiny bit of normalcy.

"Will your dad let you help Lena with the foster kids once skating season ends?"

"No. He thinks it's a waste of my time." Maria, my favorite, bursts ahead of everyone. "Who knows? What Dad thinks didn't stop me before. Working with them is so amazing."

"I knew you'd like being back here—especially with the kids you enjoy so much. You just needed a little push."

Maybe she's right. Jump back in. The knots in my stomach twist even more at the thought. I don't know what to expect. That's what makes it so scary.

The song ends and a voice comes across the PA system. "We have a celebrity in the house today—reigning World Champion and Olympic competitor, our own Docia Sikorsky, is in the bleachers. Let's hear a round of applause!"

The voice is Jack, the grandpa-like man with the sweet face who drives the Zamboni and announces during public sessions. Heads turn. *I wish the bleachers would swallow me.*

Lily elbows me in my side. "Stand up, Docia!"

I do as I'm told and wave at everyone. They applaud and cheer, and someone yells "She's still our champion!" The foster kids wave, and Lena nods up at me. Some people go on with what they are doing and pay no attention to the rest of the crowd. A few get up and walk away.

I sit back down next to Lily. If only I could fade into the crowd.

"They think I'm a loser. A fake like that woman said."

She pulls me closer. "Don't be silly. You can never make everyone happy, so ignore those people. How about the cheers from everyone else?"

"They're just being nice. Can we go now?"

I've considered the rink home for most of my life. Now it's foreign. The foster kids must experience something like this—stuck somewhere between wherever they came from with no idea where they're going. No sense of who they are or what they can be.

Lily grabs both of my hands. "Listen to me, Docia. You did nothing wrong. You worked hard to win Worlds and the Olympics. You deserve to be a champion. You *are* a champion."

I stare at the worn bleacher floor to escape her convincing eyes. "I don't feel like one."

"Believe me, only a champion could do what you've done."

Lily can't motivate me this time. She lets go of my hands and waves across the room.

"Your hot guy?" I glance over my shoulder and try to forget the whole scene. Then I see the curly black ponytail that can only be Diego's. He hands someone a pair of skates over the rental counter. I turn back around as quickly as I can before he sees me. "That's Diego!"

"I know." Lily grins. "He works here now."

"So, where's your guy? Everyone else seems to know we're here."

Lily wrinkles her nose like she does when she wants something. "Well, he's not actually my guy."

"You brought me here to see Diego? I can't face him. Not now. He hates me." I head down the steps in the opposite direction, ducking behind the bleachers. "I want to go home."

Lily follows close behind. "How do you know he hates you if you won't speak to him?"

My eyes are glued to the ground. *I would hate me.*

"Docia, stop!" I walk through the exit and toward the car where Lily grabs my arm. "You can't hide forever. It's time to face this."

"You don't understand." Heat rises to my cheeks and the tears start. Lily puts her arms around me, and I manage to speak between sobs. "I don't know what to do."

CHAPTER TWELVE

Violent shaking rouses me. "Docia. Wake up! Docia! You're supposed to catch up on your schoolwork."

I half open my eyes to see Mom, hands on hips. "Go away. Asleep." I squeeze the sofa pillow I hugged since Lily dropped me off.

"Not anymore." She clicks the lamp switch on and I feel the outside chill when she sits on the edge of the sofa. "Mr. Fuentes called when you didn't send your assignment. What's going on? You know those assignments need to be in before we leave for New York."

Why does she have to be the only mom who still keeps a perky tone even when I'm in trouble? I bury my face in the corner of the sofa cushions to shield my eyes from the lamplight.

"You can't disappoint him."

"My interview with Joy went long, and I forgot. I'll send it tomorrow."

"They've already made exceptions for you to not go to school every day." Mom leans over and strokes my hair. "Any more late assignments and he might give up on his star student."

Yeah, right. I'm not star anything anymore. I pop up on the sofa and stand with the blanket wrapped around me. "Let him give up on me." I walk toward the stairs. "Everyone else has."

"Docia, we're in the middle of a conversation." Her tone is no longer cheery. "Why did you talk to Joy again without mentioning it to me?" I continue up the stairs. "Don't make me tell your father."

"Go ahead." I stop on the landing. "What can he do?"

"He's trying to help you." Her voice switches from authoritative to desperate. "He's still your father. He cares about you."

"Funny way to show it."

"That's not fair, Docia. He has given up so much for you."

"Yeah, like what? And ruined my life in the process. You're not even my real parents. I'll find them so you don't have to worry about me anymore."

There's no usual cheerful response. In fact, Mom says nothing. Her mouth goes from gaping open to shut. The muscles in her face tighten when she clamps her teeth together. Then she walks away, leaving me looking down from the top of the stairs.

I slam my door, lie on my bed, and squeeze my stuffed penguin, Fred. The fiery orange sun peers through my window and hovers above the horizon. As it slips away, the words Lily said as we left the rink replay in my head. "It's time to face this."

How can I? I've done nothing on my own. Mom tells me when to study, when to eat, when to sleep. Lena makes every skating decision—when to practice and how long, ballet, strength training, programs, music. And Dad's like a symphony conductor who directs it all. He tells me what to think, who to trust, what to strive for. I always do as I'm told. When I do, everyone's happy.

They lied to me. Ripped away everything I knew. My parents. My country. Everything I am. They left me on a giant empty stage for everyone to stare at. The imaginary crowd laughs at me, "Look at the fake. What a freak!"

I squeeze Fred as an ache sets into the pit of my stomach. How do I know who to trust anymore? Who can help me show I did nothing wrong? Prove I'm not an imposter?

•　　•　　•

I open my eyes to see the sunset has transformed into clear dark blue. Stars scatter across the sky like lit birthday candles waiting for someone to make a wish and blow them out.

Olympic gold has been my birthday wish since I can remember. Every year, Dad asks, "What'd you wish, Docia?" I always answer, "If I tell you, it won't come true."

My dream came true, for a few minutes at least. After all the birthday candles, now I find out it wasn't even my birthday. *The joke's on me.*

I peer down the hallway and start down the stairs in pitch darkness. In the kitchen, Mom's phone shows a message. I press play and hear, "Hi Adele. It's Kimberly. I'm afraid I have bad news. Your trip to New York City day-after-tomorrow is canceled. The programs' producers say they had to get other guests on ahead of you. Oh, and next week's photo shoot for the new endorsement is on hold. Hope to have better news next time. The agency's in your corner. Can you please pass this along to Docia with my regrets? Take care."

I poke the erase button—again—and spot an open bottle of wine on the counter. "Of course they don't want a fake champion."

I should be used to messages like this by now. I look toward Mom's closed bedroom door. She washes down sleeping pills with wine every night and is always out 'til morning. Maybe a little wine will wash my problems away too.

I grab the bottle and take a big swig then hit play on the recording of the Olympic free skate programs. The red liquid tickles my taste buds and warms my chest as it slides down my throat. "Wow, they're all good."

I watch program after program and drink the wine. Even "that little thing from China," as Dad says, is more graceful than he thinks.

A drop trickles down my chin that I wipe away with the back of my hand. "The judges picked me! *I'm* the Olympic champ!"

I fast-forward through my program and giggle at the cartoon-like jumps and spins. The silly audience claps to the music and my fast-motion bows make me laugh out loud. I hit play to slow the recording to normal speed when I see myself clasping both hands over my mouth. I can still hear the announcer's voice, *"This year's Olympic gold medalist is Docia Sikorsky!"*

The empty wine bottle I set on the coffee table wobbles and rolls to the floor in slow motion.

"I have to tell Joy right now. I *am* the Olympic champ!"

As I stand, the room twirls around me like when I first I learned how to do a scratch spin. I grab the sofa arm to steady myself.

"Okay, I'm good." I focus on the coffee table and reach for my phone. I scan through my contacts and hit dial. A man's voice says "Hello?"

"Oh, hi, is this Joy's phone?" A nervous giggle comes out.

"Yes, this is Steve, her husband. Is this Docia?"

"Ha! How did you know?"

"Your name popped up when the phone rang."

"Oh yeah." I laugh again. "Will you tell Joy I'd like to speak with her? Please?"

"Docia, are you okay?" Joy says. "Do you realize what time it is?"

"Sure, it's nighttime. I need to tell you something."

"Can it wait until tomorrow?"

"Uhm, no. I need to tell you now...because I totally forgot to mention it this morning."

"You're slurring, Docia. Have you been drinking?"

"Just a little wine while I watched the Olympic performances."

"Do you want to entirely end your career?" Joy asks.

My grin falls into a pout. She sounds like Lily the last time I almost ended my career.

"No, I want to tell you something. It'll help your story."

"It can wait. What's gotten into you? This is so unlike the Docia I know."

"I just want to tell you I'm the Olympic champ. I really am. I watched the programs from Moscow again. They gave me the medal. They picked *me*!" I point at myself, even though she can't see me.

"You're right, they picked you, Docia."

"Then why did my agent call to say my appearances are canceled?" The euphoria turns to sorrow, and the tears start. "Why don't they want me?"

Joy sighs. "Docia, let all this blow over. You'll feel better after you get some sleep."

I lean my head back on the sofa and close my eyes, the glimmer of the gold medal burned into my retinas.

CHAPTER THIRTEEN

The wine bottle that rolled off the coffee table is gone but my stomach churns a reminder. I rub my throbbing head. How did I get here?

"Joy." I exhale a deep breath and hope the pounding will leave with it. What did I say to Joy—her husband? "Oh my god, I'm so embarrassed."

I swing my sock-covered feet over the side of the sofa as my first step to facing the world. Sitting up takes more effort than three back-to-backs. And my head. I close my eyes to rest before I pull myself all the way to standing.

"Need water." I drag my feet across the floor to the kitchen and hold my stomach to will the hurt away.

The cool liquid quenches my dry mouth and I fall into a chair. "Ouch!" I pull my phone out of my back pocket and lay my head on the kitchen table to steady the room. The vegetable-shaped hands on the clock above the window show almost seven o'clock. In my old life, I would've been skating for more than an hour already. The thought of the grueling schedule makes the room move even faster.

Mom's door is closed. Good, she's still asleep. I close my eyes and wonder what kind of idiot I made of myself last night.

My phone flashes.

On way over...with coffee

Lily? This early? I bury my face in my folded arms and try to figure out how to face another day until a tap on the front door disturbs my rest.

It takes two blinks to clear my eyes when Lily walks in loaded with coffee. "It *is* you. Why so early?"

"Some of us have to go to school." Lily blows an air kiss and walks to the kitchen. "Sorry, hands full. Joy texted me about what happened last night. I was worried," she whispers. "Is your mom up?"

"I don't think so. She's in her sleeping pill stupor again." I stop at the edge of the kitchen and watch Lily juggle the three cups over the countertop. "Wait. Why were you worried? I'm fine."

"Because Joy said you sounded drunk." Lily shakes her head. "I remember what happened the last time you got drunk."

"Yeah, so. This time I have a reason. It's another day in Loserville with nothing to do but think about everything I've lost. Kind of getting used to it."

"What if your mom finds out?"

"She won't." I step back and wrap my arms around myself. "What would she do? She does the same thing."

Lily tilts her head. "All the more reason for you not to."

We both stop and gawk at my mother in her bathrobe with dripping hair. "Well, good morning, girls. I didn't realize there was a party for breakfast. What's the occasion?"

Mom's eyes meet my wide-eyed stare while my heart pounds a fast rhythm. "Lily brought us coffee."

"How sweet. Maybe this is a good omen for my interview this morning. Investment firm jobs are pretty scarce these days since all the big scandals," Mom takes the warm cup from Lily. "What a nice way to ease into the day."

Lily looks at me and my eyes shoot to the floor. If Mom gets wind of what I did last night now, it'll wreck her interview.

"Why are y'all looking at each other so funny? What's going on?" Mom sits and takes a sip of her coffee. She glances at Lily and back at me. "Docia?"

Two sets of eyes burn into me. I take a quick breath. *What do I do? What do I say? Or rather, what do I* not *say?* "It's nothing. Lily thinks I need to get out. See people."

"She's right honey. You do. And you also need to get back on the ice." She gives me a wrinkled forehead mom look and heads to her room. "Well, as much as I enjoy the company, I need to get dressed. Thanks for the coffee, Lily."

Lily glares back at me behind Mom's back. "Good luck with your interview, Mrs. Sikorsky."

"Thanks. I need it." Her voice trails off.

After Mom pulls her door closed, Lily grabs my hand. "What are you doing? I'm worried about you."

"I'll be fine." My eyes drop to the floor again. "As soon as I figure out what the hell to do to fix all this." We sit in silence while I search my empty brain for ideas. A place to start, at least.

"I do need to worry about you since *you* don't seem to." Lily plops into a chair. "I've been thinking. Joy's a journalist. She must have contacts. She knows where to go for information and what questions to ask. Since she covers international skating, she probably knows some people in Russia. Maybe she can help you sort out this fake adoption thing."

My eyes brighten. "You think so?"

"It can't hurt to ask. It sounds like your parents could use some help."

Lily's right on all counts. My mind wakes up for the first time since I've been home. "First, I need my birth certificate and adoption papers." I pace across the kitchen. "But how do we get hold of this alleged birth certificate they talked about in Moscow?"

"I don't know, but we'll figure it out." She lifts her arms for a hug. "I know things will get better."

A rush travels through me and I raise my hands. "Please don't hug me or I'll totally come unglued."

Lily stops. "Okay. I'll save it for later."

"I need to be strong." I stand up straighter. "And learn to be on my own."

Instead of a hug, Lily squeezes my shoulders. "You *are* strong, Docia. It's just... your dad hasn't given you a chance. Now that he's away, you can prove it. You can show them how tough you are."

I swallow Lily's words and think about all the god-awful choices my parents have made for me. If I can't trust them, who's left? I take a deep breath and exhale.

Mom slips out of her room and walks to the garage.

"Bye Mom," I call after her. "Good luck."

She responds with a weak, "See you later."

I need to be tough for Mom and me. "I hope she gets this job," I say softly. "Without my endorsements, we need the money." Then the sound of my phone startles me. Lily and I both look down at the caller ID to see Lena's name.

It continues to ring.

"Maybe answer?"

I stare at the phone and take shallow breaths at the thought of speaking to Lena, the woman who's like a grandmother to me. I know what she wants. The thought of it scares the hell out of me.

"I'll call her back." I think it's the truth.

Lily puts her hands on her hips. "You *can* get back on the ice, you know. It might help."

My head tells me Lily's right, but so much has changed.

"Do you think a few days and a little misunderstanding will make you forget how?"

How does she always know what's in my head?

"I promise I'll call her. Really. I'll talk to Joy too."

Lily grabs her keys and phone. "I've got to get to cheer practice, or I'll be in the biggest trouble. I'm behind you, Docia. Whatever you need." She starts to hug me again but stops herself. "Text you later?"

"Thanks, Lily."

She jogs down the sidewalk to her car while I think about Lena and what she must be going through. Coaching me has filled so much of her life. Now I'm stuck. Not able to compete. What will I say to her? What about Mom and Dad? They count on the endorsements. How will we get by?

CHAPTER FOURTEEN

I sink into the sofa and stare at the message notification from Lena on the screen. I know she wants me back on the ice—like today. After that disastrous visit to the rink, I can't. Not yet. If I tell her why, she'll say I'm ridiculous.

I dial Joy's number. If I can fix the mess, I'll skate again.

"Hi, Docia." Joy's voice reminds me of what an idiot I made of myself last night.

"Joy, hi. I, uh…" I know precisely why I'm calling but can't get the words out. "I…uhm…want to apologize…uhh that I bothered you and your husband last night.

"I understand, Docia. You've had a rough week."

The understatement of the year. "And, uhm, I have a giant favor to ask."

"Certainly, Docia. Ask me anything."

"Lily and I wondered if you could use your contacts to help me dig into this adoption scandal. Maybe figure out the truth?"

Then silence. Oh god, I must have said something horrible last night. "Joy? You there?"

"Yes. I'm sorry. Of course, I'll help."

"It won't be much—some of your reporter connections might dig up these Russian records. Maybe who's behind it?"

"I'll do whatever it takes, Docia. Everyone deserves to know the truth." Joy sighs. "You see, I was also adopted. I never found my birth parents. That's why I'm honored to help you."

Now I feel like a selfish kid. "Wow, I had no idea."

"It's fine. Really. Not being able to find my roots is one reason I became a reporter. I've had a long time to get past it."

Wow, she truly understands.

"I think I know who to call to get the ball rolling. Let's work on it together. Maybe Lily too?"

"She's already all over it." Then my stomach fills with dread. "Wait, what if we prove they're right? What if I am ineligible? What will I do then?" I sink further into the cushions. *Can I trust Joy?*

"Don't go there yet. If they are right, we'll deal with the news the right way."

I hear her words, but my stomach still flutters. "Thanks, Joy." I hope she doesn't let me down like everyone else has. "Can you promise me one thing?"

"What's that?"

"Please don't mention this to my parents. At least until there's something concrete?"

"Docia—" Joy answers.

"It's important. I don't want them to screw this up too."

"Okay, we'll call it research for the article. I'll trust you to decide when to tell them. I'll make a few calls. Let you know what I find out."

"Thank you, Joy."

"We'll get to the bottom of this, Docia."

Even though I can't see her smile, I feel it.

I lay my head back and close my eyes.

My phone startles me from a deep sleep. I answer with a groggy "Hello?" and hear Lena's voice.

"Time to get back on the ice, sweet Docia."

"Hi, Lena."

"We meet at the rink tomorrow. You must not lose your conditioning."

Nope, even Lena can't bring my confidence back. "A few more days and I'll be ready."

"No, no, no. Must not wait. Worlds are soon and you must be ready."

"Why?" I pace. "I'm not eligible to compete."

"Because you will be. I know you will compete."

A sharp pain hits my gut like someone planted their fist in it. Why does everyone refuse to admit I'm a loser? "Come on, Lena. Do you not remember what happened?"

"It will pass."

"Thanks for your optimism. I don't know when I can get back out there."

"Tomorrow, Docia. Must be tomorrow. My Docia does not question."

"No. I'm sorry Lena. Not yet. I'll call you. I'll be ready soon." I end the call and slam my phone down on the back of the sofa before Lena has a chance to say anything else.

I'm not her "sweet Docia" anymore. My face is on fire.

"Why does everyone have to tell me what to do?" I pace from one end of the living room to the other. "They always butt in. Can't they let me figure things out for a change?"

The stack of books on the kitchen table catches my eye. "I'll show them!"

I yank the calculus book out of the pile and slap it open to the bookmark. No one needs to ride my butt and tell me when to study, when to skate. They treat me like I'm some three-year-old who doesn't know when to eat and sleep.

The garage door opens just as I finish the last problem. *Great. Here comes the next set of orders.* I keep my head down in my book and mentally dare Mom to tell me what to do.

Instead, she's quiet. No perky greeting. She doesn't even prance over like she usually does to see what I'm up to.

"Hey. How'd it go?" I ask, head still down, but I sneak a glance.

"Fine."

Since when does Mom give one-word answers?

She takes off her shoes and jewelry at the little desk on the edge of the kitchen like always when she first gets home. This time, there's no smile. No pleasantries.

"So, do you think you'll get the job?"

"Maybe," she answers as she takes food out of the fridge and clanks utensils.

"Do you want it? Tell me about what you'd do on this job."

Silence.

"Come on, Mom. I know there's more to say than maybe."

"I'll have to see what your dad thinks when we talk to him in the morning."

She stops and stares at the pile of food on the counter. Almost like a fairy flew over with a blanket of happy dust, her grin reappears. "Of course. I'd love to get this job. It would be great experience."

Where did that attitude change come from?

"The break from work has been nice, but considering our situation, if your father was home things would be better—more back to norm—"

"Normal? Better how?" I slam my book closed and walk into the kitchen to face her. "Wake up, Mom. He's the reason my career's in the toilet. He's why we're broke."

Her happy face fades and she goes back to peeling carrots.

I fold my arms so tight across my chest my breath goes shallow. Mom continues to whack at the carrot until there's just a tiny stick left. Then I see it. A tear.

She stops, backs into a corner, frozen for a moment in an empty stare. The carrot peeler clanks on the tile floor. She slides slowly down the cabinets, and tears flow.

"Docia, I *have* to get a job. This job. *Some* job. We have no income." Her tears turn to sobs. "We have to eat. We have to pay the mortgage."

I wrap my arms around her and we sit on the floor rocking together.

CHAPTER FIFTEEN

Mom finally lifts her head off my shoulder. Black streaks paint her porcelain cheeks. I brush them away with a kitchen towel. "We need to get you some waterproof mascara."

The corners of her mouth curve into a slight smile. "When did my little girl get so grown up?"

I shrug. "You don't have to be an adult to realize we need income to survive. Someone has to make money if I'm not." She looks like she's still waiting for my real answer. Does she want the real answer?

"I grew up when I got tired of everyone telling me what to do."

"What do you mean?"

"What and when to eat. When to study. When to skate. What to wear. What to think."

Mom reaches her hand out and touches my cheek. "That's what made you a champion."

"Not everything turned out so great."

"Docia, I'm not sure you understand everything—"

"I'm not finished, Mom. I want to make my own decisions. I may screw up, but they'll be my messes. I'll be the only one to blame."

"I understand, sweetie." She looks up at the happy expressions that stare back from the family photo on the desk. "I'm not sure your dad will know what to do if he's not directing. He'll need time to adjust."

"Dad will have to get used to it. I'm not a puppy that grows up but stays by its master's side for life."

Mom looks into my eyes, hers still glistening with tears. "I'll see what I can do, but you'll have to be patient with us." She cups my chin in her palm. "Oh, and I saw the empty wine bottle. Pull that again and your independence will be cut very short."

•   •   •

I watch the minutes change on the digital clock next to my bed and hope my eyes will feel heavy again. Five-o-eight...five-o-nine...the time Dad always got me up for the first freestyle session every day. The moon shines a spotlight on my skate bag. "This is ridiculous. If I can't sleep, I'll skate."

I tiptoe to the garage and grab Dad's keys. *I can do this.*

The car almost steers itself along the route I've ridden to the rink hundreds of times. I turn into the deserted parking lot and drive next to the still-dark neon sign to the side of the building. Jack told me once after running the Zamboni how he catches kids sneaking into the rink through the boy's bathroom window, so I park near the spot.

My skate bag barely squeezes through the shrubs. I jimmy open the loose window and drop my bag onto the floor inside. Then reach my leg through the opening, kick the toilet seat down, and plant my feet on it. I'm out of the stall now, so the worst part's over.

Outside the boy's dressing room, I stop in the dark rink and breathe in that damp, musty, beautiful smell. I follow the hallway around and reach up to flip the big switch. Soft lights hit the ice and catch the gentle morning fog that hovers a few inches above the surface. The compressor hums in the background.

I sit on the bench and take my skates out like I've done thousands of times. While one skate rests on my lap, I remember the day Diego gave me the green caterpillar soakers for good luck before sectionals in Chicago two years ago. That day was a lifetime ago.

Am I ready?

I pull the soakers off the blades and shove my feet into the boots. Then I methodically lace them like Lena taught me when I was little. The pristine white leather is still polished for the Olympic performances. "Ready as I'll ever be."

I slip the skate guards on each blade and hop on the rubber-covered floor to get the feel of the boots again. The quiet rink comforts me. It's more welcoming since it's empty.

Instead of sprinting onto the rink right into fast warm-up laps, I step onto the glassy surface and make a smooth arc on my outside edge. No matter what happens, I'll be okay.

I speed up into crossovers in s-patterns around the rink. The cool air whips by my face. My muscles awaken one at a time with the memory of each movement. I turn to skate backward in the same s-pattern to follow the choreographed warm-up I always do. I automatically move into position and sweep my right leg forward to start a series of perfectly arced waltz jumps. My tension falls away. Even I can do the easiest jump well.

Next, I set up for a single Axel. I pull my shoulders around and then lead with my right hip. When my feet leave the ice, I hear Lena's voice in my head. *"Check landing Docia! Chin up!"* I wind up for a scratch spin. Then a sit spin and a layback. After each spin, I check the pattern my blades make to be sure I've stayed centered. It works so far.

With a little more confidence, I build speed for my signature triple Lutz. Set up for the blind entry, reach my foot back, and plant my toe pick in the ice. My body turns and feet leave the ice. It's not enough. I pop it, rotating out of the jump. Not even a decent single.

I lap the rink and pull the bottom of my cami up to wipe the sweat on my forehead.

You can do this. Concentrate.

Again, I stretch my leg back. My body follows my hip into the jump, pulling in tight to complete the almost three revolutions. I fall short. A little off edge and land on my butt.

"Crap!" I slide across the ice. My voice echoes back at me against the cold, gray walls.

I crawl back up and glide over to the boards jiggling my legs to shake out the hurt. Lena's voice still resonates in my head, "Relax. Let body do jump."

I catch my reflection in the scratched Plexiglas that surrounds most of the rink. Her words run through my head again and again. "Concentrate leetle *solnyshko*. Concentrate."

I've always been Lena's little sunshine. What would she think now?

I lap the rink and begin the step sequence from my free skate into the triple Lutz. Stick the landing. Don't be a loser. I repeat the same mistake and fall again on the same hip. The pain shoots up my side as I skid across the ice until my legs collide with the boards.

Heat rises to my face. I've lost it. A champion would never skate like this. They're right.

"I'm a fake!" I slump like a rag doll and stare blankly at the scratched boards that outline the rink and let the frigid ice numb my sore hip and broken pride.

A gentle touch on my shoulder startles me. When I turn, Diego is squatting next to me. "You okay?"

I casually wipe my face and hope he thinks the tears are sweat. "I'm fine. How long have you been here?"

Of all the people to show up and see my epic failures, it has to be Diego.

"Not long. I open the rink for the six o'clock freestyle session before school."

The giant clock on the wall shows about ten minutes before the rink opens. Coaches and skaters are the last people I want to see after such a disastrous skate, so I plant my legs underneath me and start to pull myself up. Halfway to standing, a pain shoots from my hip down my leg, so I reach for the boards.

Diego extends his hand.

"I can do it. You think I've never fallen before?"

Why did I say that to him?

"I know you can." He turns and walks across the rink. "You can do anything."

His words leave me frozen.

I glide across the rink and step off while the clock hands move closer to the start of the freestyle session. I yank at my laces and pull my skates off so I can slip out through the boy's dressing room.

"You don't have to climb out the window," I hear from the other side of the wall. "Front door's unlocked."

I peer around the corner and catch Diego's eye. "Thanks."

He smiles that smile. The one like I'm the only thing in his world. Then he goes back to clearing last night's rental skates off the counter. Checking pairs. Wrapping laces.

Like everything's the way it was before.

CHAPTER SIXTEEN

I feel more defeated as I drive toward the sliver of dawn that peeps over the horizon. The rink shrinks in my rearview mirror. More cars surround me as people start their days. Everyone else gets up in the morning knowing where to go and what to do. I drive to spend another day alone in a house.

The house where that fraud girl and her fake family live.

Diego makes me feel like everything will be okay no matter how bad things get. He still believes I can do anything.

I slip into the kitchen and ruffle my hair to look like I just rolled out of bed. I sip a glass of orange juice and open *Sense and Sensibility* to the next chapter. A little after seven o'clock, Mom opens her door and shuffles out.

"Oh, you're up?" she says.

"Yeah."

"And studying? Already?" She scoops coffee beans into the grinder. "That's the Docia I know."

Yeah, right, I'll never be her again. The rumble from the grinder gives me the few seconds I need to compose myself.

"We're still talking to Dad this morning, right?"

"Yeah, between seven-thirty and eight. He'll be happy to see you with your schoolwork."

"Whatever." I eye her nightgown. "Uhm, we're on camera, right?"

"It's just your dad. Oh, you're right. It's already afternoon there. Be back."

As soon as she closes the bedroom door, I text Joy. *Will talk to my dad soon. Anything I should ask?*

I watch the screen for her answer. *Which Russian agency did he work with on your adoption? And good luck.*

"Much better." Mom slips out of her room, dressed this time. "I hope your dad's made some progress so he can come home soon. There's so much to do here to get you back on course."

Like I give a crap what course he wants me on. Mom pours more coffee.

"I'll take some." If only it were something stronger than coffee.

Mom shakes her head. "I swear. I go to sleep one night and wake up to a different daughter every morning these days. When did you start drinking coffee every day?"

Where's she been?

"Mom, since I started going to coffee shops."

"Look at the clock, it's time to call your dad," Mom interrupts and reaches for her laptop. "Will you start the session? I'll be back in a sec."

She reappears from her bedroom donned with tangerine lipstick.

"It's trying to connect." I motion for her to squeeze into the chair at the kitchen table with me.

"It'll be so good to see his face. It's been too long." Her hands quiver. "There he is! Jerry? Can you see us? Jerry? Can you hear us?"

"Yes, loud and clear. It's good to see you both. Docia, how's my favorite girl?"

"I'm good, Dad. How are you?"

"I'm okay. I'm so ready to get away from these idiots. I miss my girls."

"We miss you too, honey," Mom says. "Are they still treating you well? Do you have what you need?" The screen freezes and Mom looks at the keyboard and then at me. "Jerry, you there?"

"Yes, yes, I'm here. They treat me fine, but I still can't get my passport back."

"Your passport? When did that happen? Why?" When I glare at Mom, her eyes get bigger, and she shrugs.

"It's nothing." Dad shakes his head. "These people haven't a clue what they're doing or who they're messing with."

Mom squirms on her half of the chair. "The State Department says they're working on it. I'll call again today."

"Can you push harder? I'm ready to leave so I can get things back into shape at home. If I were trying to get you home from this God-forsaken place, I'd already have you on a plane."

Mom lowers her eyes to the floor. He's such a jerk.

"I'm trying—" Mom says.

Dad's face wrinkles as his voice grows louder. "There's got to be more you can do, Adele."

Mom sinks back in her chair and says nothing.

"Dad, what's happened since we left Moscow? What do they tell you?"

"Not a damn thing. They just say they have some proof that your adoption wasn't legal. They haven't produced a thing."

"Who's in charge of adoption over there? Who did you work with to get me?"

"It was a representative from an orphanage and some lawyer. I can't find either of them."

"So, who has the supposed proof?"

"Someone from the Ministry of Education and Science, but I'm not sure he even exists. I can't get him on the phone, and he's never in the office."

"What's his name?"

"Dimitri Bogachev—with a b."

I write the information on my English Lit notes.

"Peanut, why are you asking these questions?"

I squirm in the chair. "Dad don't call me that. Remember Joy, the reporter I told you about? She's helping figure this out. I am too."

"I'll take care of things, and your adoption records are no business of hers. Why are you involved when you should focus on your skating? Is Lena getting you ready for Worlds?"

"Yeah, we'll start this week, but—"

"But what?"

Now's the time I wish we were on a phone so he can't see me.

"Come on, Dad. You know the chances I'll go to Worlds are pretty slim."

Dad's face goes stern. "Docia, never talk that way. Those morons will reinstate you and you'll be at the top of the podium again where you belong. You train like I've taught you so you are ready." He shakes his head and clenches his jaw. "I wish I was there to keep you motivated."

He couldn't "keep" me anything except for more annoyed.

Mom reaches over and squeezes my knee. "Honey, I'll keep her motivated until you're back safe and sound. Get home soon. The attorney is making the right connections over there to get your passport back to you."

"I certainly hope so. Do I have to do everything? Docia has got to get back on top where a champion belongs."

"I know, dear. He says it should be a few more days." Mom blows him a kiss.

"So, was I bred to be a champion too? Is that why you picked me all the way over in Russia?"

Mom looks up at me. Her mouth gapes open.

"Docia, you will not speak to me that way. Ever." The shrill scrape as he pushes his chair backward echoes through the speakers. "What's going on there? Clearly, everything's fallen apart."

I pop out of my chair and lean toward the camera, so my face fills the lens. "Yeah, and *you* started it all. You made up my entire history. When did you decide to keep the truth from me?"

"Docia, sit down and shut your mouth," Dad barks back.

"Not this time." I walk away like I wish I had done a long time ago but stop and lean on the wall around the corner to hear his reaction.

There's a long silence until I hear Dad speak. "Adele, get rid of that reporter."

"Honey, it's okay. She's been fantastic with Docia. I think it's been good for her to tell her story."

"What? Tell her story? I forbid Docia to speak to that woman again. I'll go directly to the Embassy to straighten this mess out once and for all. I'll get myself on a flight tomorrow. I've got to get back there before you let everything I've worked so hard to create fall completely apart."

Silence.

CHAPTER SEVENTEEN

How stupid was I to let Dad play me my whole life? I slide down the wall out of Mom's sight and bury my face in my hands. I was just a dumb kid. How could I have known?

When I look up, Mom is standing in front of me, arms folded. Her face is twisted into a scowl like I've never seen.

"Oh stop, Mom."

We lock stares.

I walk upstairs. "Dad's so dramatic."

Mom doesn't say a word, but her stare burns into my back.

My frown glares back from the dresser mirror and my history book stares up at me. *What's with everyone?* I pound the middle of the cover with a clenched fist. *I'm the one whose whole life's been yanked away.* This time my scowl has an eerie resemblance to the last look on Mom's face.

I swipe the book off the dresser and collapse on the bed. Then I read all the way through next week's assignment until my phone beeps. I grab it and roll over onto my back to read Lily's text message.

On way to pick you up

K anywhere but rink, I respond. *All I need is more drama.*

I sit on the edge of my bed and take in the contents of my room. Medals. Trophies. Stuffed animals. Photographs. Everything's about skating. My whole life is skating.

Or was.

I fall backward, sink into the poufy comforter, and scramble to think of anything else I enjoy. One memory that doesn't involve skating.

I grab my wallet and tiptoe downstairs. The door's click when I open it breaks the dead silence in the house. I shout through the house at Mom, "I'm going out with Lily."

I sit on the curb at the end of the sidewalk and the sun's rays warm my face. Then I notice a silver car parked a few houses down. Something sticking out the window makes me focus closer. When I stand, the black thing that hung out the open window disappears. A camera lens? Heat rises to my head and pushes me toward the heap of junk.

"What do you think I am? I'm not some freak to photograph whenever you want!" As I jog down the middle of the street toward the car, the red brake lights illuminate and it lunges forward. "Leave me alone!" I holler into the trail of gray smoke from the tailpipe. My chest heaves as I catch my breath.

Lily pulls up, leaves the door open, and runs to me. "Are you okay?"

I back up. "No." I look down each end of the street to see if anyone else is lurking.

"Docia, what happened?"

"It was one of those paparazzi vultures." I point in the direction of where the car sat. "I can't even walk in my front yard without the world knowing." I fall to my knees on the grassy median. "Lily, everything's such a mess. Dad's pissed. Now Mom's unglued. I can't deal with it."

She kneels and wraps her arms around me. "Docia, that photographer just wants to make a buck off of you. It means noth—"

"But it does. I can see the headlines now. 'Skating has-been with nothing to do but sit on her front curb'."

Lily cradles my chin in her hands. "Who cares? Besides, I have good news. If you'll get your butt out of the middle of the street, I can tell you."

I reach for Lily's outstretched hand, and my anger cools.

"What are you waiting for? Get in the car."

I relax into the seat where it's safe. "I must look like a lunatic. I hope the photographer didn't catch me like this."

"Me too," Lily answers and starts down the street. "Waterproof mascara next time?"

I can't help but giggle since I just said the same thing to Mom. "Where are we headed? And please don't say the rink."

"No rink today. I promise."

"Then what's up with the goofy grin?"

"Joy and I dug up something I couldn't wait to show you. We'll grab a coffee at our place at the mall and I'll tell you all about it."

"Great. Another rink but with tons more people." I sink into the seat. "Do you have a disguise I can wear?"

Lily lets out one of her big laughs. "And cover up that beautiful face? You have nothing to hide. We're not going there for the rink."

I believe her, but I don't answer. She doesn't mention that we might run into fans or haters, but it could happen. It probably will. The dread takes over like a dress that's too tight.

"And after the good news, you can help me find an awesome new top for this weekend." Lily turns into the parking garage. "And you could use a new moisturizer to brighten up that beautiful face."

"See, everything's changed." I slam my wallet onto the car floor. "Shopping can't even help. If you don't find your awesome new top, you can borrow something of mine. I won't need them."

"Don't sit there. Mall. Now. Let's go." Lily reaches for my wallet and drags me across the parking lot and into the building. "Time to face the world again."

I groan. "So, what's this big news?"

"Well, Joy and I got hold of the document that got you disqualified."

"Document? What?" I turn my back to the line in the coffee shop and whisper. "Those people are staring at me."

"They should stare at you. You're a star," Lily says. "I learned about the document through my old coach. You know, she's friends but not really with Stacy's coach. Then Joy got hold of it with the help of her press credentials. It's a birth certificate." She clutches her purse to her heart. "And I have a copy with me."

"Mine?" I grab the two mugs of tea and walk to a table.

"That's what's so strange. It's in Russian, of course, but it's in such bad condition you can hardly read it. They say it's yours."

Lily pulls a folded piece of paper from an envelope in her purse and smooths the poor copy on the table. I try to decipher a phrase, a word, even a letter. "I have no idea what this says. All I can see is a bunch of faint Russian letters that run together."

"I know. Joy says it looks like an authentic birth certificate, but you can hardly read the mother's name. The birth date is smudged. The original is almost as bad."

"I lost a medal? My whole identity? Based on this? How do they know it's mine? And that the birthdate is even right? Especially if you can barely read it?"

"Exactly." Lily nods. "That's what we have to prove—that this document is wrong, and you are old enough to compete."

"And how do we do that?" I wave the foreign document in the air. "Everyone's already convinced I'm guilty."

Lily takes the paper and lays it on the table. "We dig. We ask questions. Find proof. All the stuff I'm learning in my journalism class."

"You're right. We don't take their word for it." I stare into my mug to look for answers in the tea leaves. "Thank you for your help, but who cares? It doesn't matter anymore."

I walk to the waist-high glass wall and peer over at the rink from my third-level vantage point. The sun shines through the glass ceiling and makes patterns on the bright white ice while little girls and boys in beginning skating classes learn bunny hop jumps and how to fall.

I don't see Lily walk up next to me, but I can feel her presence. A little blond girl in a white skating dress circles and aims to center her scratch spin in the middle of the pink, yellow, and purple flowers painted in the ice.

"Docia, we'll get your medal back."

"Thank you, Lily. I'll talk to Lena to see what she knows." My eyes move to the second level where shoppers cross in both directions toward their various missions. "Is this proof or a bunny trail? I'm not sure I can take another dead end."

"Maybe Lena can tell you *something*. She's known you almost as long as your parents."

As quickly as I forgot the hurt, it returned. "Yeah, which parents?"

"Remember our first lessons here?" Lily asks as she rests her elbows on the rails.

"How could I forget? It's where we met."

"I wonder where that coach ended up. We were a bunch of little kids, but he treated us like we were each the next champ."

"I know, right?" I look down on the rink and still see myself plowing through waltz jump after jump, trying to do the biggest one in the class. "He was so funny."

"Even before Lena came, I knew you'd be a star."

Engrossed by my drama, I notice a familiar red ponytail bounce near the rails on the second floor, Cameron is attached to her like Velcro. They stop. While she peers down at the rink, Cameron finds me and gazes over like he did that day at the lake. Those eyes used to seem sexy and mysterious. Now they remind me of a snake's beady stare. He blows a kiss that sucks the air out of my lungs.

Warm saliva fills my mouth while my stomach churns up the creamy tea and rejects its contents on the floor behind the concrete wall.

Lily grabs my elbow to steady me. "Docia, are you okay? What happened?"

"Cameron and Stacy." I dab my mouth and Lily follows my glance to where they stand. On top of Dad continuing to betray me and Mom doing nothing and paparazzi following me.

"Oh. Looks like he officially dumped Jennifer." She rolls her eyes. "Good thing you're so over him. I'll grab some water and something to clean that up."

Determination slowly replaces the heaviness in me. People are so wrapped up in new shoes and the latest phone they have no idea the guy looking over the second-floor railing almost ruined my career. The thought causes a burn so deep my chest feels hot to the touch. My bones and joints tense up like they have been replaced by steel rods. Wonder what he'll do to Stacy?

More people walk past. Do they have any idea what it's like to lose all that's important? To know everyone has lied to you just for fame? Like you're a piece of property? Your entire future hinges on a smudged piece of paper?

Do they care?

It's so out of control. Like when your Axel takeoff is completely wrong. Rotating in the air and anticipating the inevitable crash. The crash you hope to have the strength to pick yourself up from and keep moving. You fly through the air and know your landing will be off edge. Your butt hits and you slide wherever momentum takes you. There's nothing you can do until physics—or the boards—stop you. Sliding out of control through each day wondering what the next bombshell might be. When the next crash might happen. Trying every way you know to untie the knots in your stomach.

Your failure is in front of the entire world. They replay it on TV and all over the web and write about it in newspapers and magazines while reporters stick microphones in your face and ask stupid questions like "what were you thinking when you hit the ice?" and "how will you get over losing your medal?" and "will you continue to skate?"

Photographers chase you down and try to catch your tears in the prize-winning shot. Skating experts analyze. Reporters suspect the pressure of it all might make you crack. While you try to untie the twisted mess of lies the people you called your parents have told you your whole life. The people you trust without question. The teenage parents you thought gave you life didn't and the country you call home really isn't. The birthday you've celebrated forever is wrong and the only passion you know is out of reach because someone says you're not eligible.

They will know I'm still a champion.

CHAPTER EIGHTEEN

Lily shakes me to knock me out of my bizarre world then wraps her arms around me. "How did things get so off?"

"Don't know." Lily stares down at Cameron and Stacy. They're kissing like it is a performance for us.

"It's not just them. It's everything." I hug her tighter before I let go.

"I don't feel so much like shopping now. Nordstrom can't fix this one."

"Don't worry about it. Between our two closets, we'll find something." I try to make myself think about clothes and parties, but instead, I obsess over strange people huddled over smudged documents discussing my fate.

"You know what I want to do?" I rub my arms to help calm myself. "Figure out this birth certificate thing. I'm tired of avoiding this mess. It's my life and I want to fix it."

Lily's face shows that glimmer of hope that always fills me with courage so I grab her hand. "Let's go to Joy's."

•   •   •

"I don't think she's home," Lily rings the doorbell again.

Joy answers the door in jean cutoffs and no makeup with her glasses halfway off the top of her head. "Docia, Lily. Come in."

"I hope you don't mind that we stopped by," I say. "I'm so ready to get control of this mess."

"Not at all. Perfect timing. Come in. Have a seat. My editor's letting me focus on this story for now, and I found out more information." Joy sinks into a chair and catches her glasses as they slide off. "I believe others in Russia were involved in the adoption besides your birth mother. And it appears she was trying to defect to another country."

I devour every word. "Defect? Wow. Anything else?"

"That's all for now. I don't have names. I've hit a wall and could use your help." She slides her glasses to the top of her head. "We found that bad copy of the document they call your birth certificate, but nothing more."

"Yeah, I showed her," Lily says. "It's more confusing than helpful."

"I know. I emailed your dad. He told me to butt out and in a not very polite way."

"That's my dad. He only wants you to know what he wants you to know. Story of my life, but it's my life. I don't care what he says."

"Everyone over there wants cash for anything—a document or piece of information," Joy says. "Even to recommend another contact. The magazine doesn't have much budget to pay people for every little thing."

"Money?" I ask. "Pretty impossible to come by at my house these days." I slump down into the chair next to Joy. "This is hopeless. We should give up."

"We will not give up." Joy turns to hide her face. "There's got to be something."

"You okay?" Lily asks.

Joy nods and brushes a tear away. "Yeah. I'm fine."

"I hope those tears aren't for me. I'm definitely not worth crying over."

"Yes, you are, Docia" Joy says. "Everyone deserves to know the truth. We will figure this out for the sake of all adopted children who want to find their missing puzzle piece."

Now I feel like a selfish kid. "You're right, Joy. What can I do—that doesn't cost money?"

"Good question. I have a hunch Lena knows something—or at least she can point us to people who might. People who won't ask for stacks of cash. Do you think she would come here and talk to us?"

The scene after the medal ceremony replays. The stern look on the Olympic official's face, the mean man in the brown coat, Stacy, and her coach. Lena watching over it all.

"What do you think, Docia?" Joy asks.

"I think she will. She won't ask for money, but she'll use the opportunity to get me back on the ice."

Lily shakes her head. "Would that be so bad?"

"Yeah. Tragic." My stomach tumbles. "She'll realize all those years of coaching me were wasted when I fall on my butt on the simplest jumps."

"Docia, come on. You're the Olympic gold medalist," Lily says. Her brown eyes cover me with warmth. "You have to skate. You were *born* to."

Joy leans back in her chair. "What about Worlds?"

"Not as long as I'm suspended." My eyes drop to the floor. "But Lena wants me to be ready." After this morning's disastrous skate, there's no way I'll be ready—even if I am eligible. "Just in case." I fake the confident look again.

"That gives us a goal," Joy says with a warm smile. "Worlds is where you need to be."

Before I can talk myself out of it, I reach for my phone, dial Lena's number, and explain the situation.

As I expect, Lena answers without hesitation. "If you want me to talk, you must skate. I will come now, then you practice after studies are finished tomorrow."

A chill travels down my spine as I think about what we might learn from Lena. "Okay, I'll skate tomorrow. We will see you in a minute."

Lily and Joy trade smiles.

Why does everyone else believe in me?

"What's wrong, Docia?" Joy's happy expression fades. "What did your thoughts go?"

"Oh, sorry. I was back on the podium with the Olympic gold," I lie. "That was my goal. I never looked beyond..." My thoughts fade into the void where my life is stuck.

Joy reaches for my hand. "Let's focus on now and getting you back on track."

What track? I have no chance to live the life I hoped for.

      •   •   •

Lena unwraps the turquoise scarf from around her head and Joy takes her coat. "Thank you so much for coming."

"I am happy to help if I can, especially if it will get my little Docia back on the ice," Lena says.

"Please sit down. I'd love to get the coach's perspective of Docia's career—and what's happening now."

Lena pinches my cheek like she's done since I was three. "What's happening now will all be over soon. No one can keep Docia down."

"May I record our conversation?" Joy asks.

Lena's eyes grow large. "What will you do with the recording? It reminds me of people who are not nice in my home country."

I don't blame her for the question. There are not-so-nice people here too.

"Oh Lena, I'm sorry. No one else will hear this. It's just to make sure I capture your words as you say them."

Lena nods and the recorder's red light appears.

"You've coached some of the world's best skaters. How does coaching Docia compare?"

"Docia has a gift. She learns fast and always does as she is told. She has everything to make a champion." A glow beams from Lena's face like the one when I first met her. Back when I had the first recollection of my new family and skating. The first memory of loving something.

"What was on your mind while you watched Docia's winning free skate in Moscow?"

"She reminded me so much of her mmm...." She stops. "I mean, one of my students from many years ago."

My ears perk up. "Lena, what did you start to say?"

"Nothing, little Docia. Do not worry," she mumbles in Russian. Joy tilts her head.

Maybe I'm cynical, but for once I don't believe Lena.

"What can you tell us about Docia's adoption? Do you know what agency they worked with? Was it the normal process?

"She found a family who loves her and recognized from the start she is a talented girl." Lena shifts like she wants to get comfortable but can't. "I know little about who Mr. Sikorsky worked with to find her. He knew people."

Come on, Lena. Tell us more. If anyone can get answers, Joy can.

"How did she end up here in Houston and skating?" Joy slides her glasses down to her face. "How did you come to be her coach?"

"Her father contacted me in Russia. He offered to help bring me to the U.S. to coach his daughter. 'My little star,' he used to say. So, I moved to Houston to coach Docia."

That's one thing Dad did right, but move a coach all the way from Europe to coach a three-year-old kid? Few parents would do that.

"You must miss home."

"No, I have nothing but my sister left in Russia. My family is here with Docia now."

My heart breaks when I think about how I've avoided her since Moscow. Before I can stop myself, words tumble out. "What about the student I remind you of?"

Lena's face drops. "Uh...umm...she is no longer in Russia."

"Where is she? What is it that reminds you of me?"

"I couldn't say where she lives." Lena's face softens into a sad smile. Tears well up in her eyes. "It is uhh харизма. How you say in English?" she mumbles to herself.

"Charisma," Joy says.

CHAPTER NINETEEN

I build speed with alternating crossovers around the rink and glance at Lena who pretends not to watch. Then I graduate through each easy jump to spins. *It almost feels like normal.*

But it's not.

Lena did the interview with Joy, so I kept my promise to get back on the ice. Lena's happy now until she discovers I'm a complete disaster. That all the work she's done coaching me is wasted.

I set up for my quad Lutz. Shaky, but I'm still upright! I do a bigger Lutz. Lena looks away. Should I try the quad Lutz-double toe combination? I hesitate, make another lap around the rink, and set up. Stacy's face flashes through my head and I pop the jump. Stop it! Stacy will not break my concentration!

I ignore the salty taste of sweat. I also avoid Lena and skate one more lap as I search my memory for a positive thought to help me refocus. So much for Dad's pep talks.

More back crossovers, catch a strong edge, and wind up for the jump. Up. Around. Down. Check. There's my Lutz. Up. Around. Down. Check. Then the toe-loop. I let out a long breath.

"That's my girl!" Lena's hands are clasped in front of her chest. "Do again. I put music on for free skate now."

"But Lena, I'm not—" I shout back. She continues to walk to the deejay area.

I circle around again and prepare for a layback spin. Hips forward, back arched toward the ice. I softly curve my arms and fingers and angle my leg behind from the hip like Lena taught. Fears of failure tumble off with the inertia of the spin.

Lena's staccato hand claps echo through the building. "In position, Docia."

I close my eyes and circle the center of the rink until I reach my starting spot and take my pose. The first notes play. They pull me back into the zone. My body takes over and moves through the choreography, each step, hand position, and element I've learned, practiced, mastered. It all comes back. Automatic.

I start the relaxing glide through the spiral sequence and final jump. When I finish my footwork, I glance over at Lena. She watches every move and nods.

I got through it. Upright.

"Good Docia," Lena says from the side. "Now do it again."

Back-to-backs already? I nod and get in position. Don't overthink each element.

I try to get back in my zone. The magic from Moscow isn't here but I finish with only a couple of baubles.

I'm physically drained.

Lena squeezes my arm and hands me my guards. "Not bad, little Docia. You get back in top form with more practice so you are ready for Worlds."

I nod automatically but then stop. "Wait, Lena. What makes you think I'll be at Worlds? I'm suspended. Not much will change that—unless you know something I don't."

"Docia, do not give up. I know you will compete again."

My eyes narrow. "How do you know?"

"Faith." She sits next to me and watches me unlace my skates.

I pull one boot off wishing I had a little of her faith. "When you spoke to Joy, you started to say something. Something about who I remind you of when I skate. Who is it?"

"Is nothing. Just old woman mumbling about the past."

She stands up a little too fast and grabs the wall to catch herself.

"Lena," I hop on one foot after her with my other boot in hand. "Who was it? I want to know." She turns around and I see moisture in her eyes. "You're the only one who tells me the truth."

I sit back down without taking my eyes off her, but she turns away. My bare foot rests on the bench so my sock doesn't soak up the melted ice that muddies the squishy floor. She takes my other boot and slips it over my foot. "Let's go to my house. I have something to show you."

"Now?" My mind spins with possibilities.

She nods, and I follow.

CHAPTER TWENTY

We drive up to Lena's house. Inside, I weave my way through the cluster of chairs in her small but cozy living room. Embroidered doilies and knickknacks clutter every surface with a musty odor of old things. It's home here, like a grandma's house. I walk straight into the kitchen to her kettle.

"Tea?" I ask. She nods then disappears to the back of the house.

A few minutes later, her voice sings from down the hall. "Come, come Docia. I must show you something."

I glance at the two china cups ready with tea bags then stare at the vacant light on the kettle. *Come on, boil.* "On my way," I answer along with the shrill ding from the kettle.

I balance the delicate cups on their saucers and walk toward her voice. Lena sits by her bed next to an old flat-top trunk covered with a pink and blue flowered tablecloth.

"I've never noticed this before." I hand her the tea and kneel on the floor as she opens the trunk. "What is all this stuff?" The air fills with the musky odor of old paper.

"Is like scraps book."

I nod and set my tea down safely out of the way before reaching in to pick up a cardboard folder. Inside is a faded black-and-white photograph of a little girl skating. Her curly blond ponytail flows behind her.

"Is this what you want me to see?"

"No, no," Lena chuckles. "Is only me."

"Lena, you were so cute." She's focused on pulling something else out of the trunk.

"This is what I want you to see."

She hands me a framed photograph I recognize immediately. "That's Anna Ivanova. Your former student."

"Yes," she answers and hands me a photo album.

I flip through photos and Russian newspaper clippings. "Are all these about her?"

"Yes, is all about Anna."

"Why haven't you shown me these before?" I stop on a photo of Anna in her amazing spiral position, the sky-blue skating dress glimmers against the white ice like a butterfly drifting. "Tell me about this one."

"Anna's first Russian national competition." Lena's face beams with pride. "She did well. Took home silver."

I look closer at the photo. The sparkle from her pendant catches my eye.

"She's wearing a cross necklace like the one you gave to me. Did you give one to all your students?"

I take in every detail—the crowd's hands frozen in applause positions, the bright banners in Russian splash the boards, and the warm smile on Anna's face. Her gray eyes sparkle almost as much as the pendant that dangles from her neck.

Lena remains silent.

When I look up, she's staring into the trunk. Her face is still. Firm. She grips her knees like she's bracing for a plane crash.

"No Docia, I gave this Russian Orthodox cross necklace only to one— most special Anna."

"You gave one to me too..." I gaze at the photograph while pieces of my life mentally fly together like a jigsaw puzzle. "Do I have Anna's necklace?"

Lena's knuckles are white now. "Yes. Anna wanted you to have it." Lena takes a few quick breaths. Her stare never leaves the trunk.

This makes no sense. "How did Anna know I existed?" I remain fixated on her face. Not blinking. Waiting.

"She wanted her daughter to have it."

Time stops.

I suck in a mouthful of air.

"What?"

Tears escape Lena's tired eyes. They slide down her weathered cheeks. I look into her crystal blue irises with hope they will tell me something.

"Anna is your mama."

The room whirls like I'm stuck in a never-ending scratch spin.

"I don't understand. You told me my parents were a couple in Moscow who couldn't take care of me." I close my eyes and grip the edge of the open trunk to force the room to stand still.

Make the lies stop.

"That is what your father told me to tell you." She places one hand on top of mine.

As hard as I try to remain strong, every ounce of control seeps out of me. First, my hands go limp. Then my arms. Caught between rage and disbelief. My chin rests on my chest and my eyes stop on a photo of Anna with a baby in her arms.

"Is this me?"

I force my eyelids up enough to see Lena nod.

A whisper slips out instead of the scream that builds in my chest. "Why didn't you tell me?"

"I wanted your father to tell you. When you were old enough."

"My adoptive dad?"

Lena nods.

"But he didn't."

"Please Docia. He would not let me."

Big deep breaths so I don't pass out. In. Out.

Lena reaches for my hands. "He thought you would not look to him first if you knew."

Will he ever learn he can't control people? He cannot control me. "You should have told me anyway. What else has my father kept from me? Who's my real father?"

"Please, your real papa does not know about you. In time he will." Lena wraps her arms around my shoulders and holds me. "I am sorry, my sweet Docia. I tried."

Part of me longs for the closeness, to feel her heartbeat next to mine. Another part of me wants to push her away and run. Get as far away from her, from everyone, as fast as possible. Dad told me more times than I can count how I should know my enemies. I never imagined they would be the people closest to me.

Lena's hug loosens. I reach for the cross that I haven't taken off since the Olympics.

"Before she died, Anna asked me to keep the necklace for you. She asked me to watch out for you. Make sure you are cared for. She loved you very, very much. More than life. More than anything, she wanted me to get you to America so she could meet you there as soon as she could defect. No matter what it took, she wanted you to have freedom."

We sit. The room is silent except for the faint hum from the refrigerator down the hall. I stare into the trunk, my life playing backward in my head.

Moscow... recovery and accident...winning Nationals...Christmas with my parents... meeting Lena...learning to skate. I don't remember life before skating.

"Tell me more. Please." I scoot closer in hopes the answers will come faster. "Who was my father? How did I end up here? I remember nothing before Mom and Dad. I want to remember Anna holding me. Being my mother. Please, I have to know everything."

Lena's hand shakes as she reaches for her tea. "There is so much to tell. So much she did to keep you safe until she and your father could be together. To get you where you are today." She reaches for a large white book underneath a pile of photographs. "Let me show you."

I pull the chair close, and she opens the scrapbook to an image I know well. "This is my favorite picture of Anna," I say. "She looks so happy with her Olympic gold medal." The gold glimmers against the black *Swan Lake* skating dress—the same one she wears in the bronze statue at the Olympic rink in Moscow. I haven't seen this image since winning my Olympic gold. Now I understand how she must have felt.

"Yes, she was thrilled. It was her dream to win." Lena gazes at the photo. "Something else made her very happy at the Olympics. She saw the boy she loved."

My eyes grow larger than the setting sun. "My father?"

"Yes. He was a pairs skater from another country. He and Anna met at one of the European competitions. They could only see each other when they traveled; when the Russian officials were not able to watch her so closely. They planned to marry after she left Russia. She dreamed of being a family with you in America."

"Where is he now? What happened? When can we contact him?"

"Slow down. We will get to that," Lena turns the page to Anna in the middle of her famous layback spin. "This was a few weeks later at Worlds."

"Yes, I've read about this. She won the gold there too."

"That is correct. She was also pregnant with you."

CHAPTER TWENTY-ONE

My breath freezes in my lungs. Anna carried me in that tiny body? I walk to the other side of the small room and back. "I still don't understand why no one told me. Why was it such a secret?"

"Sit, Docia. I will explain." Lena sips her tea and stares into the cup. "Sit. Please. Where to begin?"

Lena waits but I no longer want to sit.

"Suit yourself," she says. "Post-U.S.S.R. Russia was a very different place than America. People were not free. As an athlete, Anna's life was not hers. Some people thought having a baby since she was not married would embarrass the country."

"That's crazy. She could skate after she had the baby...I mean me."

"Yes. It sounds simple, but it was not. She would have been shamed. Her career would have ended, and your life would have been in danger. So, we...."

The room is dead quiet except for my breathing that sounds like I've sprinted a mile. I fix on Lena and wait for her next word. "So, you did what, Lena?"

Her hands grip so tightly her knuckles fade to white. "We kept you secret, even from your real father. A team doctor risked his life to help us protect you and Anna. Even today, your mama and papa do not know who your biological father is."

"What about you? Were *you* in danger?"

"Yes, but I stayed to take care of you."

Lena's gaze follows me as I sit cross-legged on the floor. "What about when she started to show? Can't keep secrets for long in what skaters wear."

"Anna finished the season strong with gold at Worlds. She trained through spring and summer."

"I can't imagine doing a triple Lutz with a baby bump." Or how Anna risked her career. For me.

"She was small, and you were very tiny," Lena chuckles. "Then at the season's earliest competition the doctor helped us—how you say—fake an injury. It was during late-night practice when no one was there. We created an injury so serious Anna had to have surgery and recover in Switzerland where the competition was."

"And no one found out?"

"No one. The Swiss would not allow Russian security to guard her like they usually did. Russian sports officials eventually started to pry. They wanted Anna back in Russia. It was very hard to keep your father and Anna apart, but she knew she could not see him."

"Why? Why couldn't she have stayed in Switzerland and had me there?"

"She did. The Russian officials were afraid Anna would defect. Then they could no longer control her. There was one thing they could not control. You. You came early."

I sit back and try to process each word. She's talking about me. My real mom and dad. My birth. What question do I ask first?

"Hardly anyone knew about you since you were born in Switzerland—the doctor, me, and a couple of other people you need not worry about." Lena sits back in her chair. Her face looks peaceful. "After you were born, we drove you both back to a small town in the north part of Russia near Saint Petersburg with my sister. It was a very long drive—almost two days. We could protect you there until Anna could defect. You were such a beautiful little thing."

I shift back and forth between resentment and curiosity. I should be angry. "Lena, you look pale. Do you feel okay?"

"So sorry." She rests her forehead on her hand. "I have never told this story. It is very emotional."

"Please, tell me more."

"A few weeks after you were born, just before Christmas, Anna went back home to Moscow. You stayed with my sister. So many adoring fans greeted Anna when she arrived. Half of the season was already gone. She was miserable missing you and the man she loved. She could not speak of you to her love and could not see either of you. I never imagined harm might come to my Anna."

"I'll never understand how something so horrible could happen." We sit in silence since we both know the tragic story that is now skating legend. I never dreamed how much the story would mean to me one day. "I'm sure she had walked back and forth between the rink and the dorm hundreds of times. How could some crazy driver slide on the ice and hit her? Why that day? Why Anna?"

Lena shakes her head. "She lived for the ice and ice caused her death. Losing her still breaks my heart. They say an accident took your mama away." Lena lets my hand slip out of hers. "I always suspected something else; someone else. Maybe..."

But she stops. "Maybe what, Lena?"

"Nothing. Crazy old woman's imagination."

"No, Lena. You're not crazy. What do you mean?"

"I believe the government found out about her boyfriend...and caused..." While Lena talks, her breath shortens. "...the accident."

"Lena, are you alright?"

She falls back in her chair and color drains from her face.

"No, not so good." Her breath slows. "That is why we took you away."

I jump from the floor. "I'll get you some water."

Then her neck goes limp.

"Lena. Lena? Can you hear me?"

What do I do?

"I'm calling 9-1-1." I hit each number as I say it. The three tones seem to last for minutes each. "Come on, answer," I whisper into the phone.

A male voice on the other end says, "9-1-1. What is your emergency?"

All the years at the rink with accidents and blood and limbs that bent in directions they're not supposed to go in push me into automatic crisis mode.

"My coach needs an ambulance. She got really weak and is having trouble breathing. Please hurry."

"Help is coming, ma'am. What is your name?" The calm voice on the other end says.

Nothing prepares me for the thought of losing Lena. I squeeze her hand. "Lena, you will be fine. The ambulance is on the way." I forget the phone is still to my ear.

"You're doing good, ma'am. Keep talking to her. I'll stay on the line with you. What is your name?"

"Docia. Docia Sikorsky. She's my skating coach." My eyes never leave hers. "Lena, you have so many stories to tell me about my mother and father. You have to help me get ready for Worlds."

A tiny smile appears, and her lids grow heavy.

"Lena, please look into my eyes."

The man in the phone speaks again. "Docia, a few more minutes and the paramedics will be there. You're doing great. Make sure there's nothing that obstructs her breathing. Keep talking to her."

"Lena, the ambulance is almost here. You'll be just fine. Everything will be okay," I stroke her smooth hair and repeat the words as much to reassure myself as to comfort her until I hear a knock on the door. Lena perks up for a moment then relaxes again.

"Lena, I'll let the paramedics in. I'll be right back."

The red and blue lights flash through the windows. A few neighbors watch the chaos from their front porches.

I step back against the wall and watch as two men in scrubs work on my coach, my second mother, my confidant. One wraps a blood pressure cuff around her arm while the other puts oxygen to her nose. "Ma'am, do you have a heart condition?"

Lena shakes her head no. "High blood pressure?" She shakes her head again. "Do you feel nauseous?" This time she nods yes.

One of the paramedics turns his head toward me. "How long has she been like this? Did she have any earlier symptoms?"

My heart pounds. "Maybe for a few minutes. I called as soon as she started to look sick. Yeah, she seemed a little dizzy once this morning."

"Okay. You did good. We will take excellent care of her. She's your skating coach?" he asks as they lift her onto the gurney.

"Yes," I nod. My mind races back over the last few days. What if I caused this? I should have practiced like she asked. All those questions I—

"Would you like a ride to the hospital with us?" the other man asks.

I reach down next to her bed and grab Lena's purse. "Yes, I have to stay with her."

CHAPTER TWENTY-TWO

I turn around in the front seat of the ambulance so I never have to take my eyes off Lena. When my phone vibrates, I ignore it and cling to Lena's purse. The driver's radio buzzes but I don't hear words. Does he even notice I'm here? Lena lies motionless. The oxygen mask is massive on her small face. Two paramedics talk to each other as one inserts an IV into her wrist and the other sticks wires to her chest. The two words, heart attack, are all I hear. As long as her chest rises and falls, she's alive.

We pull up to the hospital and I fling the door open, jump out, and run to the back. As soon as the two men lift her out of the truck, I wrap my fingers around the hand without the IV. People rush around tending to her like I'm invisible, but I continue to squeeze Lena's hand as they wheel her through the emergency entrance.

"Sweetheart," a nurse with soft brown curls around her tan face says. "We need to take your grandmother for a while."

She must see my desperation.

"Someone will keep you updated. I promise."

I lean down close to her face, "You're going to be okay, Lena," I whisper. "I love you." She gently squeezes back as her hand slips out of mine. Then she disappears through the swinging gray doors.

I wish she were my grandmother.

I stop at the edge of the waiting area. The burnt orange vinyl chairs are uninviting. The room smells of stale coffee and sadness even though it's empty. I continue to walk and end up outside under the overcast sky. My phone vibrates again. There's a screen full of texts from Mom.

Come home!

Surprise for you!

Call me with a line of emojis.

Where are u? Need u here now!

I hit the button to dial her back and barely let her say hello. "Mom, come to the hospital. Lena's—"

"Docia. There you are. I need you home. Now."

"I can't. Lena's in the hospital. They think she had a heart attack. She needs us."

"Oh dear. What happened?"

"She collapsed so I called 911. Mom, I'm scared."

"Sweetie, I'm sure she'll be fine. We'll visit her later, but I need you home now."

"I can't leave her," I plead. "She doesn't have anyone else."

"Right now, you need to come home. Lily can bring you." Mom sighs. "I need to go."

I stare at the silent phone and then through the hospital window. All I see is emptiness. Exactly how I feel. The only person I trust fights for her life and Mom has one of her emergencies. She acts like the president of the United States is at our house.

I walk back inside to the information desk. "Is there any news on Lena Porenchova?"

She shakes her head. "Not yet. They'll let you know as soon as there is."

"Thank you, I'll be right outside."

I drag my feet back to a corner, sit on the concrete, and call Lily.

"Lily? Can you come to the hospital? Lena's here."

"Oh my God, of course, Docia. Grabbing my keys. Is she okay?"

"They don't know." A bit of tension slips away at the sound of Lily's voice. "I'm here by the emergency room."

"Be there in ten minutes."

"Thank you."

My butt goes numb against the cold concrete, so I rest my head on my knees and wrap my arms around them to stop the chills.

"Please let Lena be okay. Please let Lena be okay." I rock back and forth and hope someone hears me. "Please let Lena be okay."

"Docia, come inside. It's freezing." I look up and see Lily's outstretched hand.

"I'm so glad you're here. They haven't said a word about her yet."

"Let's ask."

The same lady is at the desk. "I'll check on her for you and let you know if there's news."

Lily takes my hand as we walk back to my spot outside. "What happened?"

"Anna's my mom."

My hand slips out of Lily's. "Anna? The Russian skater?"

I gulp and nod. "Lena was showing pictures of her when she was pregnant with me when this happened. She passed out right in front of me." Speaking the words makes it real. The surprise. The lies. Now Lena.

My face feels hot and the first tears after the day's events ooze out. "Anna's my mom but she's gone. My real dad still doesn't know about me...and now Lena."

"Oh, Docia. I don't know what to say."

She slides down next to me on the pavement where we sit in silence.

Lily rests her hands on my shoulders. "How do you feel about Anna being your mom?"

"I don't know how to feel. She's always been one of my favorite skaters, but my mother?" I remember the look on Lena's face after I won Olympic gold. "I'm scared for Lena."

"Me too. Once we know she's okay, we'll figure out everything else."

"And on top of it all, Mom wants me home. I can see her now." I stare at the intersection of cracks in the pavement where a tiny tuft of grass found life. "'Come home now, Docia. Do you hear me?' She acts like she doesn't care about Lena."

"What's up with her?"

"Who knows. She asked me to call you for a ride home."

"We'll go after we hear about Lena." She leads me to a couple of the ugly orange chairs inside.

The automatic doors open and the lady from the desk walks through with a woman in scrubs. I jump out of the chair. "How is she?"

"Hi, Docia?" The nurse asks.

I nod.

"The doctor said your grandmother's fine. I'm one of her nurses. She had a bad scare but she's okay."

My tension unwinds a notch. "Can we see her?"

"Not yet," the nurse says. "She needs to rest. Why don't you come back in the morning?"

"Yes ma'am." I'm helpless. It's like I'm back in order-taker mode. "Call me if anything changes? Or if she needs something? I'm the closest to family she has here in America."

"We will. I'll make sure of it."

Lily drapes her arm over my shoulders while we watch the nurse disappear through the doors. "Let's see what your mom's big emergency is."

Still gripping Lena's purse, I follow Lily's lead toward the exit but don't take my eyes off the hallway where I know Lena is until we turn the corner and head outside.

CHAPTER TWENTY-THREE

Through the car window, the blur of scenery whizzes past. Rain pelts the asphalt from a cloud starting to crowd the sun. "I hate hospitals."

"Who doesn't?" Lily asks.

"They remind me of my accident." Each light pole that rushes by looks like the nurses and doctors who scurried around all tall and stern while I was flat on my back. The sun's rays peeping through remind me of the blinding florescent lights over the bed I was stuck in for weeks.

"I wonder if Anna had me in a hospital." I catch Lily glancing over. "What did she think about me—about having a baby? How could she leave me there?"

Lily steers around the last curve on my street. "Did your mom say anything about people coming over? Look at the cars outside your house."

"What the...." My entire body goes stiff. "No, she didn't. Those aren't just cars. They're TV news vans. Let me out down the street. I'll slip in the back."

Lily pulls over in front of a neighbor's house. "I'm coming with you."

"I *need* to do this by myself." I grab Lena's purse and step out of the car.

"Docia, I'll wait for you here," Lily yells after me.

I turn back to the car again. "This one's for me to handle. Call you later. Promise."

Without waiting for Lily's response, I run through the backyard to the French doors that lead into my parent's room. I slip my key into the lock and stop. I don't know these people anymore.

I step inside in the middle of luggage strewn around the room. "What?" I whisper. "Is Dad home?" I crack open the door to the rest of the house and peer into the living room. Dad standing in front of the medal wall is visible through the narrow slit—with a boom microphone above his head. I open the door a tad more to see what body is attached to the hand and who's asking questions.

"What do you say about the controversy around Docia's medal?" the slick-looking man in the dark gray suit asks.

Dad looks puffy and even shorter next to the reporter I don't recognize. Now I see the TV camera and hear Dad's words.

"There's no controversy. It's drama a competitor dreamed up to push Docia off the medal stand. It's as vicious and unwarranted as that Nancy-Tanya attack but with lies instead of a pipe."

I slap my hand over my mouth to muzzle the gasp. *What is he doing?*

"But Mr. Sikorsky, she doesn't have the medal anymore."

"It's her medal. I don't have to prove anything. I worked hard to prepare..."

Enough.

I transform into a fireball I can no longer restrain and push the door open. The camera finds me across the room. Adrenaline rushes in a way I haven't felt since my two Olympic programs.

"Dad," I hiss louder than I intend. "This isn't the best time for interviews—"

"Baby girl," Dad interrupts and opens his arms like he expects me to run to him. "Your daddy's home safe." Then he turns us both to the mic and camera. "See what a star she is?"

I will not be part of his show. I duck underneath his arms to avoid the hug. Now I'm frozen in the middle of the room with a camera and strangers' eyes on me.

"I'll have that medal back in our hands soon."

"What will you do, Dad, lie more?" I can't stop the words from tumbling out.

Mom shrieks my name in a shrill whisper.

I take a deep breath, remember my media training and paint on a sincere smile. "I'm glad you're home, Daddy, but this isn't a good time for an interview," I repeat.

He grips my shoulders. "Docia, we have guests." His soft but firm tone would have commanded obedience from the former Docia. "I need to finish here. Then we can talk."

"No, Dad. Today's been so enlightening that it's time to talk now," I respond with equal firmness. "If you don't want these reporters to leave, I'll speak for myself to them."

"Whatever you have to say can wait, Docia." His eyes drill into me. "And I'll tell you all about Moscow later."

"Did you even listen?" I push his hands off my shoulders. "Today I found out I'm not the person I thought I was. I learned the people I've trusted most have totally betrayed me." I catch my breath and look from the reporter wearing the suit to Mom to Dad.

Dad grabs my arm. "Docia, stop this nonsense right now."

"Don't 'Docia' me." I twist my arm from his grip. "You lied about everything. For my entire life. Lena's the only person who's been honest. Here's one more for you." I sweep the room and stop on each speechless face. "I'm not even American."

The room is quieter than the rink at five o'clock in the morning until the reporter drops his stunned stare and approaches me with the mic close behind. "If you're not American Docia, what nationality are you?" he asks.

Dad steps toward the mic, but I don't move.

"I'm most qualified to answer that question," I say.

Mom's chin drops.

"I was born in Europe. My mother named me Tatiana Ivanovo." Everyone's eyes are on me. "Anna Ivanovo is my mother, and my biological father doesn't know I exist."

There, I said it. The story's out. I'm on camera with the truth. It feels good. No one can twist the truth into what it's not.

The room is still silent.

"I don't know yet how the adoption happened since I was a baby. I am an American now. I also won the Olympic gold fair and square."

No one says a word until the gray-suit guy whispers to the camera operator.

"I'll prove I was qualified to win that medal to the world. If you need more answers," I point to Dad, "I'm sure my dad will be happy to fill you in, if you can believe him, or maybe Mom." If she'll ever have the guts to stand for anything.

"Docia, what are you—" my dad starts to say.

The reporter hands me his business card. "Let's talk tomorrow."

Without another thought or look or word I shove the card in my pocket, walk to the front door and through it.

CHAPTER TWENTY-FOUR

As soon as my feet hit the sidewalk, I'm in a full-blown sprint. With Lena's purse still tight against me, I ignore the giant raindrops that beat down on me. I don't look back.

I run. Away from this strange place I've called home. Away from people I thought I knew and trusted. Where? I don't know. I don't care.

Away is all I want.

I blink the rain away to soothe the burn in my eyes. The houses and driveways and mailboxes and parked cars blur past. The momentum keeps me reaching one leg one in front of the other. Concrete pounds under my feet.

Suddenly one leg stops while the other continues. I hit the soft ground that cushions my fall and lie still while the rain stings my skin. My legs sprawl in two directions. A tinge from the old injury shoots up from my ankle. All I see is thin brown grass and mud.

I squeeze Lena's purse to my chest. Closer. Tighter. I won't let her go.

When I raise my head, I realize I've run to the cemetery where I've spent hours jogging laps every day—right in front of the small grave marker with two names. Babies born on the same day and died the same day a few months later. *At least I had a chance for life.*

I sit up on my knees that sink into the mushy moist soil. "Please let Lena be okay. Please let Lena be okay," I pray.

A gentle touch on my back startles me so much I lose the grip on the small purse. I can barely hear my own weak scream over the rumbling thunder.

As I look up, worn black cowboy boots caked in mud greet my gaze. Then Diego's light brown eyes full of concern.

Everything is already a bit better.

"It's not exactly jogging weather." He squats down to my eye level. "Lily called. I thought you might be here. You're the only person I know who jogs around a cemetery to clear her mind. Are you all right?"

"No," is the only word I manage to get out between sobs.

He kneels and wraps his arms around me like he used to do. "Everything will be okay." He holds me tighter. "Lily filled me in."

My breathing follows the rhythm of his steady heartbeat. "She did?"

He nods. "You'll get past this."

"I know. I have to."

He loosens his grip so now I can see his warm smile. "Thank you for rescuing me. Again."

He wipes away the mix of rain and tears that drip from my chin. "This isn't a rescue. It's what friends do."

I can't help but smile. "I've missed you."

"I'm right here."

Our eyes meet. The same feelings return that make me want to know how his lips would feel on mine, but I look away before he figures out what I'm thinking.

I hug him again. "Will you help me sort all this out?"

"Of course," he answers. "What do we do first?"

Knowing Diego is still my friend adds a foot to my height. "Will you take me to talk to Stacy? I have a hunch she knows more than we think."

Diego nods. "She's teaching a class at the rink. It should wrap up soon." He reaches his hand down to mine and guides me up. "Let's go, Skate Princess."

I always loved it when he called me that.

"Pretty far from a princess, Hockey Jock." I look down at my jeans. "I'll get mud all over your car."

"Doesn't matter." He laughs. "You've seen my car."

He never forgets how to make me smile.

CHAPTER TWENTY-FIVE

During the familiar drive to the rink, I lower the visor in Diego's car to assess the damage. Why bother? I'm drenched.

"You know you look like her," Diego says.

"Who?"

"Anna."

"I haven't thought about that." I pop the visor up, now too self-conscious to look at my reflection. "How so?"

"Your eyes and cheekbones. Your lips." He smiles. "She always looks happy in photos and a bit sneaky, like she's up to something. Just like you."

I'm not sure what to say, so I continue to stare out the window.

"You okay?"

Neither of us says a word through two traffic lights.

"No, I'm not." It feels good to express how I really feel for once. "I'm ready to take charge of my life for once. I want to know my story. Who I am. Where I came from. I want to get to know my real father. If I make a mistake, I want it to be mine. Not my dad's or mom's or Lena's, or reporters', or fans', if I have any left. I won't blame anything on Anna."

Diego reaches for my hand.

"I'm almost as old as Anna was when she got pregnant."

"I'm glad you're carrying on her memory." Diego turns into the rink parking lot.

"What do you mean?"

"Skating." He pulls into a parking space. "You skate a lot like Anna too. Good you're not having a baby though."

I laugh. No one can break the tension like Diego. "Can I leave Lena's purse here?"

"Sure. Want me to go with you?"

Stacy's car is two spots down. "I've got this."

I step out of the car and take long strides toward the main entrance. A group of younger skaters loaded up with their bags stand in a cluster. They look at me, but I keep walking.

I have a mission.

A few people call my name as I pass the skating dress display and the trophy window with the photos of Stacy and me with our last few medals. I wave and continue forward.

My sights are on one person.

I stop among the benches in front of her. "We need to talk."

"Docia, hi...uhh, you're soaked," Stacy says. "How are you now? I heard you've—"

"Not here for small talk." My voice is calm and controlled. "It's time for you to spill it. What did you have to do with this whole medal mess?"

Her eyes are huge. "I don't know what you mean."

"I think you do."

"Really." She looks around like she's searching for someone to rescue her. "I only know what I read."

"I don't believe you." My breathing is deep and even. "You were with your dad and coach right next to the Olympic officials."

"Docia, we had just skated. We were all there."

"No, reporters were interviewing the other skaters." Determination explodes. "I had just accepted my gold medal, and you had finished in sixth place. Why did you need to talk to the officials then?"

"Are you accusing me of something? You already won Nationals and the Olympics and have a famous mom." Stacy stops and fidgets with her top.

"My mom's not famous. What does my mom have to do with this?"

The interview hasn't aired yet.

"Nothing," Stacy answers, her eyes dart around. "I meant she's supportive and has gotten famous because of you."

"I'm calling you out. Do you lie as easily as you breathe?" I step a little closer and lower my voice. "How did you find out?"

Her face is blank as she twists the bottom of her cami around her finger.

"Come on. How do you know who my real mom is?" This time I speak louder and fight the urge to yank that annoying red ponytail. "I will haunt you until you say it."

Stacy's eyes lower toward the squishy tile floor. "My coach," she whispers.

"What?"

She looks up at me. "I overheard my coach talking to my parents about it a couple of months before the Olympics." Then she lowers her face again. "He told them the only way I could medal is if you were disqualified."

"So, they cooked it all up." I could hate her, but I'm surprised by my calm.

She nods.

"Thank you for the truth. Finally."

I start for the door but feel her watching me. Diego's smile greets me outside. He reaches his hand out to mine. "Where next?"

"Joy's house."

"Did you find out what you need to know?"

"Yeah." He follows me to the car. "It was her coach and parents, but Stacy didn't stop them. Now I need to figure out what her coach knew besides who my real mom is and how they all found out."

"Amazing how some people can be so vindictive." He pauses before he slides into the car. "Go easy on her though. She's going through a rough time."

"Stacy's going through a rough time?"

He nods. "She's pregnant."

CHAPTER TWENTY-SIX

A zillion thoughts run through my head. "Pregnant?" I ask. "Sounds like more made-up drama."

"Believe it," Diego says. He's focused on the road as he turns out of the rink in the direction of Joy's house.

"How?" Then I knock my fist against my head and catch a hint of a smile from Diego. "Duh. I know *how*. I mean *when*? She was training for the Olympics until a few weeks ago." He shakes his head. "And who?"

"Cameron," he answers.

The word falls like a rock crashing through the bottom of my stomach.

"He's been all over her since you blew him off after your accident. Brags about what a big man he is. He says they only did it once."

My stomach does a triple Axel. "I was so into rehab and training I didn't notice until at the mall today. Wonder if he pumped her full of booze like he did me?" I can't even say his name. "He pressured me to have sex that day at the lake."

Diego clinches his jaw.

"I didn't," I answer even though he didn't ask. "I wouldn't." *I'm not that stupid.*

Diego parks in front of Joy's house. "I know."

"He almost ruined my career. Now he's doing the same to her." The thought of Cameron touching me like Diego makes me nauseous. "Dad thinks he's perfect. 'That kid's going places,' he used to say. Yeah, Dad, he's going to family court when Stacy sues him for child support."

Dad thinks Diego's a loser? Great judge of character.

I sit in the stopped car for a moment until I can push the image of Cameron's hands all over Stacy out of my mind. "What does a sixteen-year-old athlete do with a baby?" As much as I despise Stacy, I can't help but feel sorry for her. "You're coming in with me, right?"

"Seriously, Docia. You think I'd miss this?"

As we step over the rain puddles on Joy's sidewalk, I smile for the first time since I saw Lena at her house this morning.

Before my finger reaches the bell, the door flies open. Lily grabs Diego and me by our hands and pulls us inside. "What are you doing here, Lily?"

"You've got to see this interview with your dad on ESPN," she says and drags me to the blaring TV. "Hurry. It just started. Wait, that's your house."

I gawk at my dad's face on the screen, too out of words to respond any other way.

Lily slaps her hand over her mouth and says through her fingers, "So *this* is what you walked in on?"

Then my face is on the TV screen. Diego puts his hand on my shoulder and Lily grabs my arm. Joy appears from around the corner. She looks at me then the television then me again like she just realized I have on the drenched version of the same clothes from the interview, still carrying Lena's purse like a security blanket.

"Look at you telling them how it is," Lily says.

Joy throws her arms around me. "What a day it's been for you. How do you feel...besides soaked?" She steps away when she notices the damp spots now on her shirt.

"Drained. Now that we know where I came from, I'm ready to get my life back." The heat from the towel Joy pulled out of the dryer warms the chill. "First, I need to call Stacy's no-good coach."

"Why him?" Lily asks.

"According to Stacy, he started the whole scandal to disqualify me. To save his job." My mouth curls into a Grinch-like grin when I tap his number from my skating club directory.

On the other end is a high-pitched male voice. "Hello?"

"Mr. Zilinsky? This is Docia Sikorsky."

"Oh, Docia. Hello." His voice cracks. "What can I do for you?"

"We need to meet. How about tomorrow morning? I have some questions for you."

"Questions? For me?" he asks. "I can't imagine what I could say that would be of any interest to you."

"A lot. Let's start with this. What do you know about my adoption?"

"Well, I only know what I've read—and what you said in that ESPN interview just now."

"I think you know more." No one can stop me now. "Would you like to answer my question, or shall I call that ESPN reporter and tell him what Stacy told me?"

Silence. I wrap the towel tighter and wait. His heavy breath on the other end lets me know he's still there.

"Well?" I ask.

The six eyes fixed on me grow bigger with every word.

"I don't know what Stacy might have told you." He coughs and clears his throat. "Like I said, all I know is what I see in the news. You know Stacy. The stress from the games and no medal has gotten to her."

"Yes, I know Stacy. Maybe that ESPN reporter can get more answers than I can. Thanks for talking to me."

I reach into my pocket and pull out the reporter's crumpled card as I end the call.

"What did he say?" Lily blurts out.

"A big fat nothing." I stare at the soggy card. "Denies he knows a thing."

Diego shakes his head. "I'd believe Stacy over that spineless jerk."

I nod.

"What's wrong?" Joy asks.

"The card is so soggy I can't read his number."

"Remember, I'm a journalist too," Joy says with a reassuring smile. "Be right back."

"He's got to know you won't let this go," Lily says. "I mean, it's too important to stop now."

"Exactly," I answer. "The old Docia might have."

"What will you say to that reporter?" Diego asks.

As Joy reappears, my phone rings. I expect it to be Dad with one of his famous talks. Can't wait to hear his next one after what I said on TV.

"You answering or what?" Lily asks.

I crinkle my face the way Mom always scolds me for doing. "It's Mr. Zilinsky." It rings again. "What could he want now?"

"You might find out if you answer," Diego says.

"Hello?"

"Sorry to bother you, Docia. It's Mr. Zilinsky."

"I know. I recognize your number." *Is he serious?*

"Actually, I do have something to tell you." He pauses but I still hear him breathing. "Am I on speaker? Is anyone with you?"

"Yes. My friends are here." I roll my eyes toward them. "There's nothing you can say to me that they can't hear."

"I don't know, Docia. I'm not comfortable talking in front of anyone else."

"They'll know everything as soon as we hang up. Why not let them hear it straight from you?"

"Well, if you put it that way." He fidgets on the other end. "Okay." His voice cracks mid-word. "I'm sorry, this isn't easy."

My heart pounds. We glue our eyes on the phone like we can make him speak faster.

"After it looked like you'd recover from your accident in time to compete in the Olympics, I poked into an old rumor."

"What rumor?" I ask.

"I heard years ago that you were a skater to watch. You were young. People started to notice you at the novice level. I didn't think about it at the time. I mean, no one cared where you came from."

"Right." I turn my head around to loosen my tense neck. "And, for the record, I was adopted and I'm American now, so it shouldn't matter."

"It does matter." He sighs. "The Olympics have rules, you know. Athletes have to be fifteen to compete. That's that."

"I *am*!" My leg shakes. Why doesn't he get on with it? "Almost fifteen-and-a-half, to be exact. No one can prove I'm not."

"Your Russian birth certificate says you're fourteen."

For a moment sheer panic strikes, especially when Diego shakes his head. *Proof I'm not qualified?* A thought shoots through me like a rocket. I motion to Joy for a pen and paper. "I've seen my alleged Russian birth certificate but how do we know it's real?" I say into the phone, even though I have no idea what the document says.

Joy hands me a notepad. *Lena said I wasn't born in Russia!* I scratch on the paper.

"How do you know it's real?" I ask again.

"What do you mean 'How do I know?'"

"I want to know if you can prove that birth certificate is authentic."

"Of course it's real." His voice is agitated. "What are you implying?"

Calm trickles down my spine because I know the truth, and this isn't it. "There was no formal record of my birth."

"Well, there was. The birth certificate may not have been written on the day you were born, but they record all births in Russia."

I scribble, *Should I tell him?*

All three heads nod.

I breathe in a lungful of air then exhale all my doubt. "I wasn't born in Russia."

"That...can't be," he stutters. "But, but of course you were born in Russia—in Moscow exactly as your birth certificate says. They said it was authentic. I...I have to go now."

Still holding the silent phone, I slide down the wall to the floor. "No. Way." I want to ask so many questions, but the thoughts and words bounce around in my head like corn popping. "I don't know what to say."

"You did it Docia. You proved Zilinsky didn't know if the birth certificate was real but used it to disqualify you anyway." Lily crouches down and wraps her arms around me. "The liars have finally told some truth."

"Lily, I can't breathe."

"Oh, sorry." She loosens her grip. "You know me. I get a little carried away."

"She's right, Docia," Joy says. "You got the truth out of them. You're not in the clear yet though. We still need tangible proof."

All my excitement slips away.

"But first," Joy continues. "I'll make hot cocoa. We need to celebrate. This is big."

"I'll help," Lily says and follows her into the kitchen.

Diego sits on the floor next to me and brushes my hair to the side. My head falls onto his shoulder and I go limp. "I'm so exhausted."

He reaches his other arm under my knees and carries me to the sofa.

"This is hopeless. What will I say to Dad?" And that's all I remember.

CHAPTER TWENTY-SEVEN

"Welcome back, sleepyhead," Joy says softly.

The sun peeks through the blinds creating a blurry glow around her as she holds a cup out to me. The inviting steam floating off the top reminds me of the early morning ice before anyone else arrives at the rink.

"I've never slept as much as I have since Moscow." I reach for the mug from underneath the fluffy blanket.

"You fell asleep before you got to drink your cocoa last night," she whispers.

Across the coffee table, Diego is curled up on the other sofa. His breathing is slow like he's in deep slumber.

Joy glances at the still figure. "He wouldn't leave you, and Lily will be back this morning." She puts the warm mug in my hands. "I texted your mom last night. She was worried. She told your dad you're at Lilly's."

The warm, sweet liquid sooths my dry throat. As safe and comforting as it is to be here with my friends, I have to face Dad. I've heard so many of his lectures I could give a few of my own right back. Tell him how important honesty is—especially with people you love. Remind him there's more to life than winning. I'd remind him how trust trumps any gold medal. It would be the anti-lecture—the exact opposite of what he's told me my whole life.

"Your dad's not happy with me at all."

Can Joy read my thoughts? "He'll get over it." I take another sip and lick the foam off my upper lip. *What choice does he have?*

"What will you say to him?"

"What I wish they had told me years ago. The truth." How else would I handle it? "I'll tell everyone else who asks what actually happened too."

"I think I have the proof you need for any doubters," Joy says. "After you fell asleep, I called my friend who works for the Associated Press in Moscow. He used his credentials to get into the Russian government department that manages family services."

"What did he find out?"

"A lot. He had one simple question for them. Show me the birth record for Tatiana Ivanova. They all knew exactly who he was talking about, but they passed him around to different people in the office." Joy folds her arms. "Every one of them tried to stonewall."

Joy walks around the sofa and sits next to me. Why can't my parents be honest like this? Act like they give a crap about someone besides themselves?

"He was at the ministry all day, but he kept one thing from them. He didn't let on that he speaks fluent Russian." She reaches out for my mug. "Here, let me get you a refill. Are you hungry?"

Food is the last thing on my mind. "More cocoa would be great."

"Coming right up." She takes my mug and I follow her to the kitchen.

"My friend heard the ministry employees argue about how to get rid of him since there was no record of the birth at all. When he called them on it—in Russian—they finally admitted the truth. They wrote a letter that explains the paper that disqualified you is false. No one can prove you were born in Russia, which means they also can't challenge your adoption. No one can prove the birthday you celebrate isn't yours."

"Do you have the letter?"

"Yep. He texted me a photograph of it and he's overnighting the original with the signature."

I perk up, a whole-body smile.

"Don't worry, he scanned it too," Joy says. "It won't mysteriously disappear or get all twisted around by some desperate skating coach."

"I'm going to that TV reporter and I'll speak for myself." I stretch my arms and legs. "This is my life, and I will control it." A sense of resolve like

I've never felt before flows through me. "I hope my publicist is still my publicist though. I need her right now. Lena too."

I pace back and forth to the window. Restless. Ready to confront Dad. Face everyone else. I'm ready to be me again. It doesn't matter where I was born or who my parents are. "And I really need to change clothes."

Joy laughs. "I have an idea. There's way too much for just an article. How about I write a book to tell your story? We can do it together."

A whole book about me? "Would anyone read it?"

"Your story? Absolutely. It's good. Too good to make up. Think about the other adopted kids—and adults too—who would be interested."

Wait until Dad gets hold of this. He probably has a book started already filled with a bunch of his speeches and BS that never happened. His book would be fiction.

"It would be fun to work with you on it." Still pacing, my heart revs when I picture Dad's finger wagging in my face when I see him next. "Let's keep the idea between us for now. I don't want my dad to take over and turn it into a circus."

"It's our secret until you're ready."

"And mine too." Diego sits up on the sofa. He watches me pace like a tennis match. "A book's an awesome idea. It's the only way you can be sure the truth is told."

"It's almost over. I can't believe it." Six months ago, I wasn't sure I would be healthy enough to compete. Now I'm an Olympic gold medalist with a whole new past.

"It's a matter of time before we have the proof in hand that will clear up this scandal." Joy reaches over and holds my chin like Lena does. "And you've handled yourself beautifully throughout the whole mess. Better than most adults would."

"Well, most of the time."

She doesn't answer, but her smile does.

If I can get through this, there's not much I can't do. The room feels small. I have to get out so I can breathe. So I can take control of my life.

"Hey Joy, before the chaos starts, would you mind taking me to the hospital? I need to see Lena."

"Of course," she answers.

"I'll take you," Diego says. "I'd like to see her too."

"Joy, thank you so much. For everything. I don't know what I'll ever do to repay you."

"You already are by helping our fellow adoptees."

Diego drapes his arm across my shoulders as we walk down the sidewalk to his car. "You're a little wound up today," he says.

"I know. I can't help it." Normally I would love to have him so close, but his arm feels like a weight that holds me back. "I'm tired of standing still."

"Joy's cool. She helps you get stuff done."

"I don't know how I would've gotten through this without her. I'd probably have Dad's car wrapped around a tree somewhere."

He stops shy of the car door and steps in front of me. "Why do you say that?"

"Oh, nothing. Something stupid I did."

He'd totally lose respect for me if he ever found out about that night I downed most of a bottle of wine.

"I'm glad Joy was there for you." He leans forward and his lips gently brush mine. "I'm sorry I wasn't," he whispers. Then he does it again, this time he lingers a bit longer.

He holds the tiny maroon door open for me but I'm frozen, wondering if those really were his soft lips on mine.

"So, are you coming to the hospital?" he asks.

"Oh, sorry. Guess you unwound me a little."

As I get in the car, my eyes stop on the MG emblem that peeps out from between his fingers on the gearshift. I go back to that day—the one when my dad kicked Diego out of our house after my accident and told him to never come back. His reason? *Because Diego is a good-for-nothing dreamer who will hold my daughter back.*

But he is coming back. Today. If Dad says one word about Diego....

"Are you okay?"

I snap back to reality. "Uhm, yeah. I was thinking about how awful my dad's been to you. How can you stand to speak to me?"

"How could I not speak to you?" Diego laughs. "I thought the kiss freaked you out."

My face turns warm.

"Docia, your dad has nothing to do with you and me. Zero." He turns into a parking space at the hospital. "You know that, right?"

My dad's had everything to do with every person and part of my life until now. "He did. Not anymore."

CHAPTER TWENTY-EIGHT

Hospitals ruin people's lives. Like the day the doctor told me I may not skate competitively again. Dad's words still sting. *That good-for-nothing, long-haired hippie put my daughter here.*

Diego and I walk quietly together down the fourth-floor hallway. I gently push Lena's door open and cross my fingers until I see her outstretched arms. *If any lives change during this hospital visit, I want Lena to be healthier.*

"Lena, you look so much better." I leave her purse I've carried around since yesterday on the bedside table and reach my arms around her. I bury my face into her pillow to catch the tears before they drip. "I was so worried about you."

"Thank you, my sweet girl, for taking such good care of me."

Her hug isn't as strong as usual, but I stay in her arms until I compose myself. It's where I always feel safe.

"And Diego, it's so nice of you to visit."

Lena reaches out to him, and Diego cradles her hand between both of his. "I want to help my favorite coach and skater get back on the ice soon." Then he grabs my hand. "She's got competitions to get ready for."

"Yes, we will be back at the rink soon." She looks serious for a moment, like when we left Moscow.

"The doctor says I had a heart attack. They did a small procedure this morning to unblock arteries."

Hearing Lena say it was a heart attack is like someone punched me in the stomach. "They're sure the surgery fixed it?"

"Do not worry about me. I will be fine."

Lena's face is peaceful, but I'll never forget never seeing Grandpa for the last time after the same thing happened to him. I can't think of life without Lena.

I won't.

"The doctor says I can do short sessions at the rink in about a week if I feel like it."

"Just a week?" My stomach feels normal for a moment then it flips upside down. If we start training for Worlds next week, I'll have to live up to the world champion title. "Are you sure you'll be up to it?"

Am I sure I will?

"I had better be. My doctor has no choice. I told her I would be at the rink anyway. She was very impressed when I told her who my star pupil is."

"Yeah right." I roll my eyes. "I'm sure your doctor has no idea who I am."

"Remember, you are on magazine covers now," Lena answers. "Everyone around here knows who you are. They support you."

That girl in the magazines is the one Dad created. Not me.

"They're not the only ones," Diego said. "Docia, tell her what happened."

"I know. One of the nurses showed me the interview on her phone." Lena cups my chin in her hand. "I am so proud of my brave girl. Young woman, I mean."

"It's not over yet. I haven't talked to Mom and Dad since the interview." I drop my gaze to the floor. "Diego's taking me home when we leave here." I can't think about Worlds until I clear things up with them.

"We already know you have what it takes to win the Olympics. You can tell your parents how you feel."

"Thank you, Lena. I'll try." Yeah, but a triple toe loop doesn't shush you or ground you until you're twenty-five. "I'll come back and visit as soon as I can."

I've made it this far. Nothing will stop me now.

CHAPTER TWENTY-NINE

Diego rolls to a stop in front of the house while I sit in the passenger seat gazing into the lit kitchen window. The dread of stepping inside the door I've walked through my whole life into the only home I remember spreads like poison ivy.

They're likely scheduling my life. Mom is at the kitchen table writing out my practice and school schedule for the week. Dad paces back and forth barking out "one hour of cardio" and "one hour of ballet" and stews over who he blames for "my daughter's breakdown," like he told the reporter after I walked out of the interview last night.

My hands and feet are heavier than concrete. I try to lift my arm to unhook the seat belt. It won't move. I breathe in then out and mouth, "You can do this."

"Now or never. You know what to say. Walk through that door and say it."

"Will you come with me?"

"That wouldn't be smart. Do you want to start World War III?"

"I know." A shadow crosses the kitchen window. "This is between my parents and me."

I shove all doubts and questions and conversations in my head away and push the car door open. "Here goes."

"Hey."

I turn in the seat to face him. "Yeah?"

"They'll still love you."

Diego is usually right, but how can he be so sure? Mom and Dad probably think I'm daughter-zilla.

I force one foot in front of the other and walk right in. They're in the kitchen as I expect, but not writing instructions and pacing. They're at the table eating and talking—even laughing.

Neither of them looks up. They carry on like I'm not even here.

"Oh, hi sweetheart," Mom finally says. "Grab a plate. Your dad's giving me the details about Moscow."

I make a plate of food and sit down. Dad's voice is nothing but buzzing in my head. He still doesn't look at me. I push meatloaf and steamed carrots from one side of the plate to the other. Will he let this whole thing go? I chew one bite but taste nothing.

When their plates are empty, I pick up the dishes to take them to the sink like always.

"Thank you, Docia," Dad says. It's the first time he addresses me directly. "What happened last night will never happen again." His voice is calm, but his eyes pierce all the way to my soul. "I did not teach my daughter to treat her father that way. Especially after everything I've done to make you a star."

"*Your* daughter?" I slam the plate on the marble counter and shatter it. "How could any father lie to his daughter for her entire li—?"

"Go to your room!" The veins on Dad's temples pulsate. "I will not have this conversation with you."

"I'm. Not. Finished." Words fly out like projectiles. "*You* did nothing to make me a star. All you did was set me up to *fail* after I worked my tail off to win the Olympics."

"You're fifteen," Dad barks. "You know nothing about working your tail off. You'll never know what it took for me to get you—all the Russian red tape. I had to hide your past from you. It's the only way they would leave you alone."

"I don't care what you had to go through or how old I am, I deserve to know the truth!" I gasp for breaths and nearly hyperventilate. "Why did you lie? Why did you ruin my dream?"

Mom walks toward me. "Docia, your father only wants the best for you."

"Mom, get a clue. The only best interests Dad thinks about are his own. Not yours. Not mine. Not anybody's."

Before the last word escapes my mouth, Dad strikes his hand across my face.

Everything. Stops.

Breathing.

Talking.

Movement.

Thoughts.

I hold my stinging cheek and glare at Dad. All I can think about is getting out. Away from these people.

I run to my room and lock the door. A cool washcloth on my cheek doesn't stop the hurt. *I hate him!* Why did he have to adopt me? Why did he hit me? My real father would never do that. Lena could have taken care of me in Russia. All the damp cloth does is catch my tears. *Why can't he let me be me?*

No one knocks on my door or yells from the kitchen. I curl up in a ball on my bed and stare at the stars in the dark blue sky that remind me of camera flashes across the stands in the rink.

CHAPTER THIRTY

The clock on my nightstand says three in the morning. I'm wide awake so I slide out the window with my skates in my backpack. I crouch below the garage windows and grab the key from behind the right front wheel of Dad's car. With the gear in neutral, I guide the car as it rolls down the driveway like I saw in a movie. Halfway to the street, I start it. *They'll never notice I'm gone.*

I throw the car into drive and press down on the accelerator. I hate my dad. I'm pretty sure he and Mom hate me right now. I fix my eyes on the dark street ahead while the familiar houses pass by. The right turn then the left. Maybe I can teach skating. Lena might let me live with her while I train. Then straight along the long stretch down the usually busy road. I can have more time to work with the foster kids.

The neon sign comes on against the night's blackness and triggers me to start the left turn into the empty lot, careful to not clip the curb. Damage Dad's car and I'll prove to him I'm still a kid. I can pass my driving test when I live with Lena.

Once I sneak through my secret entrance and turn on the lights, the rink's musky odor hits me. Skates hugging my feet with the freedom of speeding across the ice relaxes me. This is my home. I improvise to imaginary music. Feel the melodies between the jumps and spins that flow from my body. I'm free. No one rink side tells me to slow down or check out of my back sit spin better. I'll stop when I want.

"That was beautiful."

My heart jumps up my throat and comes out as a squeaky scream, "Who's there?"

"It's me, Peanut."

My heart settles back where it's supposed to be when he steps out of the shadows. "Dad, you scared me!"

"I'm sorry. I heard the car when you left and figured you'd be here. I see that window's still broken."

"Yeah." So much for freedom.

"You've practiced driving." He steps near the rink's edge into the light. "That was very nice—what you just skated. Is that a new program? Looks like you've practiced a lot of things."

Yeah, like being away from you. "No, I just made it up." For once, Dad looks nervous with his hands stuffed in his pockets.

"Sorry I startled you. I'm sorry for a lot of things." Now he rocks his weight back and forth between each leg. "Your mother let me have it for allowing things to get where they are."

Will he ever change? At least Mom stood up to him. I glide around the middle of the rink staring down at the smooth surface. Why can't the ice tell me the future like a crystal ball?

"Your mom wanted to tell you about your past a few years ago. Lena's wanted to for years. I wouldn't let them."

Is he speaking the truth for once?

"I thought knowing your real identity would distract you from our goal."

"Dad, it's not about *you*. Haven't you figured that out yet? Do you realize how bad you've screwed things up?" I fold my arms in front of me to hold back the adrenaline. "My career. My credibility. They're shot. How can I ever trust you?"

"I know now. I never meant for things to get like this." Now he's standing on the edge of the ice.

I glide around the middle. Take deep breaths.

"You have to trust me." His voice has a tinge of begging.

But the sting of his hand across my face last night still ripples through me. *He can't* tell *me to trust him.* Breathe. In and out. "I don't know." The picture of Lena's weak smile in her hospital bed flashes across my memory. "It's too soon."

"Give me a chance?"

I don't know if I can.

"Let's go home," he says. "It's late."

I continue to circle slowly but I crave to skate hard. "Okay," automatically comes out of my mouth. "No, I'll stay and skate." The words feel good. They're my words. My thoughts. Out loud. To my dad.

"You need some sleep." Dad reaches out with my skate guards. "Come on."

"No. You go ahead. I'll be home later." Home, or whatever that place is.

He gives me his I'm-serious-do-it-now look.

"I'm not leaving yet. Not until the first freestyle session starts."

Still holding my skate guards, his hand drops to his side. His opens his mouth like he's about to respond. Instead, he nods, carefully puts my guards down, and walks into the darkness.

I feel five inches taller like I could push the Zamboni across the rink.

After a couple of warm-up laps, I swipe my phone to my program music, then skate my Olympic long program.

It's magical. Jumps are light. Landings are strong. Each spin is centered. Fast. The choreography flows. I tap through the footwork. If Lena were here, she'd cross her hands over her heart like she did that night in Moscow. Then tell me to do it again.

At the spiral sequence, my favorite part when I know the hardest stuff is done, and when I look up into the stands for Mom and Dad. They're not there. No one's there. Not Lena or Diego or Lily. Not even a single fan.

I'm alone. The emptiness crashes into me like the weight of ten Zambonis.

My knee buckles underneath my perfect back spiral and I crumple to the ice. A couple of tears fall into the light cloud of moisture that rises from the rink and freeze when they hit the ice.

"Damn him." They're the only family I have. I've already lost one set of parents. I can't lose another. Face this alone at fifteen? Going it alone is way better than someone I trust betraying me. I bang my fist against the ice. "I don't deserve this!" The sound bounces off the empty rink.

The slight sound of my music plays above the echo of my voice from the earbuds that have fallen onto the ice. The final pose is here. The crowd roar is now. Neither happens.

I pick myself up and glide over to the door. I know better than to skate more when I'm out of the zone. Out of habit, I reach for my skate guards that sit where Dad left them arranged perfectly symmetric and controlled. I walk away and leave the guards there.

While unlacing my skates, I imagine Lena hovering as she shares what I did well and need to work on in our next practice session. She would have a fit if she saw me walking on my blades without guards.

I love Lena. She's like family. She isn't though.

I yank one boot off then the other and stuff them in my bag.

Dad has to accept me on my terms.

I pull the lever down to turn off the lights and walk through the darkness to the men's locker room.

We're it. All each other has for family. We have to make this work but letting me be me is the only way I'll still like myself.

With the car key in hand, I stuff my bag through the partial opening and pull myself up through the window. A flash catches my eye on the pavement next to the car. It's a shiny penny under the streetlight. I pick it up and rub my thumb over the smooth ridges. Every time Mom finds a penny on the ground, she picks it up. *Keep this in your bank and it will bring you luck*, she would say. Each time, she repeated the story about the penny in her shoe that her family passed down for generations. It was in her shoe when she and Dad married. She always told me I was the good luck the penny brought.

The date stamped on the penny is this year. My Olympic year. My independence year. I drop the penny into my sneaker. I need all the good luck I can find.

CHAPTER THIRTY-ONE

My mind bounces between the sting of Dad's palm and our encounter at the rink. Do I even want Mom and Dad to still love me? I slam on the brakes just shy of a delivery truck when its bright red lights flash on like exploding fireworks. "That was close," I whisper, my heart still pounding.

I turn into the almost empty hospital parking lot. An ambulance is under the covered area. People rush around it. It's almost six in the morning. They will let me see Lena soon. I recline the seat and close my eyes.

A slamming car door startles me awake. The bright ball of light that tips over the horizon reminds me I've napped in a parking lot for more than an hour. The screen on my phone is covered with messages from Dad. *Where are you? Call me. Come home. Now.* I stuff the phone back in my pocket and walk to the hospital entrance.

"Come in," I hear when I knock on Lena's door. It's closer to the strong voice I'm used to. She looks like the Lena I know.

"You're here early," she says between a sip of juice and a bite of fruit. "Did you skate the morning freestyle session?"

"Yes, I did." She doesn't need to know it was before the first freestyle. Nor does she need to know I went early to get out of that strange house. She definitely doesn't need to know what happened with my parents. "It was good. I went through my Olympic program."

Lena sets her fork down and puts her hand to her heart. "Was it as beautiful as when you won the world over in Moscow?"

"It felt good." It did for the first time in a long time. "I wish you could've been there."

"Did your quad-double entry work?"

"My version did. But you're much more important. How do you feel? When do you go home?"

"Much, much better. Doctor says I can go home today if all goes well."

She has no idea how relieved I am.

"And I'll be at the rink with you next week."

I'm getting used to being on my own, and I like it. This is Worlds though. What if I get to go? I need Lena for that. "It's hardly worth the bother since I can't compete."

"You will compete. I promise. Speaking of Worlds, I have a surprise for you."

I see that twinkle back in her eye. "Hope it's a good one. I've had more surprises than I can handle."

The only surprise I want right now is to get my medal back. Oh, and to get those idiots who started this whole scandal to admit they were wrong.

"Some skaters are organizing a show to support you and all adopted children who want to find their birth parents."

"A show? For adopted kids and me?" My heartbeat jumps into my throat. "Why? I thought most of the other skaters hated me."

"Why would you think that? How could they?" Lena says. "They want you back on the ice. They want rules to be fair for everyone. They don't believe medals should be taken away on rumors."

"I don't know what to say."

My lack of response brings Lena's laugh back. It's not as jolly as usual, but close. "How about say you will skate in it?"

"Where is it? When?"

Maybe my career's not over. I scoot to the edge of the vinyl chair next to her. These skaters are buried in training for Worlds. How will they have time? Oh my god, what will Stacy think?

"So, are you interested? It will be in Moscow next week just before Worlds. I also hear your real father will be there."

Yeah, I'm interested. I try to answer, but nothing comes out.

"Of course, your parents have to approve."

"I wouldn't miss it for anything." For once, I'm making my own decisions. "I'll make sure I'm there."

"That's my girl."

"You said my real dad will be there. Does he know about me yet?"

"Not yet, but soon."

"Will you at least tell me what country he's from? There are like twenty-five pairs men who competed the year Anna won the Olympic gold. I couldn't even begin to guess."

"Your papa is from Italy."

I'll get to meet my real dad. Then my lungs deflate like a balloon stuck with a pin. "But...I have no money. The sponsors all left. How will I get there?"

Lena reaches over and lays her hand on top of mine. "Your friends took care of that too—for you and your parents."

My parents. How will Dad screw things up for me this time?

"You look unhappy. Do not worry about expenses."

"Okay." I force a smile. "You concentrate on your recovery. I can't go without you. I won't."

"That is bull. Is that how you say it?"

I can't help but laugh. "I promise I won't worry about you getting well, Lena. Seriously. I'll just practice."

"Docia, you are a strong and exceptionally talented young woman. There is nothing you cannot do." This time she grabs my hand like she'll never let go. "You've been through a lot—more than most see in a lifetime. My grown-up Docia handled everything with sportsmanship. Maturity. Grace."

I close my eyes to keep the tears from falling. Hearing her say how much I've been through. Acknowledge it. She makes the whole drama real.

"People are behind you. No matter what has already happened or might happen in the future, those who love you most will stand by you. Always. Even your parents." Lena's voice is barely above a whisper. Her pause makes me look up to see her comforting smile. "I hope you never forget that."

I sit on the edge of the bed to hug her. "I won't." That's when the tears start. She doesn't let go until they stop. Her steady heartbeat soothes me.

"What's my real dad's name? Do you know how to contact him?"

"His name is Luca Baresi, and yes, I'm working on finding out."

"I know, but when?"

She sighs. "Be patient leetle *solnyshko*. Okay, perhaps it's time for you to go home." I sit up on the bed to see Lena's stern look. "Your parents are worried."

"Dad called?" *Of course he did.*

Lena nods. "Drive carefully."

I shake my head and turn toward the door. "Yes, Lena. You rest and get well."

"Okay. Docia?" I turn to face her as I reach the doorway. "I didn't tell your parents about the show in Moscow."

"Thanks."

CHAPTER THIRTY-TWO

When I walk into the house, Dad's at the kitchen bar pulling the zipper strip to open an express-delivery package. "This came for you."

"For me?" I grab the cardboard envelope and fall into a chair. "Then I'll open it."

Dad's so close behind me I feel the warmth from his body. This time it doesn't bother me. There are more important things to think about. I can barely make out the word Russia on the hand-written return address. Inside is a single piece of paper. Even though it's in Russian, I know what it says.

"So?" Dad's breath brushes the top of my head. "What is it?"

"A letter."

"I can see that." He reaches out to take it from me, but I pull away. "From whom? What does it say?"

"The Russian ministry that handles family services. They wrote a letter that explains there is no official record of my birth. This confirms they can't prove I was born in Russia like those people behind the scandal claim. That the birth certificate they had in Moscow was forged."

"Where did you get this?" He snatches the paper. "I knew nothing about any letter. How do you know it's real?"

His face is red, but it's not nearly as flaming as mine feels. "Be careful. It's important!" I take the letter back and smooth it on the table. "Trust me, it's real, and it didn't exist until yesterday."

"How...where did it come from?" He examines the words on the page.

"A reporter Joy knows in Moscow went to the ministry office. When the people there admitted there was nothing that could prove where and when I was born, he persuaded them to write the letter." This time, you will not intrude. "It's over. No one can prove I'm not fifteen."

"You can get your medal back," Dad says. "All our hard work paid off, Peanut."

Really? I give him a sideways stare.

"Okay, all your hard work paid off," he answers. "Better?"

"It's a start." At least he noticed. "That's not all the good news. Where's Mom?"

"Oh, she's off doing something unimportant as usual."

"Just because it's not something *you* told her to do doesn't mean it's not important." Instead of answering, he sits in the chair next to me and stares at the letter.

"Please be nicer to Mom—whether she's in the room or not."

"I am nice to her." He doesn't look up. "How do you know what this letter says?"

I ignore his question.

"We'll see if it stands up." He slides the letter back into the envelope. "There are enough people who want to see you fail. If there's a tiny crack in the proof, they'll find it."

"Thanks, Dad." I shake my head and stare at the ceiling. "Your confidence makes me feel so much better."

"Get used to it." He returns his scrunched forehead I-mean-business face. "If you plan to be the new, independent Docia Sikorsky, Skating Star, you'll encounter doubters a lot. This world's full of people who want to tear you down. Look at what happened when they sabotaged me at NASA. Then those idiot administrators at the school where I was teaching did the same thing. Now you, with everything I've done for you."

He'll never get it.

We turn to the door when we hear paper crumpling and Mom's cheery voice, "I'm home! Any word from Docia?" She appears around the corner loaded down with more than an armful of grocery bags.

"Hang on, Mom. I'll help you."

"Thank God, Docia."

I take two of the bags.

"I mean, thank God you're home. You had me worried sick."

"You knew I was fine. Dad told you I was at the rink."

"There's no need to roll your eyes at me. A mom has every right to be worried when her fifteen-year-old daughter disappears in the middle of the night."

"Okay, okay. I get it. Dump the bags then come sit down. I have news for you and Dad."

Mom's returned look says it all before she speaks. "What more could you possibly say?"

"It's good. I promise."

I know exactly what to say, but making the words come out in a way they'll be supportive is entirely different. Their stares don't help.

"A group of skaters is putting on a show in my honor in Moscow." The words spill out.

"That's crazy." Dad stomps to the window. "Why would they do that? What do they want from you? And when—with Worlds so soon?"

"Because they're my friends who want me to compete at Worlds. They want fair rules for everyone, and they want to raise awareness about adoption." Do I sound as confident as I feel? "It's this weekend, and I'll skate with them."

"Why would you fly back to a country where they wouldn't let me leave?"

"Because I want to." Excitement builds with each word. "Skating is everything to me."

Dad paces across the kitchen and waves his arms. "Who told you this nonsense?"

"Lena." The only one around here who treats me like a human.

"It sounds wonderful, Docia," says Mom, the supportive one. "I can't think of a thing wrong with the idea."

"So, we're good. I'll go."

Mom walks toward me, beaming. "What thoughtful friends there are in the skating community. I had no idea. Of course, you'll—"

"I'm not convinced." Dad steps on Mom's words again. "How do you know the Russian government isn't in on it? They may want you back to skate for them."

"Because my biological father will be there—and he's not Russian."

Dad's face turns pale and expressionless. Is he that intimidated by someone who might compete with him?

"Skaters from around the world will perform. You're both welcome to go, but Lena will be there as my guardian if you can't. Remember, you signed something to allow that. And please don't cut Mom off."

Mom and Dad look at each other and then at me.

"I'll be in my room."

"Docia, wait." Dad's voice is much weaker than usual. "Of course, your mother and I will go with you." He walks over and embraces me in a bear hug that lifts me off the ground. "Family sticks together."

He used to pick me up like this when I was little. I enjoyed it then. He made me feel special. Safe. Now it's smothering. I may be small, but I don't want him to treat me like a kid. When my feet are safely on the ground, I step away from him.

"But every family changes. Kids grow up and learn to think for themselves."

"Honey." Mom walks over to join Dad, "Look at all she's been through."

I can always count on Mom to be on my side. If Dad would only listen to her.

"Just like I've taught her," Dad says.

Exactly how I would expect him to answer. Let him take credit for anything good.

"I'll call you for dinner," Mom hollers after me.

In my room, I leave the precious letter on my desk and curl up on my bed cuddling Fred and stare at the spot on the wall where my Worlds photo was before I broke the frame. Maybe I'll be able to put it back soon. Until then, the spot is empty like that place in my heart. The one where skating goes.

CHAPTER THIRTY-THREE

I grab my phone, type in Luca Baresi, Italy, and pairs figure skating. At least I have a name and country to narrow the search. The screen displays photographs and videos and pages and pages of information about him. He was a big deal. Did he fall in love again? Do I have brothers or sisters? Wikipedia says he's married and has one child, but nothing more about his family. Would they ever accept me?

I click on an Olympic performance video. His intense blue eyes are like mine; like the Mediterranean is creeping up a sandy beach next to his olive skin and dark hair. He's tall and graceful gliding next to his petite partner, strong and controlled with the throws and lifts. How will he feel about a surprise daughter?

Car doors slamming interrupt the program music. I roll over and peer out the window. It's an ESPN news truck. "What the...?"

I toss Fred aside and run downstairs. "Dad? Why is that reporter back?"

"Well Peanut, if you have a big show to kick off your comeback, the world needs to know about it."

"I didn't ask for media coverage. Did you even plan to tell me?"

"Sweetie, calm down," Mom answers. "I don't see any harm in it."

"There's the doorbell. I'll handle it," I say.

Dad starts down the hall behind me. "We'll do it together."

"I. Will. Handle. This." I block him with my hands on my hips to make me look bigger. "I mean it, Dad. I won't move until you agree, or I'll send them away."

We stare each other down. I won't back off. Stubbornness is one good thing I learned from Dad.

"Okay." He nods. "We'll see how you do solo on this interview."

We both pretend to not race to the door. By the time we get there, Mom has let the camera operator and reporter in—the exact team we just talked to. Was that yesterday when everything unraveled even more? My life became everyone's business? On camera? In front of the entire world?

I take a deep breath and extend my hand to greet the reporter. "Hello again, Mr. Ramirez."

"Hi." He shakes my hand then Mom's and Dad's. "Thanks for calling us with your news." Today he's dressed in jeans and a Polo shirt rather than his suit. "You caught me before I boarded a plane to an assignment. Give us a few minutes to set up and we'll do a quick on-camera."

"Take your time." Interviews used to make me nervous, but after so many, it's no big thing. I catch my reflection in the entryway mirror. "Mom, would you please help them set up in the living room by the competition photos? I need to run upstairs and get something." And change these stinky clothes.

I shoot Dad a stern glance and mouth, "Do not say anything."

He responds with a shrug.

In my room, I throw on my favorite red sweater and leggings and top it off with a belt and black boots as fast as I can so Dad won't say something wrong down there. I do a once-over in the mirror and straighten my ponytail. "Not bad for forty-five seconds." I trample downstairs, letter in hand.

"I have a letter to show you," I say to the reporter. "It proves the Russian birth certificate those people used to start this whole scandal isn't real."

Mom straightens the drapes and Dad isn't even in the room.

"Oh? Let me see." The reporter reaches into his shirt pocket for his glasses and takes the letter. "Hmmm, it looks official. I'd like to authenticate it. Mind if we snap an image of it?"

"Sure, go ahead. An Associated Press reporter in Russia secured the letter." By now he's already put his phone in position to shoot a photo, and the camera guy scans the page.

"Ready?" The reporter straightens his shirt. "You on your own for this interview?"

"Yes, I am."

Dad is in the doorway looking on.

"This is Frank Ramirez reporting from Houston Texas from the home of controversial skating star Docia Sikorsky with a new development in her Olympic birthday scandal. A letter has surfaced that proves the claims her Russian birth are false. ESPN will authenticate the letter so more to come. Docia, how do you feel about the latest developments?"

"Relieved."

Dad leans against the wall, arms crossed. He doesn't look angry or happy or anything. He just listens.

"I don't remember where I was born. Like many adopted kids, no one tells us the whole story about our parents. I only want the truth and to skate."

The reporter moves the mic back to himself. "Of course. Your friends and fans in the skating world want the truth too. I understand there will be a big skating show this weekend."

"That's right. Skaters around the world want the rules to be fair for everyone—and for all adopted children to have a chance to find their missing puzzle pieces." My ponytail bounces on my neck when I nod. "The show will air live from Moscow on Sunday. All the big names will be there, along with a few surprises."

The show feels real now. I hope the shiver that worked its way through me isn't visible on camera.

"You can tune into the show this Sunday morning at eleven eastern time on ESPN 2," Ramirez says to the camera. "Docia, we hope you're back on the ice and the medal podium soon."

"Thank you." I finish the shot with a smile until Dad's slow applause distracts me from the lens.

"Nice job." He walks toward me. "You should have said more about those yo-yos who are trying to smear your reputation; all the work we've done."

"I said everything I wanted to say." Mom's face tells me she agrees. "I have no interest in dragging this out any longer. Just let me skate."

I reach out to shake the journalist's hand. "Thank you, Mr. Ramirez. Will you come to the show?"

"We'll have someone there and I'll continue to cover your story as details unfold. Good luck to you."

My phone on the coffee table lights up. "Excuse me." My publicist's name pops up. "I need to get this. Thank you so much."

I answer the call while Mom and Dad show the news crew to the door. "Hi, Kimberly. Great timing. ESPN just finished an interview."

"About the Moscow show?" she asks.

"Yes, the show and one other development."

"You've been a busy girl. If you handled it like the last one, I'm sure it went beautifully. I have some news for you too."

"Good news, I hope?"

"Yes, very. Vera Wang called our office. They've already started the design for your new skating dress for this weekend's show. They'll email design choices to you tomorrow morning."

"Are you kidding? Vera Wang? Is designing a dress for me?" I think back to winning Nationals in one of her dresses.

"The sponsors are coming back, my dear. Wang is one of them. She said she would donate the dress to 'my favorite skater' her office said. You just need to plan a stop in Manhattan on your way to Moscow for a fitting and to pick it up."

I blink to stop the tears. "I don't know what to say."

"You don't have to say anything. You've worked hard to earn support. I'm sure you'll look stunning." Kimberly is silent waiting for me to respond.

"Yes. I'll be there."

"I'll let her know. Talk to you soon."

I touch the end button on my phone and drop down onto the sofa still in shock. Only another skater like Vera Wang gets how important the dress is.

"Mom, want to stop in New York before Moscow?"

CHAPTER THIRTY-FOUR

I never thought my life could get weirder.

The familiar stuff around my room is unfamiliar. It's all hers. The little girl who always did what she was told. The one who was never allowed to have a thought of her own.

In a few days, I'll be in Manhattan to pick up my amazing new Vera Wang dress on my way back to Moscow for a show my friends created in my honor. I'll meet my real dad.

That obedient little girl will be nowhere near New York City—or Moscow.

I've already competed in the Olympics. How hard could organizing this trip be? Dad decided to be considerate and stay home until Saturday to fly with Lena. Another break from being in charge will do Dad some good. Help get him out of practice.

Without Dad in New York, Mom will be fun.

How about a surprise skate in Rockefeller Plaza? I pick up my phone to redial Kimberly.

"Hi, Docia," Kimberly's cheery voice comes across the phone. "More news?"

"Ha, not yet. What do you think of this? Since I didn't get my Rockefeller Plaza guest appearance after the Olympics, would they let me do it on Friday morning? I'll already be in Manhattan."

"Great idea. They'll love the show and adoption theme with the reunion with your real father angle. I'll call my contact there."

"You like the idea?" I haven't had a chance to have many of my own.

"Love it," Kimberly says. "Wait a minute. Did your dad put you up to this call?"

"He doesn't know." Yeah, and when he finds out, he'll crap all over it since it wasn't his idea. He won't want me to do the interview with just Mom there.

"I'd hug you if you were here, Docia. Call you back with the details when I know them."

"Thank you, Kimberly." I end the call.

I wish Diego could be with us. It won't matter that we'll be at the same place where my life fell apart. He'll get to meet my real dad. He'll help me feel strong when I'm not.

Then my phone rings. It's Diego. "I was just thinking about you. It's like you heard my brain."

"Maybe I did," he answers. "Your life changes on the hour these days so I have to check in before I see your news online. Someday I'll read a story that you're running for governor."

"Ha! No chance of that. I've had enough politics for a lifetime. Can I talk you into going to New York with me this weekend on the way to Moscow?"

"I heard about the show. That's pretty cool."

There's a short pause like he's waiting for me to speak.

"I wish I could." He sighs. "If I had the money, I would."

"You'd come all that way for me if you had the money?"

"Without a thought. You sound surprised." Diego laughs. "It's not like I can cough up a few grand overnight. Your dad would never let me come with you anyway."

That's what I expected, but I still hoped for more.

"Don't worry about Dad. Can you get off work? Would your parents let you? You'd only miss a few days of school. I can't make this trip without the best boyfriend in the world." Oh, I said boyfriend.

He pauses. "Docia, I'd do almost anything for you, but does it matter?"

"Yes. I'll call you back."

He barely has a chance to say okay before I redial Kimberly and explain the situation.

"I can't make any promises, but I think we can get one more person there," she says. "Oh, and I got those Vera Wang sketches. I'll forward them to you. Let me know as soon as you decide—tonight if you can."

"Wow, thanks."

Extra energy bounces inside me and looks for a way out. I don't know what to do, so I grab my laptop and stare at the screen willing Kimberly's email to arrive. I know my favorite design as soon as the message comes in. The first is pretty, peach, and flowy. It's close enough to white that Dad may even pick it and then have it covered with sequins. The second one is elegant. It's fitted and black at the top with a beautiful royal blue skirt that falls from an empire waist covered in tiny rhinestones that twinkle like stars on a crystal-clear night.

The last dress is me. The layered melon chiffon looks like a blazoned Texas summer sun dipping into the horizon. There are no beads or sparkles. The neckline drapes across the chest like a sash and does the same across the low back like the layers of a sunset covering the fitted bodice. The tiered chiffon in shades of melon will flow like the flames danced in the Olympic Village fireplace.

The dress looks like I feel. Fiery.

Without another thought, I type a reply to Kimberly.

They're all amazing, but the melon dress is the one. Please ask them to keep the royal blue and black design for me though. It's gorgeous and I'd love to wear it next season. Please tell them thank you. Seriously. Thank you. ~ d

She responds immediately.

That was fast. Nice choice. They'll be ready for your final fitting Friday morning. Go to the Wang studio first thing. Your mom knows where it is. ~Kimberly

P.S. Got Diego's travel covered. We'll email the itinerary for the three of you to you and your mom. You're good to go.

I stare at the screen and then at the wall. *Is that all it takes to get things done? It's easy. Why did I let Dad do everything for me until now?*

I text Diego the good news and send another to Lily to see if she wants to visit Lena with me.

Pick you up in ten, she texts back.

"Mom!" I yell into the kitchen on my way to the front door. "Lily and I are headed to visit Lena then the rink to go through my program after they close."

"Okay, don't be too late." She sounds like her head is in a mixing bowl. "You need to pack and get some rest for the trip."

"Got it covered, Mom." I don't, but it will take fifteen minutes to throw everything in my bag. Who can rest with all this amazing stuff going on? "Oh, and I picked out the dress design. They'll be ready for us Friday." I stick my head back inside. "And Diego's going with us."

CHAPTER THIRTY-FIVE

Mom doesn't have a half second to respond before I'm out of the house. There's no time to argue every tiny detail.

Lily reaches across the passenger seat to open the door. "Get in before the paparazzi find you."

I look down the street for strange cars and slide in.

"Or before something else amazing happens." Lily revs the engine and drives in the rink's direction.

"The hospital's the other way, genius."

"Oh yeah, sorry." Lily whips around in a U-turn and barely misses the car parked on the street. "Okay, smarty pants. Is Lena still in the hospital or has she gone home?"

"Good question." I dial the hospital number.

When I ask to be transferred to Lena's room, the voice on the other end says one of the best things I could hope for. "She was released a couple of hours ago."

Each word takes a little more weight off. "That's great. Thank you." I sit back and imagine Lena's proud face rink side in Moscow. "Other direction. She *is* at home."

"Awesome." Lily whips back around toward Lena's. "Does that mean she'll go to Moscow?"

"She *has* to," I say. "You both have got to see the amazing dress Vera Wang designed for me. It's my new lucky dress."

"You don't need luck. You've got facts, talent, and a slew of friends behind you." Lily laughs. "Besides, you could wear an old pair of overalls and hand-me-down skates and still do a killer program."

"Thanks. Glad someone thinks so."

What I especially need is for people to quit butting in. Having Lena and Diego there will help.

"You know I'd be there for you if I didn't have cheering stuff."

"Of course you would. I didn't dare say anything because they'd kick you off the squad. I can't ask you to give that up."

Lena's house is warm and inviting. Lights glow behind the curtains and a stream of smoke curls up from her chimney. The door opens to a strange face.

"Come in girls. Lena's expecting you."

"Thank you. I'm Docia, and this is my friend Lily."

The woman laughs. "I know who you are. Lena talks about you all the time. I'm Mrs. Johnson from next door." She turns and yells inside. "I'll check on you in a little while, Lena."

Lena looks small in the over-stuffed chair by the fireplace, but the flames brighten her tired eyes. "It's good to see you girls." Lily and I lean down so the three of us can embrace. "Sit. Tell me the latest."

"You first," I answer. "How do you feel? Can you come to Moscow?"

"Slow down, Docia. You talk faster than you skate." Lena pauses. "It looks good for Moscow. I will know for certain Friday when I see the doctor." She takes another short break to catch her breath, something she never did before. "I will never be completely well, but I can go back to normal life soon."

"Never totally well?" *I've never skated without Lena. Don't think I could.* Lily's compassionate look confirms the need to worry. She also reminds me I won't be alone. "I'll help, Lena. Whatever you need."

"I need you to practice your exhibition program. You must skate how I know you can on Sunday." Lena pauses again. "That's all I need."

"She's on it, Lena," Lily says. "I'll personally deliver her to the rink."

Lena lets out a jolly laugh although much weaker than usual. "What happened since this morning?"

"Well, Diego's going with us, and there's my amazing dress."

"Ahh, Diego is a kind boy, and I heard about the dress." Lena takes the phone with the first sketch displayed on the screen.

I flip through the options and stop on my selection. "This is the one."

"Docia, it is beautiful. So different from your others. Elegant. Sophisticated. Like you."

Lily pokes her head between us. "Hey, let me see...oh wow. It's goorgeeoouus! You'll look like a model. I have the perfect earrings to go with it."

Lena points to the back of the dress. "When you try it on, make sure the design does not allow the bottoms to slip up while you skate. They may forget."

Lily looks at me and cracks up. "Remember when Stacy skated half of her program at Junior Nationals with her butt hanging out?"

I nod and laugh. "I would've died!"

Lena puts her hand on my cheek. "You made the perfect choice."

I tense up at her response. People have thought for me my entire life and Lena acknowledged I know how to think on my own.

"What's wrong?" Lena asks. "You look upset."

"I'm okay. Thinking about my program." Even if I don't get my medal back, I still have my dignity if I skate well. "We should go to the rink. It closes in an hour, and I want to run through my exhibition program at least a couple of times tonight."

"I wish I could be there," Lena says. "Are you comfortable with your program? You've never performed this one before. I haven't seen you skate it since before the Olympics.

"Yeah, I can do it. Should I do the quad-double? And what about the more difficult ending?"

Lena strokes my arm drawing my eyes to hers. "I don't know, should you?"

It's not the answer I expected, but I nod. I know exactly what to do.

"And I have news for you." Lena's face brightens. "I found Luca, your papa."

"You waited this long to say something?" My attention is fully focused on her.

"I thought very hard about it and contacted him without speaking with your father first. It was the right decision."

My heart revs. "Did you?" Lily scoots forward and squeezes my arm. "What did he say? Can I contact him?"

"He was very surprised. Sad again about Anna but happy she has a daughter—they have a daughter. He is also confused." She pauses and pulls on a loose thread on her robe. "He needs time to think. He must talk with his wife. She knew Anna too. He married his skating partner, and they have a new baby girl. When he is ready, we can contact him together."

"Wow, I have a sister." I lean back on the sofa. "But what if he doesn't want to meet me? Does he still plan to be in Moscow for the show?"

Lena shakes her head. "I don't know."

CHAPTER THIRTY-SIX

"Are you going to contact him?" Lily asks as soon as we get in the car.

"I really want to." I take in an enormous breath and release it. "I need to listen to Lena though. He should be ready to talk to me."

"Makes sense. You're always so patient. I'd call him too soon and screw it all up." She turns down the road that leads to the rink. "You have another dad. That's crazy."

"I know. I wonder what he's like. Did he ever get over Anna? What do I call him?" We ride with only the road noise until Lily breaks the silence.

"So, will you do it?" Lily asks.

"Do what?"

"The quad-double and the tougher ending, silly. The things you can control."

"You'll see."

She sticks her tongue out at me. "What kind of answer is that? I'll watch you practice."

"I know. Promise you won't tell Lena. I want to surprise her in Moscow."

"Whatever." Lily breathes out an exaggerated sigh.

"Please don't spoil the surprise." I want to make this decision. For Lena and for me. "Can you stay for the *whole* practice tonight?"

Lily looks at me with gigantic eyes then focuses back on the road. She doesn't say a word.

"What's that face for? I can ask Diego to take me home if you have to leave." I hope she's not mad at me. "But I want you to stay."

"You'll see." She turns with the same face.

"I deserve that answer."

If only she could be with us in Moscow, she could protect me from my parents and meet my real father. She'd see me attempt to perform my exhibition program with Anna's grace. Each finger in its right place. Every landing like a floating flower petal.

Then Dad's voice skids through my brain and wipes away the vision. His voice echoes in my head. *Concentrate, Docia!*

I breathe faster.

Don't be a klutz! Follow through on that landing! Docia, what are you doing?

Then Stacy's red ponytail whips across my face right as I set up for the quad-double. I can't see my entry! I single the first jump and skip the second altogether.

"Docia, what just happened?" Lily's hand is on my mine. "You're about to pull the parking brake on."

My eyelids pop open to see white knuckles clutching the brake and the familiar illuminated ice rink sign. I frantically rub my face to erase the vision and wipe away the sweat from my forehead. I could swear it was red hair.

"Sorry." The word comes out as a whisper. "A little daytime nightmare."

"Docia, you will be fine." Lily pulls into a parking space.

"Yeah, that's what I thought a few weeks ago on that medal stand."

She puts the car in park and faces me. "You'll be fine in New York and Moscow and at Worlds and wherever else you decide to go. Whether you're skating or in college or caring for foster kids or whatever you choose to do. It doesn't matter if your dad or Lena or Joy or me or Diego are by your side or not. Stacy either. Forget what we say. You don't need us."

"I don't know if I'd go that far. I need some of those people. I definitely need you." For moral support. To call me out when I need it. For love. "Oh, crap. That's Stacy's car."

"So. What does that matter?"

"Because whenever she's around there's trouble. I want a no-drama practice session."

"Then have one."

Lily always makes everything sound so simple. "All right then. I will."

"See how easy it is to take control?" Lily opens the heavy glass door and the first person we see is Stacy on the rink.

Lily looks at me like she needs a reaction. Diego waves from behind the desk. He could distract me from just about anything.

We approach rink side as Stacy catches a toe pick and stumbles during her footwork. It's one of those klutzy, lost concentration moves. She glares at us. I wave and don't dare let go of my media-darling face. I scan the rest of the building. A couple of girls put their shoes back on while Cameron watches Stacy skate. "How appropriate, Cameron's in the penalty box."

Lily doesn't even look at him. "Where he belongs."

Cameron calls Stacy's name. She skates over. They exchange a few words, and he walks toward our side of the rink. No Velcro kissing this time.

"Want me to put your music on after you warm up?" Lily says.

"I'll wait until I have the ice to myself." Another Nancy Kerrigan versus Tonya Harding incident that stars Stacy and me could happen. Headlines are great, but not one that says, *Skating Star Gets Wacked on Knee Three Days Before Show*. "I don't want to crowd Stacy."

"Right," Lily laughs. "I'll bet that's *exactly* what you were thinking."

I rub my arms to wipe away the skin-crawling sensation as Cameron walks up.

"Hey."

He stops. "Sucks about your medal." His eyes almost look like he cares.

"Yeah, thanks."

Then he leans in with that smile I used to think was sexy. "You still looked hot out there." I step back and watch him walk out the door.

Lily shakes her head and mouths, "What?"

"Nothing important."

Even though Stacy's music still blares through the speakers, she stomps off the ice. She plops down on a bench and yanks the laces like a mound of fire ants has invaded her feet.

"I guess you're here to practice your exhibition program." She jerks one skate off and throws it into her bag. "Congratulations. Your show must be so exciting for you."

Lily and I catch each other's glance while I stretch.

"Actually, kind of overwhelming," I answer. "Are you performing in the show?"

"Who, me?"

I lean closer in a hamstring stretch so I don't miss her response.

"That's about the last place on the planet I can be right now." She throws the other skate in. "You're the star. Like always."

Leave me alone and mind your own business is on the tip of my tongue, but I suck the words back in and sit to put my skates on instead.

Stacy looks over. "What I'm trying to say is—" Then her face goes pale and she lunges for the garbage can at the end of the bench where I sit.

Is she coming at me?

Instead, she leans over the black container and hurls.

Lily pulls Stacy's ponytail out of her face. "Pregnant!" Lily mouths to me. "Are you okay?"

"No, not really." Stacy grips the sides of the trash can. "I guess you've heard. Everyone else has." She leans forward with closed eyes, gripping the sides of the garbage can. "I can't get through a practice without throwing up. The smell of the rink or hairspray does it every time."

I grab the towel out of my bag and hand it to Stacy.

"I heard," Lily says. "I didn't know if it was true."

She lowers back to the bench and buries her face in the towel while Lily and I sit on either side of her. Diego looks over from the lobby. I nod to let him know all's okay.

"What will you do?" I ask.

This could've been me. Images of the last year tumble through my head. Cameron's sexy smile. The accident. Hospital. Hearing I may never compete again. Working my tush off to prove them wrong.

She hands the towel back with a streak of vomit across it that makes my stomach turn.

"I don't know." Stacy's shoulders slump curling her petite body into a ball. "My parents want me to have an abortion so I can keep skating. They don't want the rumors."

I roll the towel up to hide the stain and tuck it into my bag. "What do you want?"

She rubs her tummy. "I don't think I can. I remember when we were kids how happy your parents were to have you. What if your mom had had an abortion?"

Those are the first kind words Stacy's spoken to me in years. She faces me with tears in her eyes. I'm almost sorry for her.

"I told Mom and Dad I'll have the abortion on one condition. If they leave you alone."

Stacy would do that for me?

Stacy dabs the tear away before it slides down her cheek. "I have to decide by next week before I'm too far along. It's hard. The toughest decision I've ever had to make."

We sit with only the hum of the rink's compressor. Stacy stares at a cup someone discarded next to the trash can. Lily and I exchange glances. *I don't have a clue what I would do.*

Stacy breaks the quiet. "What I tried to say before was I hope you get your medal back."

Pregnancy must make some people weird. Three nice comments in five minutes?

"And I'm sorry for the stuff that's happened." She looks me in the eyes. "You don't deserve it."

"Thank you." Should believe her? "I hope everything works out for you, Stacy."

"Hey, Docia," I hear Diego's voice behind us. "Are you going to skate or are we ready to shut this place down?"

When I turn to answer him, he mouths, "You okay?"

I nod. I'm more than okay.

"I'll skate if it's all right with you."

"I'm headed home," Stacy says as she reaches down for her skate bag. "Good luck in Moscow." Instead of looking at me, she focuses on the door.

"Thanks." *What's hiding behind this moment of niceness?* "Good luck to you too." *It's almost like we're friends again.*

Lily hands Stacy her purse. "We'll be thinking about you."

The three of us watch her take what seems like the longest walk out of the rink. A walk like it might be her last.

CHAPTER THIRTY-SEVEN

My eyes pop open but my brain is foggy. Am I in Russia? New York? Soft sheets. The Bolshoi painting Diego gave me for my birthday is on the wall. I'm in my bed in Houston.

"Crap!" I throw off the covers and step into fuzzy slippers. "Eight o'clock?"

I've got to pack, eat breakfast, and get to the rink. Did I sleep through Dad's usual pre-dawn wake-up? That's not possible. Maybe my independence is working?

I throw on my practice clothes and grab my two favorite outfits, jeans, two sweaters, and a dress, and fold them into my suitcase. Unfortunately, there's nothing new to wear this time. Shoes, boots, tights, practice clothes, undies, makeup, toiletries, and Mr. Penguin top off my packing. This trip can't happen without Fred Penguin. I do a double take at the stack of books on my desk and toss in my English Lit book.

Skate bag in hand, I run downstairs into the kitchen. "Morning!" I yell. No one answers. "Almost ready." There's no morning television or hair dryer. The quiet is unusually loud.

I scoop oatmeal and water into a bowl and pop it into the microwave then grab a banana and a glass of orange juice. That's when I see the note on the bar with a big D scratched across the top.

At a job interview. Your dad's at the gym. Be home to take you to rink about 9. We leave for airport at 3.

Love Mom

P.S. Make sure you're packed.

"Yes, Mother." With just enough time to relax and text Diego, I perch on a barstool and take a bite of the banana. *Morning! Meet here just before 3.*

See you then, he responds.

Warm oatmeal slides down my throat when it hits me this trip is happening. Diego, Mom, and I leave today. Together. The warmth continues down to my toes. Maybe we can let Mom shop so we can snuggle under a blanket on a carriage ride around Central Park. If this is adulting, I like it already.

I grab my phone again and share with my fans. *Big Apple today! Surprise waits there. Can't wait to share.*

Then I message Lena. *Heading to rink. Any chance we can talk to Luca before our flight?*

I hold my breath and wait for good news. *Not yet*, she replies.

Patience. I chug the last of my OJ and close my eyes to visualize the exhibition program I'll do on Sunday. The rink, the crowd, Lena near the entrance next to a man I don't know. My music begins and I do every bit of choreography and the quad-double so they know I didn't give up. In my mind it's flawless.

I visualize the entrance into my last spin when Mom blows in like a tornado.

"I got the job! You packed? Do I need to check over what you're taking? Will Diego be ready? I actually got the job!"

"Mom, slow down. That's awesome!" I rinse my bowl and pop it into the dishwasher. "When do you start?"

"The week after we get home from Moscow. I can hardly wait to go back to work. It's right where I should be in my career." She crumples into a chair. "But your dad will not like it. Less time to take care of him."

"I'm happy for you Mom. You deserve to do what you want." If Dad thinks he can take care of me, he doesn't need Mom to take care of him.

"I'll figure it out." She disappears into her bedroom.

"Rink soon?" I say after her. Dad comes in from the garage. "Hey, Dad."

He walks to the kitchen bar and fiddles with the mail.

Great. One of his moods. I sit at the table and pick up my phone to text Lily.

"What do you think you're doing making decisions without consulting me?" He rips open envelopes. "Your new costume? New York? Sponsorships? They're not decisions for you to make. And Diego? You've lost your mind, Docia. This is not what I taught you."

I wait for a pause. "Are you finished?"

"For now," he answers, still not looking at me.

"They're my decisions." I'm calm. Controlled. My reaction seems to throw him off.

"If this Manhattan trip, that slutty skating dress, or anything else backfires, it's all on you." Now he glares at me.

Heat rises to my head. What could backfire in New York with Mom and one of my best friends? There is nothing "slutty" about anything Vera Wang. Where's the Dad who just said at the rink he would trust me? I open my mouth to lob back, but I don't. Instead, I take a deep breath and count to ten. "It's my life." I take another deep breath. "They are good decisions."

We exchange stares until I grab my skate bag and walk to Mom's room. She's arranging what looks like work outfits. "Ready? I need to make the nine-thirty freestyle."

"Sure honey. Just need to get my purse. I should get a better one for the new job, don't you think?" She crinkles her face at her slouchy shoulder bag. "Maybe in New York."

We walk through the kitchen to meet Dad's glare.

Mom looks at me, then him "What'd I miss?"

"Nothing," I answer.

CHAPTER THIRTY-EIGHT

When Mom closes the car door, it flips her on switch. "As soon as we get to New York, we'll go to the hotel and check in. You should sleep on the plane, and it will give Diego time to do his makeup schoolwork. I hope I packed enough warm clothes."

Usually, her chatter binges annoy me. This time my brain works as fast as her mouth.

"Those poor people in Manhattan and Moscow must freeze their booties off all winter. I'm so glad we don't need all those heavy coats and wool here like they do."

She must need to breathe soon.

"Is it supposed to snow? Will you check the weather?"

"Mom." Finally, the question leaves a millisecond-long pause. "Let's have dinner Saturday night in that cool little restaurant we didn't get to go to before we left Moscow."

"Sure, if you're not too tired," Mom answers. "Thanks for the reminder. I need to pack a nice outfit to wear out at night. What do I own that's nice and warm too? And my coat is so casual. No suede if there's snow."

"Hang on. I'm looking." I think through what I packed as I check the weather. "No new snow predicted, but super cold."

"Perfect." Mom turns and beams. "Kimberly called this morning. She's working out the final travel details."

"Cool." It's almost like things were before the Olympics. "Mom, look." I point at the TV vans near the rink entrance.

"You up for it?"

Do I have a choice? I scoot up in the seat like it might get us there faster.

Mom stops in the middle of the parking lot and looks across the seat at me. "So, are you?"

"Yes. Bring it on."

As soon as we pull into a parking space, camera crews rush the car. Lenses crowd the windows like alien eyes. Mom gives me a final glance. "Honey don't forget to smile. You looked so angry in the last interview."

Yes, Mother. The day of that last interview, I was angry. I wanted to flip someone off—on camera or off.

I take a deep breath, nail my best camera expression, open the door, and step onto the pavement. Microphones are in my face from every direction. Reporters lob questions faster than I can think.

"Will you meet your real father?"

"Do you resent your mother's death now?"

"Are you mad at your parents for hiding your past? Are they going to Moscow with you?"

"Will you get your medal back?"

I'm not prepared to tell the world some of these answers. Despite the chilly wind, my palms pour out moisture until my skate bag is slippery in my hand. My camera face never wavers.

Mom walks around the car and drapes her arm around my shoulders. "Thank y'all for coming today. Your support means a lot to Docia," she says to the aggressive crowd with calm poise, opposite the chatterbox she was on the way here. "Docia's here to practice, but she's happy to answer a couple of your questions first."

She turns to me. "Sweetheart, I believe one reporter asked if you'll meet your real father in Moscow."

I tell her thanks for the rescue with my eyes. "I do plan to meet my biological father and look forward to it very much. Everyone deserves to know where they came from."

Mom gently rubs my shoulder. That answer must have worked.

She takes over again. "And this lovely journalist over here asked about who's going on the trip with you and if you will get your medal back." She skips the one about whether I'm mad at my parents for hiding my past.

It's none of their business.

I stand straighter and look the reporter in the eye as the tension trickles off. "There is no evidence that proves I wasn't qualified to compete. I hope they do the right thing and return my medal. That's one reason so many athletes support Sunday's tribute show." The reporter nods with the rhythm of my words. "No matter what happens, my mom and dad, my coach, and my boyfriend will be there with me."

I said it. I admitted Diego is my boyfriend. On national TV. I hope he's okay with that because Dad won't be. The words feel comfortable but tingly exciting like warm sand between my toes on spring's first beach day.

When someone in the crowd asks, "Who's your boyfriend, Docia?" my face feels toasty and my camera-ready face fades into a shy grin.

I can't answer. I won't.

"Time to practice," I say instead. "I hope everyone can watch the show on Sunday. I promise it will be good." They'll know soon enough. I take Mom's hand and lead her through the crowd to the familiar double glass doors where Diego's smile welcomes us on the other side. Most of the reporters scurry to their vans to file their stories.

A group of young skaters fresh off the last freestyle session stands in front of Diego. Their faces are lit like they've seen the latest Disney princess come to life. No angry mothers. Diego hands me a Sharpie and Mom takes my skate bag so I can sign autographs.

Maybe the worst is over.

A tiny girl tugs on my sleeve. "Will you sign my skate?" She hands me her shiny white boot. "My name's Jordan. I'm also adopted."

"You are? We're both special since our parents chose us." I sign my name then lean down to her level and a camera flashes. "What's your favorite jump?"

"I like the toe loop. I'm learning my Axel now and my bottom hurts. Your triple Axel is awesome."

"We have a lot in common." She giggles when I poke her tummy with my finger. "My bottom hurts when I fall on my Axel too."

One after another, they stand in front of me with pens and snaggletooth grins that drip sweetness. These young athletes make it hard to believe the skating world can be so harsh.

"Okay, girls," Diego's strong voice overpowers their giggles. "It's time to let Docia practice. Aren't you supposed to be in school?" He eggs them on. "Move it!" They giggle more. "Do I have to call your teachers?"

I wave to a chorus of "Bye Docia" and "Good luck" as the miniature fan club scrambles for the door. The group of moms that just dispersed reveals Joy sitting across the lobby. "Diego told me you'd be here. I hope you don't mind."

I cross the room and hug her. "You're always welcome."

"Nice job with the reporters."

"I'll never get used to the attention." I shake my head and roll my eyes. "I'm not that interesting."

Mom and Joy trade glances. "I'm afraid I disagree with you," Joy says. "So many people relate to your story."

"Docia. You gonna skate or what?" Diego says from the front counter.

"Yeah, sorry." I grab my skates back from Mom. "You headed to school now?"

He nods. "Catching a few classes before we leave. You ready for this trip?"

"Never been readier." The door opens and distracts us both when the gray-haired man walks in.

"There's Jack now. Better go." He leans over the counter and kisses the tip of my nose. "See you by three."

His walk is familiar, but I've never noticed his long slow sexy strides. *Now it feels different. We're different. Nothing will stand in our way this time.*

While Diego stops to talk with Jack, I glance over to see if Mom saw the kiss. She and Joy are engrossed in conversation. She knows Diego and I made up, but it feels like we're sneaking around since Dad doesn't approve of him.

I step out on the ice, finish my warmup, and signal Jack to start my music. I eek all the way through the first jumping pass. My mind is everywhere but the rink. I set up for a double Axel and for a second, I forget what jump I'm doing and fall splat on my butt and slide across the ice.

"Seriously?" I hiss out loud to myself. "That was just a double Axel."

I catch up to my music but finish the program without the usual spirit. I skate around the rink as fast as I can and lose myself in the ice. Sweat trickles down my chest. At least last night's practice was good. Reporters got their stories this morning and left. Now I can just be.

Joy and Mom are still deep in conversation and not watching, so I work through each program element—the jumps and spins and footwork sequence and end with the quad-double. I lift off so high that I slightly over-rotate the jump and have to check the landing extra strong to hold on.

"Way to go, Docia," Lily says, and I skid to a stop near where she stands rink side. "You will kill that jump on Sunday!"

"Relieved someone thinks so. I'm so glad you could stop by." I step off the ice and slip my guards on.

"I can't believe you're leaving in a few hours," Lily says with downturned eyes. "And I can't believe you'll be there with Diego and not me."

"I know. It won't be the same without you." With her, the trip would be complete.

Lily laughs. "I'll be there in spirit, and on your ears and lips." She pulls a small bag out of her purse. "Here are some earrings to wear with your dress and lipstick to top it off."

"Lily, they're perfect." I squeeze her as tight as I can. "You'll be in my heart too."

"Text me when you get to New York and all about your dress. I'll record you on TV in the morning. Let me know who shows up in Moscow and every detail about your real father. Take pics of everything!"

"I will. Joy will cover the Moscow part of the trip too."

"Looks like your mom's ready." We hug and she whispers in my ear, "You'll be fabulous."

•   •   •

The clock on my nightstand tells me there is an hour until we have to leave. *Hear from him yet?* I text Lena.

Patience, she responds, which means no.

I step into the shower and the what-ifs start. What if Dad starts something with my biological dad? What if Stacy's crazy coach pulls something else? What if the government butts in like Dad expects? What if my real dad backs out? I close my eyes and let the water wash the worries away. The warm spray massages tension from my tight shoulders.

"Docia! We leave in twenty minutes!" Mom's voice snaps me out of my meditation.

"Okay," I holler back and wrap up in a fluffy yellow towel to dry my hair. Then I slip on jeans, boots, and the green sweater with flowers on the front that Lily gave me for my birthday last year. One more way she'll be there with me.

After zipping my bag, I snap a pic and share it with my fans,
Suitcase closed. Wish I could pack all of you in it!

"Docia!" Mom calls up the stairs.

"Coming." I drag my suitcase and skate bag downstairs.

Mom's running around barefoot between her room and the laundry room with her top halfway on. "I thought I was. Here are our passports. Please do not let go of these."

"What's wrong?" If I can be calm today, she certainly should be too.

"I want to take that black cashmere sweater your father gave me for Christmas last year but can't find it anywhere." She heads back to the laundry room while she puts on earrings. "It would mean so much to him if I wear it Sunday."

Like he would notice. "It's in Grandma's cedar trunk in the guest room where you put things then forget you have them. You'll smell like a giant mothball."

"Thank you, honey." She disappears as the doorbell rings. "It will air out by then. Is that Diego?"

I open the door to see Diego in his brown bomber jacket and scarf with jeans and boots and a duffle bag over his shoulder.

He steps inside, picks me up, and spins me around like my partner used to do when I briefly tried pairs skating. I'm happy when he's around, even without the spinning.

This time I ask, "You ready for this trip?" as I see Dad pull up in the driveway.

"Yep, let's do this," Diego says.

CHAPTER THIRTY-NINE

Fabulous. Through the window, I watch Dad walk up the sidewalk staring at his phone. What will blow up this time? No, wait. Not a thing will ruin this trip. I grab Diego's arm and lead him into the living room before Dad sees us.

"What?" Diego asks.

Before I answer, Mom yells from the kitchen. "Is that your father? It's about time he got home. He's taking us to the airport."

"Yeah, Mom," I shout back.

"Oh, I get it. Dad drama?"

"Trying to avoid it," I whisper when I hear the front door slam and footsteps get closer.

"You girls ready?" Dad asks. "Diego." He barely nods in Diego's direction and walks in front of us on his way to the kitchen. "Need to hit the road before traffic."

It's like we're tiptoeing around live grenades.

"Docia, I need to talk to you," his voice barks from the next room.

Diego tips his head in the kitchen's direction. "Dad's calling."

I shrug as I head into his lair.

"I'm always with you on such important trips." He paces from one corner of the kitchen to the other with his arms crossed. "I'll be there on Sunday for the show, but that's three days away." His eyes are still focused on the floor. "Remember these things since I'm not there to remind you."

"Dad, I know. Eat foods you know. Nothing strange."

He counts off points on each finger. "Get on a Moscow sleep schedule. For God's sake, don't forget to stretch that ankle."

I let him get it all out now rather than give up valuable New York time on the phone to hear his pointless lectures.

"Do you understand?"

Now he's on finger four. I nod and zone out. *Did I pack my fuchsia sweater?*

"Don't answer any reporters' questions that don't involve skating. Nothing about your adoption or family members besides your mother and me, no matter what your mother says. I'll handle any of that from here or when I get there. Got it?"

I still bob my head up and down from the last time he asked.

"And that Diego—"

Wait. My methodical nods stop. "No, Dad." Back to finger four. "You will not handle questions about anything." He finally looks up. "This is exactly what we talked about."

"Docia, I'm—" he starts to interrupt.

"I speak for myself. I just answered those very questions for the reporters at the rink."

Dad's teeth clinch and one hand goes to his hip. "You can't handle those questions, Docia." He wags a finger a little too close to my face. "You know they always trap you into saying things you don't mean."

"I. Will. Handle. It." Oh god, I sound like Dad. "And leave Diego out of this." I take a couple of deep breaths to keep the heat to a simmer. "This weekend is important. I will not let you blow it for me."

He doesn't agree or disagree. He doesn't say a word. Instead, his eyes pierce mine.

"Time to go, Mom," I yell past him and still hold the stare. "Diego and I will be in the car." I walk out of the kitchen and a sense of calm drapes over me. It's a serenity I haven't felt in a long time.

"All good?" Diego asks.

"Yep. Pep talk."

Diego doesn't need to know I already had to stop Dad from dragging him into it.

I pull my suitcase and skate bag toward the garage door.

"Here, get your skates, I'll take the other one," Diego says.

"I got it." The independent woman act is becoming habit. I like not needing help.

"I know you do, but I want to."

Maneuvering the two bags around the cars in the crowded garage isn't easy. "Thank you." I pass the handle to him.

The winter sun almost blinds me. With New York's gray snowy days and Moscow's only eight or nine hours of daylight, these may be the last rays we see for a few days. "I can't believe this trip is happening. It seemed so hopeless." I stand in the driveway and soak in warmth. "Everything should go as planned in New York. Rockefeller Center and then my fitting. Once those are done, we have free time before our flight. Anything you'd like to do?"

"Yeah, actually the MoMA would be cool." Diego's eyes brighten. "I read about an exhibit with some of my favorite artists. One is the guy whose work inspired that Bolshoi painting I did for you."

I visualize the theater's beautiful interior. "I've never been there. Maybe Mom can shop while we do that."

I can hardly count the number of hours in the first days after the Olympics I curled up on my bed staring at the painted dancer on the painted stage and felt more alone than she must've felt. She was always there. Dancing by herself. The painting inspired me to not give up.

"I hope the Bolshoi is open this time," I say.

"What about the Bolshoi?" Dad's voice muffled by rolling suitcase wheels and Mom's heels on the concrete comes from inside the garage. "You won't have time for that this trip."

"Whatever," I mumble.

Diego smiles.

"Right on time," Mom says. "Everyone have their passport?"

"Yep, everyone but you," I answer and watch Mom's face drop while she thinks about it for a second. "'Cause I've got it."

Dad throws my bags and Mom's into the trunk and starts to close it before Diego tosses his duffle in. I look over the top of the car at Diego and shake my head. *No Dad, ignoring Diego will not make him go away.*

"Get me on that jet," I whisper to Diego when he slides into the back seat next to me.

Mom gets in the front seat and the chatter to Dad starts across the console. She carries on about everything from her friend who's getting married to the other one divorcing and what will happen to their poor children. "I dropped off your dry cleaning, honey, so don't forget to pick it up tomorrow if you need that stuff on the trip. Or you could wait until we get back. Did you pay the Visa bill?" She doesn't stop for a breath. "Speaking of when we get back, Target has a sale on spring flowers. Let's get some to spruce up the front yard and those big pots on the deck."

Dad glances back at me in the rearview a couple of times but never says a word. Mom sticks to the safe subjects. She avoids her new job, the trip, and anything about skating. She's touched that hot stove before. The best part, I get to sit in the back seat and answer no questions and listen to no lectures. Diego clutches my hand the entire thirty-three minutes to the airport.

As we approach the departure drop-off area, I wrap my hair up underneath the plain black baseball cap and hide behind shades so I can slip through unrecognized. I just want to keep the drama down. Diego grabs my bags while I give Dad a hug.

"Do nothing I wouldn't approve of." He follows with his sternest look.

"See you Sunday," I say and don't address his parting words. "Please take good care of Lena on the trip over." I hope he follows instructions better than he gives them. "Okay, Dad?"

He nods.

This time, I get the last word.

We make it to the gate just in time. I've spent so much time waiting since the Olympics, I'm waited out.

I escape people recognizing me until the flight attendant next to the gate agent sees my boarding pass. "You're that skater!" he announces way too loud to the entire group of passengers lined up to board. "I've followed your story," he says then leans so close I sneeze over his Tom Ford Noir Extreme cologne. "Those people have been so unfair. I'll take good care of you on the flight."

"Thank you," I answer while everyone we'll be on the plane with for the next three-and-a-half hours stares.

Mom's talking to the woman behind her and doesn't notice a thing, but a woman further back in the queue shoots a very disapproving look my way. The little girl with her has big curious eyes also focused on me. When the woman sees me notice, she turns the little girl around to face the other direction.

The woman and her small traveling companion are directly across from our seats. Before they sit, she stops the flight attendant I talked to before boarding. "My daughter and I need to be moved." She does not try to speak quietly. "We don't want to sit next to *those* people." She points to me. "Too much, uhm, *attention.*"

"I'm sorry, ma'am, the flight is full," the flight attendant says. "You'll have to remain in your assigned seats." He winks at me and flits up the aisle.

Mom notices and leans across the aisle. "Mom." I grab her arm. "Please don't start anything." She shakes her head and speaks to the woman anyway.

"This is going to be the longest flight ever," I whisper to Diego. I slouch, pull my cap down and sink into the seat between Mom and Diego. I pull my English lit book out of the seat pocket and open it to chapter fourteen.

"Look." I follow Diego's glance across the aisle to see the little girl waving until the woman grabs her hand and pulls it down. "Seriously?"

"What did you say to her?" I ask Mom.

"I told her she was rude."

"Mom, we're stuck here for the rest of the flight."

"Exactly why I won't let her get away with talk like that." She glances back at the woman who now has turned her back to us to block her daughter's view. "People can be equally as disrespectful to her daughter."

I bury myself in my textbook until I hear Diego's chuckle. "Bet you'll catch up on this trip." He holds the same book, but he's about ten chapters ahead, where I need to be.

"Maybe all this crap will be over once we get home."

CHAPTER FORTY

"We're about eighty miles from New York's La Guardia airport and beginning our descent," the man on the speaker says. "We've turned on the fasten seatbelt sign, and we will touch down in about twenty minutes."

My stomach feels like an out-of-control back scratch spin, not from the turbulence, but from how much rides on this trip. I close my textbook and peer through the window at the crisscross patterns of white that cover the ground below.

"It's twenty-nine degrees in snow-covered New York City," the pilot continues. "We'll see you on the ground shortly. Thank you for flying with us."

Diego's looking out too. "This trip is what you need to get your life back on track. It'll be awesome."

He always says the words I need to hear. Not too many or few. They're never patronizing or controlling. "Even awesomer since you're part of it."

We fly around the Statue of Liberty and Ellis Island. If she had lived, Anna could have had it all like the thousands of people who started new lives on Ellis Island. She could have skated and been with my father and me. She could have lived her dream in America. My life would be completely different.

My stomach tumbles faster as the ground gets closer because I have control over what happens on the trip for once.

"Let's check into the hotel then get some dinner. I'm hungry."

"Sounds good." Mom nods out of her groggy slumber. "Wake me up when we're on the ground."

"Okay, Mom." I answer and whisper to Diego. "She must've taken a sleeping pill before we left. I haven't seen her so out of it in a while."

Diego leans forward in the seat to get a good look. "Will she be okay when we land?"

"I think so." We bounce on the runway. "You and I can find the hotel if she can't."

"Mom, we're here." I gently shake her. "I'll get your bags."

"Thank you, sweetie. I'm awake." Her head flops down onto my shoulder while I reapply my disguise.

When it's our turn to walk up the aisle, Diego and I trade looks. "I'll grab the rest of our stuff if you can help her," I say.

"I'm okay," Mom says.

"I'll help you, Mrs. Sikorsky." Diego slips out and walks sideways up the aisle leading Mom to the exit.

The chatty flight attendant is at the door wishing passengers well. "Can't wait to watch your show on Sunday. Good luck." He pats me on the shoulder. "Everything okay?" he says looking over the top of his glasses at Diego guiding Mom.

"Yes, we're fine. Thanks for looking out for us on the flight."

With me on one side of Mom and Diego on the other, we stroll through La Guardia and try to blend into the crowd. At baggage claim, we settle Mom in a seat where she dozes off again. "There are the bags from our fight." I point Diego to the carousel that started to circle.

"Got it. I'll grab ours."

"I'll call the car service." I rummage through Mom's purse to find the number and the hotel address. "Mom." I shake her again. "Time to wake up. Our car will be outside in a few minutes."

Eyes wide open, she sits up hypnotized by the luggage that circles in front of her. Her lids close like window shades.

"Mom, did you take a sleeping pill before we left?" I shake her again.

"I'm awake...and a muscle relaxer," she slurs. "Your dad had me all wound up."

"Seriously, Mom? You have to walk to the car." I dive back into her purse to find the medicine bottles and slip them into my purse. "The driver is here. Diego has our bags."

"Okay, I've got this." She stands and wobbles until Diego helps steady her.

"Grab my arm, Mom." I hold my head down to avoid the humiliation of anyone recognizing me. When the cold dry air hits us outside, I'm glad I'm wearing a cap and scarf.

"There's our car," Diego says.

The sign in the window says "Scissorhands" our secret code name Kimberly came up with to dodge reporters. Knowing it's from her favorite movie still makes me laugh.

"The Hyatt at Grand Central, please," I tell the driver after he loads our luggage.

"Yes ma'am." His look at Mom lingers a little long.

As soon as we get in the car, Mom leans her head against the window. "She's out again."

"Yeah, I'm not sure she could get her boots on the right feet much less stay awake through dinner," Diego whispers. "Is she like this often?"

"Not in a while. She used to be once or twice a week back when Dad changed jobs all the time." We both giggle when her head slides down the window and bobs along with the bumps in the road. "I'm sorry you have to see this."

"Don't worry about it. We hit traffic right. Looks like we missed rush hour," Diego looks at his phone where he tracks our route. "We're almost there."

People covered up under coats, hats, and scarves step over piles of snow on the sidewalk edges as they rush to work, home, or wherever they're headed for the evening. We'll be a part of that crowd soon.

"Look, the Empire State Building." I point above the buildings as we cross through an intersection. "The sky's clear enough to see the top."

"And there's Grand Central Station, so that must be our hotel."

"Yes, sir," the driver says. "Here we are." He unloads our luggage and passes it on to the bellman while we unload Mom.

"This looks very nice." She shuffles through the heavy revolving door. "I don't think we've ever stayed here."

I eye the long flight of marble stairs. "We'll take the elevator, Mom."

When we step off, a friendly voice meets us. "Welcome to the Hyatt. We're glad you're staying with us."

I wait for Mom to step up. When she doesn't, I slip her wallet out of her purse. "I'm checking in for Liz Scissorhands and Diego Scissorhands. It's uhm, two rooms."

"Yes ma'am. I do have a room for Liz, but I don't see another room in your party." He taps on the keys and never breaks his smile. "Let me check again."

"I'm sure you must have it. These reservations were made earlier this week." Mom still shows no inclination to step in, but I won't panic.

"Could the reservation be under a different name?"

Diego shrugs. "Try Diego Cruz."

"No, nothing under that name either," the reservation clerk says. "And I'm so sorry but we're completely sold out tonight. Can you share a room?"

"No, that won't be possible." I look at Mom to avoid the awkward moment with Diego. "Mom, what do we do?"

"Aren't we checking in?"

She's clueless about what's going on. *This cannot be happening.*

"I know Kimberly reserved two rooms." I dig for my phone. "I'll call her."

After I explain the situation to a very apologetic Kimberly, she asks to speak to the reservation clerk. "Yes. Yes. That's correct," I hear on the hotel side of the conversation. "No problem." He hands the phone back to me.

"All is good, Docia," Kimberly says. "They have the three of you in a suite with two double beds and a separate living area with a fold-out sofa."

"Thanks, that will work," I answer. Diego clings to every word while Mom looks blindly around the enormous lobby, still oblivious there's a problem. "What happened to the original reservation? Did the hotel make a mistake?"

"It doesn't matter. It's fixed now," Kimberly says.

"Kimberly, please. I'd like to know."

She hesitates before answering. "Your father asked me to reserve a room for Diego at a hotel down the street. He said you wanted it that way, but I take it you didn't."

"I get it. Yes, we're good now. Thanks so much, Kimberly. I'll talk to you tomorrow."

Diego looks confused like he did when we were biology lab partners in middle school and had to dissect a frog. "What was that about? Do I have to sleep in the lobby?"

"Of course not. Follow me."

This time it's funny. Dad still tries to control my every move. I can't wait to hear his reaction when I tell him his little trick backfired.

"This is beautiful," Mom says when we walk into the suite. "Look at the view of the Empire State Building."

"Is my room close?" Diego asks, still puzzled.

"We're all staying right here. This is a fold-out sofa for you. Mom and I will sleep in the bedroom. You even have your own bathroom."

"Won't your dad freak?" His eyes almost pop out of his head.

"He'll more than freak, but he totally asked for this."

"Mom, do you feel like going out to dinner? Mom? Where'd she go?" We walk into the bedroom and find her stretched across the bed.

Diego chuckles. "I guess not."

"Seriously, Mom? You're still wearing your coat and shoes." Drama from both parents.

"Don't worry about it, Docia. She'll be fine once she sleeps it off."

"I know, but I wanted her to experience New York City with us, not take a drug-induced nap in the hotel." I pull each arm out of her coat and set her shoes on the floor beside the bed. "Mom let's get you comfortable. She won't even know we're gone." On the hotel notepad, I scratch a message and lay it next to her phone on the nightstand.

Gone for dinner. Will bring you food. Sleep well.

"I'll charge her phone so we can call her if we need to." Diego stands at the foot of the bed looking at Mom sprawled diagonally across it. "You think she'll be okay here by herself?"

"Yeah, she'll be fine. She always is." I think back to all the times Dad took me to the early freestyle sessions because Mom couldn't wake up. I didn't understand why then. "She'll be a real pain in the butt to wake up tomorrow."

I open my bag and pull out the clothes I'll need in the morning. "Okay, the fuchsia sweater or the green one for tonight?"

"You'll look great in either, but you know me. I always go for the bright colors."

I giggle as I slip into the bathroom. He'd say I look great in a tablecloth or nothing at all.

Before I pull my sweater over my head, I catch a three-dimensional glimpse of my athletic shape in the corner mirror. Am I actually this tiny? The bra does hardly anything but give me a little something up there. Does Diego like my body like this? I turn and look from another angle and yank the sweater down to cover myself. *If only I had bigger boobs.*

"All ready." I pull Mom's credit card and sixty bucks out of her purse. "You think this will cover us?" I fan out the plastic and cash like a winning hand.

"It should, and I've got more if we need it."

I grab my coat, scarf, hat, and gloves and layer up as we travel down the elevator from the thirty-fifth floor.

CHAPTER FORTY-ONE

We step into the grandiose Grand Central Station main terminal. My gaze follows the huge columns up to the intense turquoise ceiling with the zodiac splashed across it in gold. The hum of commuters fills the air.

"Diego, this is amaz…" and I crash head-on into him and stomp on his toe. "Oh my gosh, I'm sorry," I say through hands that try to cover up my full-on laugh. "Did I hurt you?"

"Yeah, all eighty-two pounds of you will destroy me." He breaks into a smile, one of the rare times he shows the slight gap I love between his front teeth. "I can hear the reporters now. 'Olympic champion unable to perform because of collision with boyfriend.'"

He said boyfriend. Except for what I said to the reporters, we've never defined what we are. That means I'm his girlfriend. I look away so he won't see the fourteen shades of red I've turned.

Diego grabs my hand. "I was kidding—about the collision part, not the boyfriend part."

"Good." How does he always know my thoughts? "I like you being my boyfriend. It's still a little strange."

"I'm okay with that," Diego answers as a group of girls approaches.

They timidly look at each other until one asks, "You're Docia Sikorsky, the skater, right?"

If I say no, will they believe me? Did they see my near-humiliating crash? "I am. Are you skaters too?"

They giggle, and the one who digs through her purse says, "Yes. Can I have your autograph?"

"Sure." I take the paper and a pen she fishes out.

"Can we take a picture?" another asks.

We cluster around the bottom of the steps and Diego takes it.

"Thank you," they say in unison. "We want you to get your medal back!" one says through the noise as they blend into the crowd.

As much as I enjoy the independence, knowing people support me helps my confidence.

"Back to the food search." Diego points past the vast space. "The Dining Concourse is that way."

We walk through the marble walkway and down a white-tiled staircase into an area that resembles a shopping mall food court. "Pizza? Deli? Stir fry?" I eye the options. "Anything but pasta. Last time we were in New York for Nationals, Dad made me eat pasta with chicken and marinara. Again."

"No wonder you hate pasta. There's a soup place and an oyster bar."

"Oyster bar. Definitely." I lead Diego to the restaurant's takeout area.

I glance at the menu. "Want to share a dozen oysters? Definitely an option Dad would never let me order."

"Sure."

"Order to go please," I tell the bartender. "We'll take a dozen oysters with extra lemon, two clam chowders, and a dinner salad."

Diego nods. "I'll take the coconut shrimp."

"Good choices." The bartender nods and slides two glasses across the bar. "Here's some water while you wait."

"Is everyone in Manhattan gorgeous?" I watch her float across the floor like a model on a runway as we wait for our food. "I feel like such a kid."

"You're as glamorous as they are." Diego shakes his head. "And you're a star."

How does Diego talk about me and not patronize me like Dad? "This is our first real date, and we're out in Manhattan." And no one decided for me. "How are they surviving without you at the rink for six days?"

Diego answers in his true style. "They'll figure it out. Same way the rink goes on without you."

"Yeah but—"

"But nothing," he interrupts. "You're the biggest star that's ever skated at that rink and they know it."

Before I counter, the server comes back. "Here are your oysters. The rest is on its way."

I pop the lid off the container. "I'm hungry. Let's eat these now." I squeeze a lemon wedge across the pearly open shells. "Cheers." I dip my tiny fork into the cocktail sauce, spear an oyster, and slip it in my mouth. I chew it a few times. It slides down my throat while Diego follows my lead. "What do you think?"

"Not bad," he answers still chewing. "You?"

"Yeah, it's good." I pick up another and think of how Dad would react. "This one tastes even better."

I take a sip of water as the bartender returns with the rest of our order. "How were the oysters?" She reaches for the empty takeout box.

"Delicious," I answer. "Thank you."

Diego grabs the takeout bag and follows me through the restaurant. We take our time going through Grand Central Terminal and back to the hotel suite.

Mom is still out cold, so I pull the bedroom door shut and watch Diego unload our food on the coffee table. "This will be a good dinner for Mom after the day she's had."

"Speaking of your mom, is she okay? You seem used to her like this."

"She's fine. I promise." I know my words bend the truth.

"Are you sure? She doesn't look okay." Diego sips his drink. "Before my mom kicked my stepdad out, she was a mess. She could hardly get up in the morning. Dad was always on her case."

Diego squeezes his fork so hard his knuckles are white. "I don't think he ever hit her—I guess he got that out of his system by kicking my ass—but he pushed her around and cut her down until she didn't care about anything. One night I came home and the cops were there. He screamed at her for over an hour and threatened to kill her. She called 911, cut her hand when he tried to get the phone away from her. The cops heard him yell through the door. She didn't tell the cops her hand dripped blood or about the death threat. They didn't arrest him. Luckily, she kicked the no-good son-of-a-bitch out a couple of months later."

"Why didn't you ever tell me?"

"I moved on. Mom's so much happier now that the jerk's out of our lives." He's breathing normally enough to eat again.

But I'm not.

He stops mid-chew. "Why are you crying?"

"You're right." I wipe the tear away. "Mom's not okay."

"He hasn't hit you or your mom, has he?" He scoots his chair out and grips the edge of the table. "I'll kick his sorry ass if he does."

"No, nothing like that. Not that I've seen." I don't mention the slap. "But it's bad. Mom checks out like she did on the plane. The first time I saw her almost normal was while Dad was stuck in Moscow. As soon as he got home, she came unglued again. Back to wine and pills." I stare at the half-eaten soup. "What do I do?" I blink back tears that threaten to fall.

"I see your dad's a jerk, but you never mentioned problems with your mom."

Yeah, I thought if I ignored her problems they would go away. They didn't. Instead, I'm going numb like Mom. *I don't want to be numb— or like Mom.*

"I've unloaded so much drama on you, Lily, and Joy I didn't want to add to it."

He reaches across the table and grips my hand like he'll never let go. "Bring it on. I can take it."

We finish our dinner. With each spoonful of clam chowder, I plot out exactly what needs to happen next.

CHAPTER FORTY-TWO

"We got you some food." I gently shake Mom until her eyes open. "You haven't eaten since breakfast. Then you can sleep until tomorrow morning."

"Thank you, sweetie." Her voice is barely audible.

"Come on, Mom." I drag her feet so her legs hang over the side of the bed. "We got you salad and clam chowder."

She sits up. "Is it time to go to dinner?"

"We've already been, Mom."

She looks around like she's trying to place where she is. "Yes, I should eat something."

"It's way more than something. This restaurant's food is amazing—one of the best meals I've had." I motion to Diego to bring it into the bedroom. "And not a bite of pasta."

Diego removes the lid from the chowder so the savory aroma fills the room. "Get a whiff of this, Mrs. Sikorsky."

"And guess what we ate." If her food aroma doesn't rouse her, this will. "Raw oysters."

Diego looks at me like I told her we just had sex.

She scoots to the edge of the bed. "You ate what? Your father would never approve."

"And you know what else?" I don't wait for an answer. "I didn't hurl. My muscles didn't shrivel up." And I feel about three feet taller than my three-and-a-half-inch heels make me.

"Aren't we empowered." By the look on her face, she's awake now. "Yes, speaking of your Dad, would you talk to him like that?"

I don't think she would like my answer.

"Diego set your dinner up on the table in our little living room. Come and get it while the chowder's still warm."

She sits and scoops a bite. "This is good. You're right, I am hungry." She grazes on the salad like a horse chewing into the first spring grass. "Picking up dinner without me doesn't mean you can set that smarty tone for the whole trip. There's empowered then there's smart-aleck." Mom uses her loud whisper like she doesn't want Diego to hear.

"I'm aiming for empowered, but with no role model for empowered behavior, I have to wing it."

I suck in a quick breath. Can I take the words back?

Mom drops the plastic spoon and splashes soup on the table. She stares at me until tears spill out.

"I'm sorry, I shouldn't have said that."

She needed to hear it, but I wish I hadn't brought it up during this trip. Like that.

"Then why did you?" She pushes her food away and retreats into the bedroom.

Diego walks toward the door and mouths, "I'll be back."

I nod, "Sorry."

He leaves me in an empty room.

Diego won't want to be here for the rest of the conversation if it goes how I hope.

I curl up in the chair, stare at the closed bedroom door, and go over what I want to say. This conversation would go so much better at home next week, but I started it when the comment slipped. I hope Mom will still speak to me. She's got to know her relationship with Dad is far from normal. She deserves for Dad to treat her better. I'm out of the house in a couple of years, but she's stuck there.

From the other room, I hear Mom rustle through her purse, then a series of bumps and clanks as the contents fall on the dresser. "Docia, where are my pills?"

"You don't need pills." I stuff my purse into Diego's duffle bag.

"That wasn't my question." She pulls the door open. "Where are they?"

Collecting Mom's lip gloss tubes that keep rolling off onto the bedroom floor gives me a moment to think. "I have them."

Mom leans on the door frame and sticks her palm out.

"You don't need a pill until our flight tomorrow."

She pokes her outstretched hand a little closer to my face. "Pills. In my hand. Now."

I don't move. "Why do you take them?"

She pulls her hand away and folds her arms across her chest. "They help me relax so I can sleep. You know that."

"You told me earlier Dad had you all wound up. That means he's the reason you're in this condition in the first place." I feel like I'm scolding an injured child. "Does Dad affect you so much you have to take pills to deal with it?"

She drops into the chair next to the dresser and retreats into a ball while my heart twists in half. It must be worse than I thought. Maybe she needs the pills. I wrap my arms around her and let her tears flow like she used to do with me after a bad practice. Girls never grow out of the need for a good cry.

"Mom, you don't need to stay with Dad." I wipe her cheeks with a handful of tissues and replay the argument about her new job they had before we left. "I see how he treats you; how much happier you are when he's not around."

She looks up and the tears flow again. "I don't mean to drag you into our problems. I didn't realize you noticed."

"It's pretty hard to miss. Don't stay with him for me. I'll be fine." I squeeze her tighter again and whisper, "We'll be fine."

We hold the embrace and exist in the silence until we hear a couple walk down the hotel hallway arguing.

"Relationships are hard," she says.

"I know. Sometimes you have to let go. You have to decide when it's not worth beating yourself up to save it."

Her face beams a real smile for the first time since Dad got back from Moscow. "How did you get so wise?"

"Learning from other people's mistakes. And mine." This time she laughs. "I'll put your food in the fridge in case you want it later."

"Thanks. I'm tired." She crawls under the covers. "Think I'll go to bed for real now."

"I'll wait for Diego to come back and go to bed soon." I hug her again. "I'm glad you're here. I wouldn't want to do all this without you."

"Wouldn't miss it." She pulls the blanket up and is asleep within ten seconds.

Relieved she didn't bring up the pills again, I tiptoe over to my bag and slip on pajama pants and a t-shirt. Quiet, even though a Learjet flying through the room couldn't wake her.

Coast clear. She's asleep, I text Diego.

Then I curl up on the sofa and message my fans, *In NYC. Tune in to Today Show Friday!*

Then the room key beeps.

"Sorry, Diego. I didn't mean to kick you out of your own room."

"That's okay." He sits next to me. "I hung out in the lobby and watched people come in from partying. How did it go?"

"I told her." Diego's calm face makes me more confident in what I said. "I actually suggested to my mom that she dump my dad. Have I totally lost my mind?"

"You did the right thing."

The skyline disappearing into the clouds draws me to the window. "I know, but it still feels bizarre. Now if she'll do something about it."

Days without Dad would be a huge change. Mom's new job. Wherever my life goes. I'd rather have these experiences without him.

"Then if she can hold it together," I say.

"If she's anything like you, she's stronger than she seems."

"Mom and I were fine while he was gone. We'll do it again."

I lean in and try to see the top of the Empire State Building that has disappeared into the clouds. Diego wraps his strong arms around my waist, his whole body against mine. He turns me around and kisses my forehead.

What am I doing? I'm in my pajamas with my boyfriend in a hotel room in New York City with my mom right next door. I push away and slip out of the tiny space between him and the windowsill.

"What's wrong?" Diego asks.

"Nothing."

I shift my gaze from the patterned carpet to the bland art on the walls to the red numbers on the clock that say ten-twenty. Everywhere but his face. Then I shuffle my bare feet toward the bedroom.

"My five-thirty alarm will come a lot sooner than I want," I say.

"Tonight was fun," he says softly.

When I turn around, he's sitting on the sofa with a pillow in his lap. "Good night." I blow a kiss, close the door between us, and crawl into bed next to Mom. I curl up and doze off.

I jolt up in bed thinking I've missed the TV appearance, but it's only one-fifteen. It happens again a little more than an hour later and twice more before the alarm finally sounds. Mom's still in deep slumber, so I tiptoe to the door and crack it to see Diego stretched out on the sofa, mouth slightly open letting out a soft, steady snore.

While it's still quiet, I step into the shower. The warm water falls on me, and I replay every detail from last night. *I hope Mom's okay today.*

Still wrapped in my towel, I gently shake Mom awake. "The car will be here in forty-five minutes."

She sits up, stretches, and scans the surroundings—from the closed door to Diego's room to the soft light from the bathroom. "I feel so much better. You ready to face the world?"

"As ready as I'll ever be."

My phone lights up with a message. It's Dad.

Are you up? Can't be late for your appearance.

If only Lena had news about my real father.

"What is it?" Mom asks.

"Nothing important." I give her a hug as she perches on the edge of the bed. "Let's get dressed. We've got a TV show to do."

CHAPTER FORTY-THREE

As soon as Mom's ready, I knock on the door to Diego's room. "Come on in," I hear from the other side.

When I open it this time, Diego's dressed and sitting on the sofa with his coat next to him. If I hadn't seen him zonked out an hour ago, I'd think he had never slept. "We're ready finally. The car will be here any minute."

Kimberly already sent my music, I'm wearing my costume, but I double-check that I have my skates while we walk down the hallway to the elevator.

"I'm terribly sorry about last night, Diego," Mom says as we travel down the elevator. "I didn't mean to have that whole episode, and I wanted to join you two for dinner."

"Don't worry about it, Mrs. Sikorsky. I'm glad you're feeling better."

"We'll make up for it this afternoon. After the show and the Vera Wang errand, we'll do whatever you two want."

The Mom who has her act together is back. Finally.

We step through the revolving door into the bitter cold. "Thankfully, I brought my wooly tights and a long-sleeved dress for the rink. I'm not sure my body would move in anything less." The dry wind hits my face like my eyeballs might shatter.

"Good thinking, sweetie." Mom wraps her arm around my shoulders. "Do a good warm-up, and the performance will be over before you know it." She walks toward the black town car with the NBC license plates.

Mom's correct. This performance will be short. It's my first chance to show people I earned that medal no matter who my parents are and what decisions they made when I was a baby.

We wait at each block between the hotel and Rockefeller Center as commuters scurry across streets, faces wrapped in scarves and buried in their phones like the people who bustled down the sidewalks in Moscow.

"Here's the door for guests." The driver pulls up to an unmarked entrance. "I'll get your bag out of the trunk. Ring the bell and they will let you in."

I pull my scarf over my ears before I step into the chill. Diego taps the buzzer and a lady with a friendly face appears on the other side.

"Welcome, Docia. Right on time. Come in where it's warm. I'm Jennifer, one of the producers."

"This is my mom and Diego." She leads us down a brightly lit narrow hallway lined with closed doors.

"Hello Mrs. Sikorsky. Welcome Diego. Please make yourselves comfortable here in the green room. Help yourself to coffee and breakfast." She turns to me. "Docia, you and I will head down so you can get changed and ready for the show."

"Good luck, sweetie," Mom says and hugs me.

"Since Lena's not here to nag you, chin up," Diego says. "And break a leg, ha, ha." He gives me a peck on the lips.

I laugh when Mom's eyes get a little big.

Jennifer leads me through a winding hallway that opens into a room filled with makeup chairs and mirrors. It's cluttered with overloaded wardrobe racks. "Here you go." She opens a door with my name taped to it. "You can change then they'll touch up your makeup and hair right over there. Are you hungry?"

"No, but some hot cocoa would warm me up."

"No problem. I'll have it out here for you."

In the quiet behind the closed door, I peel off the layers down to my lucky skating dress. It was my best practice dress when I shocked everyone and won Worlds. When I stare at my reflection in the mirror, I imagine the gold medal from Worlds. It looked as stunning on the black burnout velvet fabric as it felt to win it. Even though that medal is at home, the Olympic gold is not. I want my medal back. I earned it.

A knock comes from the door as I straighten my ponytail, which shows a little wear from the wind and my scarf. The experts out there will take care of it better than I can. "Be right out!"

I grab my Olympic jacket and walk into the area where they make people look like stars.

"Here, Docia." I follow the sound until I see a guy in green skinny jeans and retro print shirt waving in my direction. "Come sit in Stephon's chair and I'll try to add a tad more to your perfection, sweetheart."

Is he for real?

"I'll take all the help you can give me."

"It won't take much, darlin'." He steps back and gets a full view of my outfit. "Love, love, love that dress. Let's give you some dramatic eyes. They'll look great on camera with the torn-out strips."

"Please don't go too crazy." I take a sip of the steaming hot cocoa. "It's barely seven in the morning. I don't want to scare people."

With the skilled hands of an artist, Stephon sweeps on gray shadow and sparkly liner that boosts the drama level. Then he sprays magic potion in my hair to make it look like black silk draped across the velvet dress. *Dad would be pissed. I like the new look.*

"Wow, you're hired. Want to go to Moscow for the weekend?"

"I'd love to. I'm a little big to fit in your suitcase," he says. "You're good to go. Trot down that hallway to the red door. Jennifer's waiting for you. Don't forget your jacket. Lordy, it was never this cold back home in Georgia."

"Thank you, Stephon."

Jennifer greets me on the other side of the studio's red door as Stephon promised. "Twenty minutes. Would you like to warm up here or on the ice?"

"It's been a long time since I've skated outside on such a chilly day. I'll stretch here then hit the ice."

"Perfect. They'll want you to be quiet since we're so close to the set."

Quiet helps me get in my zone since I don't have my music. I stretch out my cold muscles and watch the whispering bustle of other guests and the show's hosts settle into the sofas. Monster-looking cameras with arms surround them. The rink is through the window. Once I slip my skates on, I join Jennifer who talks intensely with another woman.

"Sorry to interrupt," I say. "All ready."

My muscles are, at least. If only stretching got rid of the jitters too.

"Let's get you out on that ice," Jennifer says and leads me underneath a ceiling covered in lights and by the small, glassed-in control room with monitors and complicated nobs and buttons. "Here's how it will work. Debra will ask you a few questions—maybe two minutes. Then you start your three-minute skate."

"Okay. Do you know the questions?"

"No, sorry I don't. Standard questions. Nothing to worry about." Someone distracts her before I can push for more.

The sunken rink is surrounded by flags above at street level with the majestic gold sculpture of Prometheus on one end. The ice is hard—one benefit of the frigid temperatures—but it's bumpy. I run through my warm-up and the first part of my exhibition program. Quad-double combination or play it safe? It's an exhibition. I could take the safe route. I circle the rink and set up the jump. Landed but shaky, so I try again. Still a little wobbly. Then Jennifer's voice projects from rink side. "Two minutes! Come over and meet Debra."

Jennifer is with Debra Tate, the host who interviews the biggest stars. Her orange coat stands out like a pumpkin in a blizzard. "Hi, Docia." Her outreached hand greets me when I skate to the edge of the rink. "Nice to meet you. Thanks for bearing the cold with us."

"My pleasure. It's perfect timing since I'm already in New York."

"Let's get this done so we can go inside and warm up. Ready?" We watch the camera operator's gloved fingers—four, three, two, one.

"We are so happy to have Docia Sikorsky with us for the Today at the Rink segment," Debra says to the camera. "She is America's skating darling who's also caught in the middle of the Olympic birthday scandal."

"Docia stopped here on her way back to Moscow in her fight to regain her Olympic gold where she'll skate in a tribute show on Sunday and meet her biological father." Then Debra turns to me. "Docia, what's your favorite memory from your first trip to the Olympics?"

This question's not so bad.

I take a deep breath without breaking my TV face. "I loved Moscow, and skating alongside such great athletes on Olympic ice was such an amazing experience." *I can do this.*

"What was going through your mind during the medal ceremony when you accepted the gold?"

I look up at the faces in the crowd gathered around the rink and think back to that moment. "When the American national anthem played, I hardly know where to begin—the pride, hard work, everyone who helped me along the way, the great people I met in Moscow. How my dream had come true."

"I know many people stand by you through this whole ordeal, but some don't. What would you say to those who do not believe in you?"

Debra's bright eyes wait for my answer, but I want to back away from the microphone to keep everyone from hearing if I say the wrong thing.

Before I think another second, I blurt out what's on my mind. "As the entire world—and I—learned recently, I was born to skate. An Olympic gold isn't a right. I earned it skating almost every day since I was three." I take a breath and scan the crowd. "I thank my biological parents for my skating genes and my adoptive mom and dad and my coach for pushing me every step of the way. I'm grateful to each of you who didn't turn your back on me. Everyone else—I hope you find it in your hearts to accept that I earned that medal with hard work and dedication."

"Thank you, Docia. This gives everyone a lot to think about. Now it's time to remind the world of what you can do."

I lay my Olympic jacket that I earned the right to wear on the ledge and skate a slow circle around the rink. I stop in my starting position and wait for the music.

A small group yells in tandem, "We love you, Docia!" Words that remind me to put on a happy face.

The first note of *Rock This Town* flips a switch in me. The adrenaline pumps warmth all the way to my gloved fingers and bundled-up toes. The

Stray Cats' fast tempo sends me into swing dance mode, and I forget about having to answer questions I wanted no one to ask. The audience claps along leading into my quad-double. I'm doing it.

Setup. Jump. Land. Repeat. Wobbly but done.

The crowd's reaction makes me smile. *I wish it were always this easy.*

The rest of the program flies by until I'm in my final pose. Applause from the people gathered around the Plaza surround me. I skate around the rink and wave up to the fans. Many return the wave. It feels good to be back out here performing like I'm supposed to. It's what I love.

Mom, Diego, and I embrace as soon as I skate off the ice. "It's way too cold for you to be outside!"

"Who wants to watch a monitor when we're right here?" Diego says. His arm stays around my waist after the embrace ends. "You looked great out there."

"Thanks. It was a lot of fun—after the questions, at least."

"You answered like a pro and skated flawlessly," Mom says and hands me my jacket. "You must be freezing. All we need is for you to get sick before Sunday."

"Good job on that quad-double," Diego says. "You were way up there on the second jump."

I beam from the inside out.

"Your dad called right after your performance," Mom says. "He said you were a little low energy on your footwork, but good overall."

Whatever. My knees almost froze like popsicles out there.

Jennifer's inside the door. "Great job, Docia!" She gives me a one-arm hug and leads us back to the dressing area. "Take your time getting changed. We can have a car take you back to your hotel or wherever you need to go. Let me know when you're ready."

"Thanks for everything, Jennifer. Such fun! I'd love to come back to the show again."

"Docia," Stephon says as he runs up to my dressing room door. "You were faaabulous! And you look amazing—if I may say so myself."

"Thanks! This is my Mom and my frie– I mean boyfriend, Diego."

"Well, aren't you two the lucky ones," Stephon says.

"Thanks for taking care of my little girl. The TV makeup is stunning, but I'm sure she won't mind taking it off before we head out into the city." Mom leans in. "Her father mentioned it was a little much."

"Actually, the makeup stays so I can try it out with my new dress at the fitting. I like the dramatic look." I step through the door to my dressing room and close it behind me before Mom has a chance to argue.

CHAPTER FORTY-FOUR

Mom gives the NBC driver who waits outside the guest entrance the address while Diego loads my bag. "We'll be at Vera's studio before nine," Mom says. "That should leave us plenty of time for an outing."

"Mom, do you feel like doing something afterward?" I say as we slide into the car's back seat. I'd be a mess after the yesterday she had.

"Absolutely. I feel surprisingly good. Guess I needed that sleep."

We sit in silence and listen to car horns and the occasional person yelling across the street. Morning commuters pack the Midtown sidewalks and move almost as fast as traffic. At least half of the cars are taxis or black town cars like this one.

"Miss?" the driver says. "You looked great."

Did he say that to me?

"I'm sorry?" I wake from my window daze.

"Skating—you did a great job. I watched you from the street this morning and in the Olympics."

Mom squeezes my knee in approval. Not my typical fan, but I'll take it. "Thanks so much. What's your name?"

"I'm Walid."

"Thank you, Walid. It's freezing out there but I enjoyed it." He glances back in the rearview mirror.

"My daughter loves to skate. I've had to take her every week since the Olympics." He points out the driver's window to the tree-line park. "We skated right there in Bryant Park yesterday."

"So, skating in this freezing weather is nothing to you." It would be especially nice if he's a supportive dad rather than one who pushes too hard. "Is your daughter in lessons?"

"Not yet, but lessons are probably next. Any suggestions?"

"Yes. Good skates, even if they're not brand new. Rental skates are impossible. They never fit right, and the blades are too dull to ever catch an edge in the ice."

"Thank you, Miss Sikorsky. Good luck. This is your destination."

"Oh, we should have walked, but then we wouldn't have met you." Tall gray and beige buildings line the narrow street as far as I can see in both directions. One of the buildings holds my amazing new dress. "Let's take a picture for your daughter."

"She would like that. Thank you." He steps out, beaming as Diego takes the pic.

"And please tell her hello and keep skating."

We walk into the understated Art Deco-style building nestled along a street with rows of fabric stores down both sides. I sneak a glance at my phone and my heart revs when I see Lena's name.

Beautiful performance my Docia, her text says.

I smile and wait for news about Luca. Nothing. Lily's text comes in next. *You kicked butt out there! Have fun!*

"Hello, Ms. Sikorsky. Welcome. Vera is expecting you and your guests," a trendy girl not much older than me says. "Up one flight, turn to the right and you'll see the design room. She'll meet you there."

"Thank you." We walk toward the stairs. My bag trails behind until Diego picks it up and carries it like it's no heavier than a bunch of bananas.

When we enter the design room, she's there. *It's Vera Wang. For real.*

"Docia, Adele, welcome. I'm so happy we were able to make a dress for this important occasion. I wish I could be in Moscow to see it live."

Mom reaches out for a two-handed handshake. "We appreciate your support wherever you are, Vera. Thank you."

"You guys are awesome." I can't help but feel a little star struck. "It was a huge surprise when Kimberly called about your offer. It means so much more since you were a skater. You understand how it feels on the rink when you know you look fabulous."

When I notice Diego hanging back near the entrance to guard my skates, I motion for him to join us. "And this is Diego. He'll be in Moscow with us."

She reaches out her hand. "Nice to meet you, Diego. You must be very important to Docia to take this trip with her."

"Thank you, Ms. Wang." Diego gives me a sheepish look. "I like to think so."

"Let's get started," Vera says. "We have you set up in the changing room right over there. Sophia will help with the fitting."

I turn back to Mom on the way to the fitting room. "If we stay ahead of schedule, maybe we can stop at a couple of stores and look for a cool outfit for you to wear to your new job."

"Hello Docia." A petite thirty-something woman holds open the fabric door to my fitting space. She wears a bracelet-style pin cushion that peeks out from the sleeve of her very Wang-looking asymmetric red and black top. "We hope you love the dress. We think it will look beautiful on you."

I step inside. *Where's my dream melon-colored dress?* All I see is a black, very un-what-I-dreamed-of long-sleeve dress with a white skirt covered in sparkles. For some reason, I'm not surprised.

I stick my head through the drape cover. "Sophia, can you come in please?"

She steps into the changing room.

"Did my dad call here?"

"Yes, he told us you changed your mind on the dress design. He gave us your very specific instructions since you were flying yesterday. I hope we got it right. Do you like it?"

"Sophia, it is beautiful." I hesitate and look at the dress and back at her. "But I didn't change my mind. I never asked him to contact you."

Sophia goes pale and kneads her hands. "I am so sorry, Docia. He was very clear. We thought it was odd, but he said you would be terribly upset if you had to wear the other dress."

"Do you still have the other one?" I hold my breath to gather all the hopeful energy possible.

Color trickles back over Sophia's face. "We do. It's not quite finished but it can be in a snap. I'll get it." I follow her outside the room as she dashes out of the dressing area.

Mom looks confused. "What's going on?"

"Sophia forgot something." I lean on the changing room doorway much more relaxed than I thought I would be. "She'll be right back."

As I finish the sentence, Sophia rounds the corner, garment bag in hand and slips in behind the curtain. She hangs it on the hook and unzips the cover. It's the exact statement I want to represent the new me.

Sophia's almost blue from holding her breath.

"I. Love. It. I can't wait to put it on."

Sophia lets out a lungful of air. "Thank God." She backs out of the room. "We want you to *really* love it."

It's perfect. Like a Mediterranean sunset. I caress the soft fabric from the front to the back. Then I rip off my clothes and carefully slip on the work of art. The simple elegance. The rich color. I look older; more sophisticated. It doesn't matter that the ruching on the sides isn't finished and that part of the soft draping in the front and back isn't yet stitched. All I see is how the fabric will flow like a floating butterfly as I move through each element of my program on Sunday.

I step out of the changing room in front of the three-way mirrors and twirl like a child beauty pageant winner showing off her new pageant dress.

Diego nods.

"This is the most beautiful dress I've ever seen. It's exactly what I hoped for." I turn to Sophia. "Please work your magic to make it fit."

"Where's Mom?" Before Diego answers, she comes out of another changing room. "Wow, Mom. You look amazing." Not just the outfit, but her face glows with confidence.

"Vera insisted I select an outfit from her new collection." Then she turns and notices me. She puts both hands on her cheeks. "Docia, you look beautiful. So grown up."

"Thanks." I'm still stuck on Mom's new look. "You look amazing in that royal blue."

"And there's a blazer too." Mom steps in front of the mirror with me. "It's so tailored but also feminine. With a little hemming, it will fit perfectly."

While someone else marks the length for Mom, Sophia skillfully tucks in the sides and the back with straight pins so the dress hugs me. Diego stands to the side and takes it all in.

"How does it feel?" Sophia asks and steps back to inspect it from all sides. "Get into some of your positions and let's see if it stays in place."

I try a spiral, a sit spin, and a catch-foot spin position. "Oh, one little problem." I point to the partially exposed left side of my butt and pull it back down before Diego notices. I definitely don't want to be another bare-butt-Stacy skater when I need to be fabulous.

"We'll fix that," Sophia stands back and looks pleased. "You look gorgeous, and the eye makeup is perfect."

"Thanks to the NBC makeup artist." I stroke the soft, sparkle-less fabric as we walk back to the changing room. "I *feel* gorgeous. Can you get it ready fast?"

"What time do you leave?"

"The car will pick us up from our hotel at four o'clock this afternoon."

Sophia looks at the large clock on the wall. "We'll have your dress and your mom's suit delivered to you at the hotel by three."

"I couldn't ask for anything more. You have all been amazing. The outfit for Mom is even more than we expected." I hug Sophia. "Thank you." There's confidence in Sophia's face, and Mom never needs to know a thing.

"It's the least we could do to make up for the confusion," Sophia whispers. "We will send a repair kit too, you know, needle, thread, bits of extra fabric just in case."

"Perfect," I answer. "This will absolutely make the show on Sunday."

"Thank you, Sophia," Mom says. "Should we wait for the final alterations?"

"Sophia and I sorted out the details. Both outfits will be waiting for us at the hotel before we leave."

Diego's grin from behind Mom tells me he figured out what happened.

"Are you sure?" Mom looks at her watch and back at Sophia. "How?"

"Trust me," Sophia answers. "I'll deliver them myself."

This trip would have been so smooth if Dad hadn't thrown in his little complications.

"No need to panic, Mom. Diego and I will grab a cab while you get dressed."

"Thank you, sweetie. I'll be out in a minute."

Diego reaches out for my hand on the way down the stairs. His body next to mine adds strength, and I need as much as I can get.

He stops on the landing and turns to me. "Your Dad screwed something up again?"

I let out a slight chuckle. "How did you know?"

"I know you," he answers, "and I know your dad. How bad?"

"Could've been worse, and it's fixed now. Please don't say anything to Mom."

Even though I wanted to keep this hushed, I'm glad Diego knows. He'll back me up if I need it.

"I won't say a word. Who would want to add more stress to her world?" He starts back down toward the street. "I'll get that taxi."

CHAPTER FORTY-FIVE

"Look, Mom. It's just now ten." I slide into the backseat of the cab next to her. "Let's drop off my skates on the way." I look across the seat at Diego. "That way, Diego won't insist on lugging them around for me all afternoon."

"I don't mind," he says, "but I don't think they'll let them into the MoMA anyway." He leans up to speak to the driver. "Sir, can you please take us by the Hyatt at Grand Central Station?"

"Good idea," Mom answers absently and looks at her phone. "Your father hasn't called in a while."

Since when did ninety minutes become too long to go without talking to Dad?

"Can you believe we've already done the TV appearance, taken care of my skating dress, and you have a fabulous new outfit for work this morning? You'll be the first person in Houston wearing the new Vera Wang line."

"Hard to believe, huh?" She rubs her hand across her cheek and seems to forget what she was saying. "Vera can make anyone feel beautiful."

"You *are* beautiful, Mom. In whatever you wear."

"Thank you, sweetie. You don't have to humor me." She looks down and straightens her scarf that doesn't need straightening. "If it's not too cold, I'll wear it to your performance. I planned to wear the black sweater your father gave me. He likes it so much."

"Wear what makes you feel good, Mom, not what Dad tells you to wear."

"I'll be right back." I hop out in front of the hotel and drag my bag to the elevator and up to our floor.

I've got some work to do to bring Mom's confidence back. With a lighter load on the way down, I think back on the trip so far. It's been so much fun. Even with what Dad pulled and Mom's episode. I wrap my coat tighter before I step through the revolving door into the bitter cold.

"Diego and I discovered we have something in common," Mom says as I slide into the warm car. "We both like the artist Sigmar Polke. His art is on exhibit at the museum."

I smile, glad they had a moment.

"Before your father and I got married, I used to paint."

"Mom, I never knew that. Why did you stop?" I'll bet I can guess.

"Work and your father. There wasn't time." She stares at the MoMA as we drive up. "Maybe I'll start again," she says quietly.

Diego jumps out and opens the door for us. "These Polke pieces might inspire you," he says.

"Thank you," I whisper and squeeze his hand when I step onto the curb. A group of children in matching shirts reminds me of the foster kids at home. Diego nods toward the cluster of young girls who whisper and point at us as we approach the museum entrance.

I wave to the girls. "School trip?" They nod and giggle. "Would you like a photo?"

"Yes," they say in unison and dive for their phones.

"I'll take them," Diego says. The girls crowd around me and pose.

"Miss Docia, did you get your medal back?" one of the girls asks.

"Not yet, but I hope to soon. Thank you for asking." I hug her then wave to the rest of the girls as they follow the group to their waiting school bus.

Mom's inside, hands on her hips. "What are you grinning about?" I ask.

"You're so good with your young fans."

"I've gotten a lot more practice since Dad's been away. He's always rush, rush, gotta go." One more reason things are better when he's not here.

"Wait here," Mom says. "I'll get our tickets."

"That's not all," Diego says and reaches out for my hand. "The way you deal with your dad takes guts, on top of the conspiracy business. It sounds like a bad TV movie. Not too shabby for an ice princess."

"Hey!" I throw a playful punch into his shoulder that makes him laugh, but my pride grows inside like a summer sunrise.

I wouldn't have the will or determination to make it here without all Lily, Joy, and Diego have done—and Lena finally telling me the truth.

"Okay, Sigmar Polke exhibit is this way," Mom says and heads for the stairs.

"Wait up, Mom!" I grab my ringing phone out of my purse as I catch up with her. The word Dad flashes across the screen. I turn off the ringer and let it fall back into the side pocket. If only it had been an Italian phone number—my other dad.

Diego radiates awe in the first room. He studies each painting from a distance and then up close. I follow him as he explores each piece. Is Diego or the art more interesting? In the next room, he pauses at one group of paintings for an extra-long time.

"Tell me what you see in this painting."

"I don't know. It's hard to put into words." He steps in closer. "At first, it's just shapes. When you study it, the shapes could be a piece of something huge. They could be moving. Since it's still, we'll never know."

My phone vibrates. This time I know it's Dad without looking. I ignore it.

"He doesn't paint people very often, but when he does, he gives them life. Expression. Almost like they can feel. That's what I tried to capture with the dancers in the Bolshoi painting I did for you."

"Nicely stated," Mom says. "Even though he doesn't show us, I can almost guess what these people are doing by the motion he captures. It's so interesting how he uses dots...." Mom pulls her ringing phone out of her purse and retreats toward a quiet corner. She turns back and hands the phone to me.

"Who is it?" I whisper, but she drops the phone in my hand without answering. Jerry is plastered across the screen. "I'll talk to him later," and hand the phone back.

"Talk to your father. He insists."

"Not now. We're in the museum." He will not ruin our fabulous day in Manhattan. "Mom!"

She turns to one of the paintings, still holding the phone away like it's a grenade about to explode. I look to Diego for help, but he's engrossed in one of the artist's movies. If we talk now, we won't have to again until Moscow. I won't acknowledge any of the screw-ups he's caused. I'm saving the chaos he tried to create for him to face in person. I take the phone and hope he's given up, but the word Jerry still stares back.

"Hi, Dad."

"Hi, Peanut. I know you had a busy morning and want to make sure you take it easy and don't push it. You need to eat your usual simple protein and carb lunch. Nothing unusual or spicy. Did you get a short workout in?"

"No Dad, we're actually—"

"Your performance was good this morning—a little stiff on your footwork and your combination entrance—well, rushed, but I'm sure we can work through that next week."

"Dad."

"And we need to talk about your interview this morning. You shouldn't have answered that question about the people who have stood by you. Next time I'll cover it. Did the Vera Wang people come through with your dress?"

"Dad," I interrupt when he takes a millisecond to breathe. "We're busy now. I'll talk to you when you get to Moscow on Sunday."

He has some nerve mentioning the dress. I bite my tongue to keep from barking back.

"Busy? Nothing should keep you from talking with your father."

Seriously? He has said nothing that couldn't wait until Sunday.

"Running around the city will wear you out. Isn't your mother taking care of you?"

"Dad, we're managing fine."

"Do I have to do everything? I'll get tonight's flight to Moscow and meet you there before you do irreparable harm. You still have to prepare for Worlds."

I stop mid-breath and almost choke on his words. "Lena needs you to fly with her tomorrow. Remember, her doctor wants her to have the extra day to recover."

"She'll be fine. The airline can help her. No airline can make sure you take care of yourself."

"Dad! You promised Lena you would fly with her." I catch my breath to keep from screaming in the middle of the museum. "You promised me."

The museum docent puts his finger to his mouth and shoots me a keep-it-down look.

"Only if I can't get on this flight. Good thing I'm already packed."

I pace down the center of the exhibit room. Breathe in. Out. Tell myself to keep from hyperventilating or screaming so loud that we get kicked out.

"If anything happens to Lena and she's alone, I'll never forgive you." Then I end the call.

His name flashes across the screen. There are no words left to say.

My fierce grip on the phone keeps me from throwing it across the room. My jaw clenches so tight I couldn't speak if I tried. How can the person I'm supposed to trust most be my biggest *enemy?*

A hand is on my back then Diego is in front of me. His mouth moves but the noise in my head is too deafening to hear.

"Docia," he says. "It'll be okay."

I speak but I'm not sure sounds come out.

He wraps his arms around me and rocks back and forth. "I promise," he whispers.

"I cannot believe my dad." I look around the room for Mom. "He has got to be the most controlling, selfish person on the planet."

"What happened?"

"Most recently?" I flip through his myriad of underhanded tricks. "He threatened to dump Lena and fly to Moscow today. He thinks I can't manage myself."

"He wouldn't. Would he?"

"Unless the flight's full."

Mom rounds the corner from the next room. "Please don't let on that anything's wrong. She can't handle it." I can't deal with how she might react.

He nods and I put on my everything-is-fabulous face.

"How's your father?" Mom takes her phone back. "It will be good to see him Sunday."

"He's good." I turn away so she can't read what my face must say.

"Lunch?" Mom asks. "I hear Café 2 here is nice."

Diego looks at me with a questioning face while I nod. "That sounds perfect, Mrs. Sikorsky."

We make our way to the restaurant. After the host shows us to our table, a server walks by with plates full of pasta. My belly churns like an earthquake threatening to erupt. "Be right back," I whisper to Diego while Mom's preoccupied with today's specials.

I walk as fast as I can and concentrate on breathing instead of what wants to happen. I duck into a stall in the restroom and lean over the toilet. My face boils. My body convulses but nothing comes out. I take a couple of breaths. I know it's not what I ate since all I had was hot cocoa before the TV show hours ago. Why do I let Dad get to me like he gets to Mom?

"You okay in there?" someone asks outside the stall. "Want me to get someone?"

Yeah, that's all I need. People in the restaurant knowing I'm hurling in the bathroom. Then Mom will freak out and call Dad. I'll be under his watch stuck with pasta for the rest of my life. I jerk forward again to more dry heaves.

"I'm fine. Something I ate." I hope that calls the woman off.

"If you need something, stick your head out the door. My table is close by."

I close my eyes, lean my head against the stall, and visualize a nice meal, a relaxing afternoon, and an uneventful trip to the airport. It's the exact exercise Lena taught me to be calm and focused before a competition. I've never had to do it to get through lunch.

Once the bathroom is quiet, I step out of the stall and wash the metallic taste out of my mouth. I dampen a paper towel and dab it across my face and neck. It feels like ice dripping on a hot burner.

Avoiding the direction where I think the lady from the bathroom sits, I concentrate on a tiny spot on my sleeve to avoid eye contact until I get back to the table where the server takes our order.

The menu choices don't seem appetizing—panini, pasta, salad, pasta, pasta, pasta. I'm drowning in the slimy stuff. "Minestrone soup, please."

"And for your meal?" the server answers.

"That's all. Is there any way you can ask the chef to serve the soup with no pasta?"

She returns a blank look. "No pasta? Yes, ma'am, we can try."

After Mom and Diego order, Mom turns to me. "What's the deal with pasta today? You eat it all the time when you compete."

"It's time for a change." Change that reaches way beyond pasta.

"Okay, sweetie." She looks at me with her most concerned mother look. "You know your dad always insists you get your carbs."

I take a bite of bread from the basket. "This is amazing. It's so warm and soft it melts in my mouth." I continue to talk with a mouth full. "And it's whole grain, a perfect carb source."

Mom stares at me like I'm speaking Latin. Diego pinches my leg under the table. I step all my eighty-two pounds onto his foot. "You know a lot about fitness. Don't you agree?"

He almost spits out a bite of pizza. "Absolutely."

"Then, if I'm not too full after my soup, I'll get a nonfat yogurt with banana and berries, much healthier than the regular pasta with marinara Dad insists I eat every meal for the week before competitions."

"I'm impressed. You've been doing your homework."

Now that Mom has heard my point, I don't feel the need to spit the bread out like I thought I might. I grab another slice, nibble it around the edges, and fish around my soup to avoid stray pasta. Mom and Diego chatter about a Russian artist's work they hope to see in Moscow.

As Mom takes her last bite, she picks up her phone. "Oh, it's after two o'clock already. As soon as you finish your soup, let's get that yogurt to-go and head back to the hotel."

"We can go now. I'm finished. Have you heard from Dad?" Mom will be the first to know if he plans to meet us in Moscow a day early.

"No, not yet. Do you need to call him?"

"Nope. Only curious."

Hopefully, we won't see him before Sunday.

CHAPTER FORTY-SIX

We step out of the taxi in front of the hotel just as Sophia emerges through the revolving door holding white garment bags.

"Good timing," she says. "Vera and I want to be certain these make it to you safely."

"Bless your heart, dear," Mom says with her best Texas charm. "You're such a sweetheart to trek over here in the freezing cold. Can we get you a coffee to warm you up? Maybe a cocktail?"

"Coffee would be nice, to-go," Sophia says.

"I'll get it," Diego says.

Mom slips him a twenty.

"And you can take a look at the designs to make sure they are perfect," Sophia tilts her head at me. "This is a pretty special weekend for you."

"The right dress makes all the difference, Sophia. Thanks for all you've done."

In a corner of the lobby outside the café, Sophia pulls down the first long zipper to reveal Mom's Mardi Gras blue. Mom's face blooms pink when she sees it again. "This is the most beautiful ensemble. I'm hardly worthy to wear it."

"Oh, stop, Mom. You're as worthy as anyone." I squeeze her hand. "You'll be the best-dressed person in the office."

Sophia lays Mom's outfit over the back of a chair and reveals my prized dress in the second bag. Aside from it being gorgeous, the flowing piece of art seems like one of Katniss' Hunger Games victory dresses. At least I didn't have to fight for my life. Though, like her, I've had a hell of a battle against one of my competitors and an awful lot of greedy grownups who should know better.

I scan the lobby for anyone who might look suspicious and tuck the masterpiece back in its bag.

"We'll carry these on the plane with my skates." I'm not sure I can take another sabotage.

"Best of luck this weekend, Docia." Sophia leans in for a hug. "I'll be one of your loudest TV fans."

"Even though you and Ms. Wang won't be there," I say in her ear, "you'll be in my heart."

Mom reaches her hand out to Sophia. "Thank you for bringing these over."

"Bon voyage!" she says as she walks through the door.

Diego puts his hand on my shoulder. "Wait here and I'll go up to the room with your mom and get our luggage," he says while Mom follows.

What did I do to deserve such amazing support? Diego. Vera Wang. Her staff. Joy. Lily. I lay one hand on top of the bags draped across a chair. With the other, I dial Lily.

"Hey! We're about to head to the airport. Mom and Diego went to the room to get our stuff."

"I miss you," she says. "You looked great on TV this morning! How's the trip?"

It's so good to hear her voice. "It's been fun. Full of surprises. You wouldn't believe it all."

Lily gasps. "Please tell me you have your awesome new dress."

"Yes. They just delivered it. It's in my hand."

"And..."

"There are no words. It's even more beautiful than I expected, and the earrings and lip stain you gave me are perfect." I gaze at the garment bag like it's transparent. "I want to get to Moscow now. Move past the BS. These few weeks since the Olympics have been the longest ever."

"After Worlds, you'll be home so I can hang out with my old friend Docia, the one who's never down."

"It's the new version of your old friend," I answer. "You'll like her. I promise."

"I already do. Message me when you get there? I wish I was with you."

"I will. Me too." *More than you know.* "See you soon."

I slip my phone into my purse and catch a glimpse of Mom's pill bottles. Lily would know what to do to handle Mom and Dad. She always cuts through the drama without pissing people off. Watching the water slide down the tile wall in the lobby calms me, but not as much as Lily does.

Diego and Mom emerge from the elevators dragging armloads of bags. "The car service texted, sweetie," Mom says. "Their driver is a few minutes away."

I put my coat on and follow the bellman with our bags. "I'll see if that's us." I walk to the black Town Car that pulled up to the curb. "Scissorhands?" I ask through the window.

The driver nods back with a strange look. "You leave from JFK, right?"

"Yes." I wave to Mom and Diego and slide across the back seat still gripping the precious garment bags while the driver loads the rest of our stuff.

"Right on schedule, but no time to spare," Mom says.

"A month ago, I never dreamed we'd be back in Moscow so soon." I turn to Diego. "And with you."

People walk down the sidewalks faster than the car moves.

"Will traffic be like this the whole way?" I ask.

"I hope not, ma'am," the driver says. "I'll get you there as fast as I can."

The fifteen miles stretches to thirty minutes then an hour before we see jets take off and land. "Are we almost there?"

"About ten minutes," the driver answers. "What time is your flight?"

"We have a little over an hour and a half," Mom answers. "But it's an international flight." A look of worry glosses over her face, and her eyes follow an ascending jet.

"We'll be fine, Mom." I show Diego crossed fingers. "I hope," I mouth.

At the airport, we go straight to the ticket counter. With no bags to check, the passport and boarding pass inspection process is quick.

"The fastest security line is down there to your right." The ticket agent points down the long corridor. "Have a nice trip, and good luck, Docia."

I turn back to her. "Thank you!"

The three of us dash to security—me dragging my skates and the garment bags.

I stop and almost cause a pile-up collision. "Look at the security line."

"Let's get in it," Diego says. "No time to stand around."

The line inches forward, minutes tick closer to our flight time. Finally, it's our turn. I stand in the machine for the scan that always makes me feel naked and vulnerable. No matter how famous, quiet, or infamous, we all have to be approved before we can get on a plane.

I pull my boots back on and reclaim the garment bags. "Where are my skates?" Diego makes it through the scanner.

Diego motions toward the TSA officials. "They're looking at them now." We watch the man point at the screen and talk to the uniformed woman next to him.

"What's up with my skates?" Something I can't do without. "They'll let me take them on, right?"

"Don't panic," Diego says.

"I always keep them with me." Mom has joined us now. "It's never been a problem before." I realize I'm hugging our Vera Wang treasures to my chest like someone might take them away too.

"Sir, is there a problem with my daughter's skates?"

The man motions for us to step aside. "Ma'am, all flights headed to Eastern Europe are on heightened security alert."

Mom smiles back at him. "Mr. Reynolds, it's just a pair of skates. My daughter has a televised performance in Moscow on Sunday."

"I'm sorry, ma'am. It's our directive. You know—the blades."

Mom still wears a smile, but I know she's agitated by the way she tilts her head from one side to the other. "We looked into this before we left Houston on Wednesday and everything was fine."

"This happened today," the man says. "Let me check."

"Mom, I can't fly without my skates," I speak in a voice that is likely much louder than I think. "I'll miss the flight if I have to go back and check them."

"I know sweetie. Let's see what we can work out."

"Mr. Reynolds, may we check them at the gate when we board?"

"No, but I'll let you bypass the security line after you go back to the ticket counter."

I look at him and then at Mom. "Seriously?"

"It looks that way," she says. "I'll wait here with our stuff. Please hurry."

"I'll go with you." Diego and I take off running with my precious skates in tow until we see the red-headed lady at the Delta ticket counter.

"Well, hello again," she says. "How can I help you?"

"They're making me check my skates. Can you be sure they get on our plane? I *have to* have them when I get there."

"Absolutely, Docia. I'll tag them for special handling. You have your contact information on the bag?"

"Yes, cell number and all." I watch her tap her keyboard and pull the big white luggage tag off the printer. She sticks it through the handle on my bag and tops it off with a bright pink special handling tag.

"They'll make it," Diego says. "At least our flight is direct."

"He's right," the lady says and bats her green eyes at us. "As long as they get on the plane, they'll be there."

There's nothing we can do but trust her.

"Now hurry to your gate. I'll let the gate agent know you're on your way."

"Thank you." I turn back to watch my skates on the conveyer and say one of those if-my-skates-make-it-I'll-study-my-schoolwork-every-day-until-I-graduate prayers.

We go to the closed security line like the man told us and repeat the scan routine. Mom is on a bench surrounded by bags on the other side.

"That was fast," Mom says. "Our gate's right over there."

"I'm parched. I'll stop and get us water. Meet you there."

Inside the newsstand, I notice the latest issue of *Sports LIVE!* with my picture in the corner. It's a teaser for Joy's article in the next issue. It's nice to read good news. I know Joy won't let Dad screw the story up either.

I set the three waters on the counter while I wait in line. When I open my purse to grab my wallet, Mom's medicine bottles rattle around. She'll want pills as soon as she has water in hand. What will I do for nine-and-a-half hours besides worry about what Dad will do to mess things up tomorrow? She won't notice a couple missing. I dig for one of the blue pills—the one with A on it—and unscrew the cap on a water bottle to wash it down. They always work for Mom when she needs a good sleep.

Most everyone's standing when I approach the gate.

"Good news," Mom says when I hand her the water as we board. "They upgraded us. It will be so much more comfortable to stretch out and nap in the larger seats."

Mom reaches across the aisle and over Diego as we settle into our seats. "Time to hand my pills back over."

"How about I hang on to them and you let me know when you want to take one?"

"Actually, now would be good. They're not yours. Besides, you're a child and shouldn't have drugs like that so accessible."

"Let's get through this trip and I'll give them back to you at home. Do you want one of the blue ones?" I unscrew the cap.

"I'll take one of each for this flight," she answers. "And both bottles."

"Both at once? Are you sure?"

Should I take both too? Maybe not since I'm not sure how they'll affect me.

"I'll keep them for now. I *need* you on this trip," I say.

"We'll talk about it when we get there." She leans her head back and closes her eyes.

After two sips of the orange juice the flight attendant served and before the seatbelt and airbag instructions, my eyelids feel heavy. I hope Diego likes the inflight movies since Mom and I will be sacked out.

It seems like only a moment of slumber when I hear Diego's voice and feel someone shake me, "We're almost over Moscow."

"Already? What about dinner? And breakfast? And the movie?" I stretch out my arms and legs and wipe the drool off my cheek. The garment bags are still draped across my lap like a blanket. "I'm so thirsty."

Diego turns to me and asks quietly, "How did you sleep so long? You didn't move."

"Tired I guess."

"You took your mom's pills, didn't you?"

Am I that obvious?

"Docia, tell me. You know I'll get it out of you, eventually."

"Well, guess I—"

"We will land at Moscow's Sheremetyevo International Airport in about ten minutes," the captain says interrupting me at a very strategic moment. "It's zero degrees Celsius and sunny at half-past noon in Moscow. We want to give a special send-off to today's passenger, American Olympic gold medal-winning skater Docia Sikorsky, for her performance Sunday."

"I'll take them away from both of you," Diego whispers and reaches across the aisle to shake Mom awake.

I took them away from Mom. I don't need him to butt into this too.

"We're pulling for you to get your medal back," the captain continues.

Mom looks over at me and beams.

Passengers applaud and start a spontaneous chant. "U-S-A. U-S-A. U-S-A."

CHAPTER FORTY-SEVEN

I never thought I'd be so happy to see Moscow, especially after Lena and I had to slip out so fast. The cab drops the three of us in front of the Ritz-Carlton that overlooks the austere Kremlin and Red Square. The crisp midday air and our luggage surround us until the bellman whisks our bags away.

"I'll keep this," I say to the tall man in the burgundy uniform. I won't let go of the garment bag or my skate bag with the hot pink special handling tag that made it safely back by my side.

"Oh honey," Mom says and slides her sunshades down from the top of her head. "Your dad texted during our flight to remind you to stretch your ankle after sitting so long."

"Already did." Maybe the drive by the Kremlin made her think of Dad. "Did he say anything else?"

"To text when we land. Do you need something from him?" She tries to walk past me through the door.

"Just curious how everything is at home." And whether we'll see him on the other side of these doors.

"He said he would see us Sunday. That's about it."

Exactly what I want to hear.

"Cool." I try to answer with no emotion even though the good news feels like the weight of our jet loaded with luggage slid off my back. Now if my real dad would contact me.

"What did you two do during the flight over? What was the movie? Sorry, I zonked out."

Diego chuckles.

"That's okay, Mom. I'm used to it." I glance at him and he shakes his head.

"You look cheery." She stares us both down as she walks into the lobby.

"What's there to not be happy about? We're here together. Tomorrow's show will be amazing. I finally get to meet my real father."

"I guess your dad's all we're missing." She looks sad for a moment.

"And Lena. We've had a blast so far." Despite Dad's little surprises. "We're in Moscow. I'm not competing. Let's have the most Russian lunch we can find then go to the Bolshoi."

"Are you up to it?" Mom asks. "Did you rest at all on the plane? You still have rehearsal tonight."

"I feel great, but I'm starved to try new and adventurous food." I'm also famished since I slept through the airplane meals too. "Mom, you haven't eaten a bite since the MoMA in New York. Check us in so we can have some fun!"

"Give me a minute." Mom fumbles around in her purse. "Don't worry. I'll get our rooms squared away."

"We'll decide on a place for lunch."

Diego and I relax in the high-backed red chairs in the lobby. "I guess she forgot what happened when we checked into our hotel in New York."

"Give her a break. She's pretty stressed," Diego says.

"Wow, you're protective." He's right.

I glance at the registration desk for signs that Dad screwed this one up too, but I'm sure Kimberly made sure he didn't. This event is all about me, but Mom also needs support. "Let's have lunch over there in the Lobby Bar."

"Do they serve food?" Diego tilts his head in agreement. "I just see people drinking vodka. That's what they do in Moscow."

We watch a server balancing a tray of burgers. "Grab that spot by the fireplace. I'll tell Mom to have the bags sent up to our rooms."

"Afternoon tea with a Russian touch," I read from the menu after Mom joins us. "Burger...not very Russian, but caviar is."

When the waiter brings our food, I gulp down a smoked salmon sandwich barely pausing long enough to chew and gaze at the caviar that stares back at me. "Mom, Diego, are you having any? I got the one called Osetra because it's a little cheaper."

"Burger and fries are all I need." Diego grins.

"Mom?" She's surrounded by little cakes and tiny sandwiches without crusts.

"Try some caviar sweetie, and don't tell your father," she whispers. I guess the food distracted her from hearing me. "He'd never let me hear the end of letting you eat caviar on such an important weekend."

I use the little spoon to scoop the tiny spheres onto a cracker. Four eyes are on me. "It's salty and strange but good, and not mushy like I thought it would be." I follow with more until the dish is almost empty. "It tastes a little nutty; just melts in my mouth."

One more new experience to add to my list.

"You're the regular little adventurer," Mom says. "What did you do with my daughter?"

"Been right here all along, but Dad never let me try much of anything new."

Mom's smile fades and she looks away.

"Well," Diego says. "If we take about an hour to tour the Bolshoi, there will be plenty of time to rest before your rehearsal."

Diego saves the day again, but I don't want to get used to his rescues.

We walk the few blocks to the theatre and follow the signs to the ticket office. The ticket windows are closed. *Not again.*

Mom knocks on the window. "Hello, is anyone there?" It's quiet. "Hello?"

There are quick footsteps on a hard floor, then a window flies open to reveal a man's stern face.

"We would like to purchase tickets for a tour," Mom says.

"English tours only Monday and Friday. Must buy tickets on day of tour." Then he slams the window shut.

Mom knocks again. "The ticket is for an Olympic gold medalist. And it doesn't have to be English."

Nothing.

"But she is Anna Ivanova's daughter." This time she speaks much less confidently.

Still quiet. *How could Moscow disappoint me again?*

"Oh sweetie," Mom turns to me. "I'm so sorry. Maybe we can do a tour on Monday before we leave."

"That's okay. It won't be our last chance." I answer. "Let's go back to the hotel and I'll rest. We can be early for rehearsal."

I walk quietly alongside Mom and Diego and tune out their art talk. That day in front of the Bolshoi wasn't the first day I ran away from Dad. Next time I'll face him head-on, no matter how bad it gets.

In our hotel room, the soft, white comforter looks inviting. When I curl up on the bed, I sink in like it's made of cotton balls and doze off to the rhythm of Mom and Diego exchanging thoughts on art. Something about a new style that's popular in Europe.

Then someone shakes me awake. "Docia, get up," Diego says. "Rehearsal is in an hour."

Rehearsal? I open my eyes and rub my face.

"I'm up." I stretch my legs and swing them over the side of the bed. "I woke up and thought we were anywhere but here."

"We're here all right, complete with the most inconvenient business hours and the air colder than the room when my dad's ex-wife is around. The museum your mom and I wanted to go to is closed for an installation."

I dig through my suitcase for practice clothes. The only things that resemble art I can think about right now are the last few puzzle pieces of my life I'm trying to put together.

"No big deal." Diego shrugs. "That's not why we're here."

"Don't forget your music," Mom says through the bathroom door.

"Got it!" I have the drill down. I've done this since I was three. I take a deep breath before walking out to avoid saying something stupid. I need Mom in my corner.

•　　•　　•

The taxi rolls up to the Megasport Arena and it all comes back. The excitement. The intimidating structure. The loneliness. The first time I stepped out of the athletes' bus in front of it a few weeks ago, my life changed.

This time, I have nothing to lose.

"Meet you rink side," I tell Mom and Diego when we step inside the arena's lobby. "I'll be a minute."

I circle Anna's statue to take in every detail of her carefully placed fingers; the curve of her legs the sculptor captured. I remember the *Swan Lake* program she performed in this costume. Anna's arms arch like wings stretching to take flight, frozen forever in bronze.

When I reach up and run my hand down Anna's cold metal leg curved into a layback spin position, a sort of energy tingles from my fingers through me. It's only a sculpture, but it's the closest I'll ever get.

"She's beautiful," Diego says. He puts his hand over mine while I trace the Russian letters on the bronze plaque at the base of the masterpiece.

"Lena told me the letters say what Anna told the poor children so they didn't lose hope. 'Always reach for your dream' then 'In memory of Anna Ivanova, the People's Princess on the Ice.'"

"I know she was famous, but I had no idea the Russian people idolized her," Diego says.

I look into her blank bronze eyes. "Lena says her kindness brought warmth every day into this cold country." My imagination fills in the statue's soft gray eyes I remember from watching her old skating videos. "I wish I had known her."

Diego squeezes my hand. "At least you skate a lot like her."

"I wish." I notice Mom watching from the corner of the lobby. She turns away when I look up and quickly sweeps her hand across her cheeks. *Is she wiping away tears?*

"Okay, let's do this. I hope people showed up." When we reach Mom, I take her hand and the three of us walk together through the tunnel to the rink.

Skaters are warming up on the ice. *They showed up.*

"The entire U.S. team, minus one." I lean against the boards to digest it all as my heart warms the outside chill away. "Look at all the others." I tick off the teams by their jacket colors—Japan, South Korea, Russia, Canada, France, Switzerland, England, Australia, and Spain. "Even the girls who won the Olympic medals."

They came all this way for me? I hope it's not a waste of time.

When Lucy sees me, she breaks away from Greg and rushes to the boards. "Docia, it's about time you got here!" She throws her arms around me. "I didn't even get to say goodbye."

Greg and the others skate over to exchange embraces.

"Stacy won't be here, will she?" Lucy whispers. I shake my head. "I didn't think she'd have the nerve to show up."

Stacy's harmless now. "Is anyone from Italy here?"

"Not yet," Lucy answers. "I believe they arrive in the morning."

I imagine what I might say to my real dad first. What did you think when you found out about me? Do you still miss Anna? When can I meet my new sister?

"Come on!" Greg says. "We were about to go over one of the group numbers."

I look toward Mom like I need approval. Before she knows the question, I answer. "Let me get my skates on."

Lucy runs through the choreography and then I join the group on the ice. When one of the Russian skaters leads a fast number, it brings new meaning. We start in teams by country, then he mixes us up so we can show unity as fellow athletes.

I laugh at myself when I bump into one of the other skaters. "Dang it, left not right, Docia!"

We move to the next number and step through the timing for each solo. We've all done shows like this dozens of times so everyone catches on immediately. Even I didn't forget how after such a long break without having to think about new choreography.

The skaters trade hugs. Tomorrow is the show. Lena will be here. So will Dad, and also my real father, I hope. If only I could talk to him before we meet tomorrow.

"Can I share a cab with you guys back to the hotel?" Lucy asks.

We walk arm-in-arm to the other side of the arena where Mom and Diego wait for us. I slow down to gaze at Anna's statue again and snap a picture to capture the memory. Her calm face frozen in time brings me peace, unwinds every muscle Dad twisted.

"I heard, and about your dad too," Lucy says. "That's trippy."

"I wish I could have met her," I say softly so my voice doesn't echo through the empty room. "At least my real dad will be here tomorrow."

Mom slips between Lucy and me. "This will be a good show, girls." She wraps her arms around us. "Everyone looks like they're having fun."

"Thank you, Mrs. Sikorsky," Lucy answers. "Docia has lots of support. She deserves that medal."

"Lucy's riding to the hotel with us," I tell Mom. "Join us for dinner?"

"In the hotel?" Lucy says. "Not sure I can handle going out on the town with the amount of sleep I've had. Maybe we could go to O2 Lounge? I've heard they serve great sushi and the view at night is sick."

"Works for me." I look down at my outfit. "We need to put on real clothes."

"We'll get a table and wait for you," Diego says.

When we get back to the hotel, Lucy and I leave Mom and Diego in the elevator. "Meet you in ten minutes," I say through the closing door. We get to our floor and Lucy walks the other direction toward her room.

I park my skate bag in the corner inside the door and dig out the red cashmere sweater Lena gave me for Christmas and pull it on over my favorite jeans.

As I walk down the hall to Lucy's door, I think about Lena on the long flight. *Dad had better take care of her like he promised.* Lucy answers my knock as she puts on an earring.

"Let's go," she says. "I'm starved."

Inside the top-floor restaurant, the glass ceiling reveals an electric blue sky. A jet flies across the splatter of stars. "Shall we?" Diego says and grabs my hand. Mom and Lucy follow. I gaze up at the large geometric-shaped lights that glow above the bar. He leads me around giant couches where I see a group of familiar faces—not only skaters but Olympians from around the world.

"Surprise!"

Lucy and Diego have ear-to-ear grins. I can barely breathe. "Did you know about this?" I ask Mom.

She nods and tears roll down her cheeks. "Kimberly told me the other day."

The group crowds around with well wishes in many accents. They're all here, everyone from the rehearsal plus athletes from other sports. I get lost in the crowd as I catch up with friends and recall the good Olympic memories while I search faces for someone who looks like the photos of my Italian dad. I've lost Mom and Diego in the sea of friends.

A hand on my shoulder makes me turn to see the cute snowboarder from Canada. "David!" I scream and hug him.

"Do you always sneak away without saying goodbye?" he asks.

"Like I had any choice." I grab Diego's arm and pull him over. "David, this is Diego, my boyfriend."

They shake hands. "Yeah, I saw you board in the games," Diego says. "Nice moves."

"Thanks, man."

"I can't believe you're here. All these other people too." I thought I'd never see David again.

"We believe in you. We support fairness for athletes," he answers. "Plus, I've got another competition not far away next week, so it worked out great."

Across the room, Mom talks to a handsome man with thick black hair who also wears a red sweater. I take in every detail of his face, but he doesn't look like my dad. Maybe a coach, reporter, or one of the Olympic officials.

CHAPTER FORTY-EIGHT

"Docia. Earth to Docia," Diego says. "Are you hungry?"

My mouth gapes until hearing my name snaps me back. "Yeah, food would be good." Mom glances over with no sign talking to this man is unusual.

Servers fill our plates with sushi from the buffet that would horrify Dad and we sit down with David. His grin is much bigger than the day I met him.

A cute blond girl joins us. "This is Tracy, my girlfriend—I mean fiancée," he says. "I asked her to marry me right after the Olympics. Sorry, sweetie. I'm not used to the f-word yet."

"Congratulations!"

"Thank you, but you're the one with the storybook life," Tracy says. "What's it like to know your mom was one of the most famous skaters ever?"

"I hardly believe it's true. I'm sad I don't remember knowing her."

Diego squeezes my hand.

"Did you compete in this year's Olympics?" I ask.

"Yes, I'm a slalom skier for Canada," she answers. "I didn't do so well this time."

"Don't sell yourself short." David reaches his arm around her shoulders. "You were in the top ten and it was your first games. Next time."

She laughs. "If I'm not barefoot and pregnant by then."

Her comment sends a snapshot of my real dad with Anna when she was barely and secretly pregnant flashing through my head. The sushi doesn't taste so good now. I sip on a glass of water and wait for the nausea to pass while David, Tracy, and Diego chatter about skiing. I thought I would get used to the loss, but watching a happy couple talk about the future like Anna and my dad should have had hurts the most.

"I'm tired," I whisper to Diego. "Will you tell Mom I'm going to the room?"

"Let's find her and I'll walk you down," Diego says.

I nod. "Thank you."

I circle the table to say my goodnights. "David, it's so good to see you. It means so much that you both came all this way."

"We wouldn't miss it," David answers.

"And we believe in you too," Tracy adds. "You should have the medal you earned."

I wave back at them and scan the crowd for Mom.

"There she is." Diego grabs my hand and maneuvers us through the people. "I'll wait here for you."

"Hi sweetie," Mom says. "Are you having fun?"

"Yes, this is amazing. I still can't believe everyone came. I don't even know some of them. Are you enjoying yourself?"

She nods and sips from her glass.

"Who was that man you were talking to?"

"What man?"

"The attractive Italian-looking one who was here a little while ago."

"Oh, he's nobody." She looks around like Dad might walk up any second. "Some guy involved with the Spanish team. He wanted to hear the latest about your situation."

"My situation isn't very funny. How did he make you giggle for the last thirty minutes?"

Her face goes red. She leans in and whispers. "He told me I'm beautiful, and he listened to every word I said." She pauses as if she doesn't believe the words. "It sounded even better with his accent. You know those Latin men."

Oh my God, Mom's acting like a teenager when the cutest boy in school first notices her.

"Your father has said nothing like that in years."

"Well, he should because you are one hot mom."

Mom shakes her head and laughs.

"I'll leave the partying to you so I can get some sleep. Will you be okay?"

"Oh, I should go with you." She reaches for her purse.

"Stay here. Have fun. You deserve it. Diego will be back down."

"Are you sure?" she looks up with a crinkled face.

"Yes. Enjoy yourself." I turn back. "Wake me up when you come in, so I know you're safe." Did I seriously say that to my mother?

"What's so funny?" Diego asks.

"Nothing." Me parenting Mom is one I won't share with anyone. "Mom's having more fun than I've seen in years. She's so pretty when she laughs." I reach up to cover my giant yawn.

"Too bad your dad's on his way."

We walk hand-in-hand to the elevator. When the door closes behind us, Diego steps in front of me and leans in. Our lips touch and his tongue tickles mine. The elevator dings two floors below. *I don't want it to stop.*

"Text me when you wake up and we can get breakfast," Diego says outside the elevator.

"Okay, have fun." I reach up on my tiptoes and kiss him before I walk away. "Goodnight," I say softly down the hall when the card clicks the door open.

Inside the room, I lean against the closed door, reminiscing on the feel of Diego's lips. I shake my head awake before I fall asleep standing up.

By dim lamplight, I unzip the bag from my new skating dress and smooth out the travel wrinkles. This time I'm exhausted and curl up in bed. I have to be ready to face one of the most important days of my life.

• • •

The sun's glow peeks in around the drapes. Right on schedule, ten minutes before my alarm goes off. I've never slept until nine o'clock on a skating day.

I stretch and look over to the other bed where Mom sleeps. She's sacked out on top of the covers still in her clothes. Her shoes and purse make a trail from the door. Looks like she had fun. If she woke me up when she came in like I asked, I don't remember. I tiptoe around the bed and throw on clothes then text Diego, *Workout then breakfast?*

His response arrives in a few seconds. *Meet you by elevator.*

I arrive first and watch him walk down the hall, Diego style. "Good morning. Sleep well?"

"Yeah, once I got your mom back to your room." He gives me a peck on the lips. "She's like a caged animal set free."

"What did she do? Or do I want to know?"

"Don't worry. She stopped anything that might have happened when she curled up in one of the booths and fell asleep. That's when I helped her up to the room."

"So that's why she slept in her clothes?"

Diego nods. "I guessed she wouldn't move all night. Probably slipped in a pill or two with her drinks since your dad will be here soon."

I grab a towel and step onto the treadmill at the end of the row. Once I program in my route, I lose myself in running and Mom. Does Dad keep her off the pills or cause her to take them? She says it's the latter. I say she needs to learn to live without the pills, and without Dad.

The miles tick by, but before the end of the route, I hit stop and step off. I dab the perspiration off my face and watch Diego finish bench pressing.

"Want to do this one?" he asks.

Normally I'd take a turn behind him. "No, I'll skip weights today. Too impatient to focus. Breakfast?"

"Yeah. Should we wake your mom up?"

"Let her sleep. I'll take her something."

"Speaking of food," Diego says. "What's that place Lena always talks about? Her special occasion restaurant she planned to take you to after you won your medal? Let's go there after the show tonight."

"Great idea! I mentioned it to Mom before we left. It's CDL, the one that has the cool staircase without nails. I'll look them up right now." I grab my phone. "I still have international calling, one thing Dad hasn't screwed up."

"Yet," Diego answers.

"Oh. Their website includes English now. Here's the phone number."

Even though I'm used to wearing workout clothes most of the day, I feel out of place in the marble and gold-trimmed lobby surrounded by people in fashionable dresses and suits. Diego would tell me to ignore what everyone else thinks. He's not wrong. I look around and realize I'll probably never see any of these people again. Maybe they won't recognize me.

"Hey, that's Lena!" I turn Diego around to face the registration area. "She's here!" I forget how embarrassed I was and jog through the clusters of people. "Lena!" When I throw my arms around her, I knock her a little off balance.

"Oh dear!" She straightens her scarf. "I thought I was being attacked."

"Sorry, Lena. You're here!"

She pinches my cheeks. "I wanted to surprise you, but you beat me to it."

"How do you feel? How was your flight?" She's signs papers to check in, so I pause until I realize something's missing. "Where's Dad?" I glance around the lobby.

"Please, in a moment, Docia."

Diego hears me and steps onto the sidewalk to see if he's still outside. He shrugs.

"Your papa had to answer some questions in immigration. He will meet us at the rink."

That'll put him in a great mood.

"Procedure," Lena says. "Long flight, but I am fine," she continues. "I rested on the plane. How are you, my little Docia? Are you ready for the show?"

"We've had so much fun, Lena. New York was amazing. The rehearsal yesterday was almost perfect. They had a surprise party last night. You won't believe the masses of people who are here from all over the world, and not just skaters. Did you hear from my father?"

Lena nods. "Before my flight, he said he looks forward to seeing you here today."

"Really? That's the best news all week!" My heart might explode. "Come and have breakfast with us."

"No, no. You have breakfast. I will rest before the big day. We will catch up tonight. First things first. You didn't answer me. Are you ready for the show?"

"So ready I could compete again."

CHAPTER FORTY-NINE

We walk into the arena with a buzz much like my final night at the Olympics, but more relaxed. Fun. It's not a competition with skaters against skaters. We're a team. Skaters against the system. No matter where we're from, we have a common goal.

Event organizers and media mill around among the skaters before they allow spectators in. A group of reporters crowds us when Mom, Lena, Diego, and I walk down the ramp to rink side. I wave to the barrage of flashes. "Look happy," I whisper to Diego. He takes the garment bag from me and slaps on a smile.

"Docia, what an exciting day for you," one reporter says. "How do you feel?"

This whole group is here because of me. The skaters, other athletes, and the crowd gathering outside give me strength. There's no one here who will tell me how to feel or what to say. "Today is one of the most incredible days of my life. My family is here." I look over at the three people I truly consider my family. "And the support from around the world is overwhelming."

The reporter nods and takes the microphone back to his lips. "And the athletes here aren't just skaters. Did you expect this level of support?"

"Never in a million years." I catch Diego's eye over the cameraman's shoulder. "There are skiers and runners and bobsledders. All kinds of Olympians. It's almost too much to take in."

"I understand your biological father will be here," another reporter says. "Have you met him yet? How do your adoptive parents feel about you two meeting?"

"This will be the first time we've met. Mom and Dad support us getting to know each other." I glance at Mom and she nods. "As you can imagine, it's a big moment. I look forward to seeing him this afternoon."

Flashes fire and TV cameras focus on me while another reporter starts to ask a question. Before she does, I interrupt. "I need to change clothes and get ready for the show, but I have one last message. Encouragement from fans has meant the world to me. This has been the most difficult month of my life. I couldn't have made it without each one of you."

The cameras capture the shot they want with my tear-filled eyes and blowing a double-handed kiss. I reach my arms around Mom, Lena, and Diego for a group embrace. This is real, not a hug staged for the cameras. A few deep breaths help me regain my composure before the embrace ends. A few tears are okay, but I don't want the cameras to catch me boohooing. It's not the image I want splashed all over the web.

"Okay, let's get outta here while we can," I whisper.

"I am so proud of you." Lena's eyes sparkle as she squeezes both of my hands. "You answered those questions like the beautiful, smart young woman you've become."

"Thank you, Lena. That means more than you know." We duck away from the cameras and microphones and walk silently while I try to comprehend what will happen over the next few hours.

We get to the girls' dressing area and Mom and Lena follow me inside like usual. "I'd like a few minutes alone. I'll stretch and dress, then I'll join you."

Diego hands over my skates and garment bag.

"Okay, sweetie." Mom hugs me. "Pop your head out if you need anything. We'll be right here."

In my quiet corner, I peel off my clothes and slip the dress on over my tights. As I adjust it to fit just right, the fiery color flashes in the mirror. I gaze at my reflection. Next to my heart is the Russian Orthodox cross Lena gave me. Instead of tucking it into my dress, I wear it so everyone can see. The gold pendant glistens on the soft fabric draping from the neck.

The beautiful Swarovski Crystal earrings Lily gave me glisten shades of purple, pink, and orange like a Mediterranean sunset. I smooth my hair back into a bun and glide on the lip stain Lily picked out to top off the dramatic eye makeup I copied from New York. All that's missing is Lily herself.

After I lace up my skates, I close my eyes and visualize myself performing the entire routine, from the first step on the ice in the middle of the spotlight all the way to the final pose. This time my real dad will be at the side of the rink when I finish.

"Whoa!" I open my eyes and hardly recognize myself.

I look like Anna.

"This is it," I whisper to my reflection. "Tons of people—and the father you've never met—are here for you. Your entire world is about to change. Make it count."

Diego watches me walk through the door with my Olympic jacket. Mom and Lena are deep in conversation. He taps Mom on the shoulder.

When she and Lena turn around, Mom's hands go to her face. "Oh, sweetheart." She wipes her cheek like when she saw me with Anna's statue. "You are absolutely stunning."

Lena's hands go to her heart. "A beautiful young woman who looks like her mother."

Diego smiles and nods.

"Now I need to skate like Anna so I don't disappoint the crowd."

Lena smooths the drapey fabric. "Skate like Docia and you will disappoint no one."

"You're right, Lena. Mom, *you* are gorgeous in your new Vera Wang. The prettiest lady here."

While her face flushes, Diego's expression changes. I turn toward his glance.

"Daddy's here, Peanut." A familiar voice says way too loudly. I go rigid. "The show can go on."

I take a deep breath to help relieve the tension so he doesn't notice. "Hi, Dad." I kneel to adjust my skate laces. "Just in time. I'm certain this show would go on with or without us."

Dad waits. He expects me to go to him, but I don't.

"Hi, Jerry." Mom kisses him on the cheek.

Dad walks over and loses his pleasant face. "Docia. Where did you get that hideous dress? You look like a tramp. That gaudy color and low neckline. And the makeup?"

He grabs my arm. His touch makes me go stiff again and I automatically pull away. As I do, the sound of ripping fabric drowns out every other noise in the arena. A piece of chiffon now hangs down my arm. The surrounding hum of activity goes silent in my head. Rage grows inside like flames engulfing a home.

"What are you doing?" I glare up at him. "The show starts in fifteen minutes."

"That is *not* the dress I ordered, and you—"

"I'm aware of that." I stop him before he says more. "It's the dress I selected."

"Docia, don't interrupt me." He starts to raise his hand to my face. I swat it down and step back out of his reach.

"You've done enough," I say in a calm but firm voice and hold my composure. "If you remember, I now make my own choices. If I want your input, I'll ask."

"You can't manage all this—your career—decisions that will affect your entire life." He crosses his arms. "You're not capable of doing it without me."

"Watch me." I back away toward the dressing area.

Dad shakes his head. "When you destroy everything I've built and your career crumbles, blame yourself. Don't come to me to fix it."

Lena gently takes my hand and leads me a few steps away. "Docia, let us look at your dress." She has the repair kit from New York. Diego and Joy watch from a distance.

Mom walks over. "Jerry, you've gone too far this time," she says quietly. "I've had enough. We've had enough."

"What do you mean, 'too far this time'?" he asks.

"Changing the dress order. The hotel in New York," Mom says. "Making such a scene."

"You women can't do anything right," Dad says under his breath.

"The way you treat me." Mom's fists are clenched and her face is stern. It's like the new outfit has given her Wonder Woman powers. "Never telling me Docia's adoption wasn't by the books. Dragging us both into your shady scheme for all these years. Do you need more?"

Her words are another slap across the face. Dad lied to her too. Between every few stitches, Lena rubs my arm and helps wipe away the tension and hurt. Mom's stern face relaxes like she just dropped a huge burden.

"You have a room at the Hyatt down the street. You can stay there as long as you like. When we get home, you need to move out."

Mom did it. She stood up for herself. Only five minutes ago, the progress I had made was unraveling. Now, thanks to Lena and Mom, it's all stitched back together.

"Docia, you're set," Lena says softly. "You are ready to go to the rink."

I take Mom's and Lena's hands. "Diego, Joy, want to go with us?"

We leave Dad standing alone.

One by one, the cluster of skaters who wait for the opening number clap. Others whistle and holler until the spotlight finds us and the crowd joins in. I can't see spectators' faces because of the bright lights, but I know the arena is full by the noise and twinkling flashes from floor to ceiling. *This must be a dream.*

"We'll be in our seats." Diego kisses me on the cheek. "I love you."

"I love you too," I whisper back. His eyes draw me in until Mom reaches out for me.

"I'm sorry," is all she says then she squeezes me so tight I can barely breathe.

"Me too," I answer when I can catch my breath again. "We'll be fine."

Then Lena holds my hands over her heart. "I can hardly wait to see you skate again. It's been too long."

"Is my father here?"

"I don't know. I have not seen him yet."

"He's supposed to skate, isn't he?"

Lena nods. "Focus on your program."

My eyes follow my family up the steps to their seats as the announcer's voice booms, "Welcome to this historic event. The world's best skaters and other Olympians are gathered in support of athletes' rights and to help adopted children around the world reunite with their biological parents if they choose."

The crowd roars. Skaters around me reach for my elbow, shoulder, or whatever they can grab onto.

He's got to show up. He can't blow this off. He's my real dad.

"In this *Right to Be* performance, we will see skaters from all over the world," the announcer continues.

Each person skates onto the ice, by nation, as he announces their name. He announces Italy but not *his* name. I roll up on my toe picks to see if there's anyone who looks like his photos.

"And the star of tonight's show is U.S. skater, who is adopted and the rightful Olympic gold medal winner, Docia Sikorsky."

I glide to center ice and meet the others to take my bow. The energy from the crowd takes over. When the opening music starts, spotlights dance across the ice and up the grandstands. Each skater knows his or her parts in the choreographed segments. The crowd claps along. Then we each do a solo element. For my turn, I skate across the ice and do a giant split jump followed by one of my famous ultra-fast back spins. When the music stops, the arena echoes the crowd's whoops and whistles. The lights catch spectators' signs and waving flags.

One by one, the booming voice introduces each solo number. I continue to search for anyone who looks remotely like my father among the blur of faces and waving flags.

"Hey, my friend," Lucy says. "Can you believe how many people are here?"

"In a million years, I can't."

"How are you doing?"

"I don't know," I answer. "There's been no event like this. Ever. It blows my mind."

We watch the other skaters, but I can't keep my eyes on the ice.

"Who are you looking for?" Lucy asks.

"My mystery father."

"Oh, him," she answers.

"He *has* to be here." I glance around again. "But if he is, why hasn't he found me?"

"Give it time," Lucy says. "Oh, there's Greg. We're up soon." She leans over and embraces me. "Can't wait to see you skate!"

"You too," I say back. "I'm glad you're here."

"A thousand Stacys couldn't keep me away."

After Greg and Lucy perform, I spot a couple of Italian skaters about to go on. "Ciao, Docia," Cecilia says. "You look beautiful."

"Thank you. I'm so glad you're both here," I say. "Have you seen Luca Baresi today?"

Cecilia and Martina look at each other. "I saw his name on the program but have not seen him," Martina says.

"We will tell you if we do," Cecilia says.

"Thank you. Skate well." I watch Martina remove her guards to take the ice and then go back to searching the crowd. I'm up after the Italians. Then it's over.

I look up in the stands to where my family sits. Mom and Lena watch Cecilia. Diego waves. I blow back a kiss right as Cecilia's music stops. Dad stares forward with his arms crossed. One last look around as I listen for the announcer to say my father's name.

"Our final skater," his voice echoes, "the reason we're all here, Docia Sikorsky."

Someone just ripped my heart out.

Applause erupts through the packed arena. I take a final glance for him and then skate over the patterns the others left. Does he not care enough to be here?

The first notes of *I am Changing*, a song from Dream Girls, one of my favorite movies, play. The music pulls me in. The triple-triple and the double Axel, then I have a moment to connect with the crowd during the s-shaped spiral sequence. My energy builds with the song. Another triple and a layback spin.

I'll surprise Lena with the more difficult ending. I tap down the middle through the footwork entrance into the quad Lutz, double toe-loop. Landed! My tight legs feel the tension from the stress as I skate to the center for my signature back scratch spin as I hear the last line of the song, "I'll change my life, I'll make a vow and nothing's gonna stop me now." I plant my toe pick for the final pose.

I gave it all I have.

Before I look up at the crowd, I totally let go of every emotion from this weekend—wonder, sadness, joy, fear, thrill, love. They all come out through my tears and laughter. As I bow to each side of the rink, the rest of the skaters rush on the ice and unite in a mass embrace. By the sound of the crowd, they would join us if they could.

How can I do the closing number? My legs are as weak as overcooked spaghetti.

A few skaters take their poses and the rest of us follow. At least it's easy and short and I make it through before my legs collapse. Each skater exits the ice leaving me for a final bow.

This bow is not final. It marks a beginning.

When I step off the ice, my family, the other skaters, and a strange man in a black suit circle me. The man reaches his hand out.

"Hello Docia." His heavy accent stirs even more curiosity. "My name is Antonio Ruiz, a representative from the International Olympic Committee. It's very nice to meet you."

I shake his hand but let my arm fall away limp. He's not my father, and I have nothing else for anyone to take away.

"I have good news for you." His voice is warm and velvety like a new kitten. "We received the letter from the Russian adoption authority. We also received signed affidavits from your coach, the physician who delivered you—and from your biological father. Even though there is no legal certificate that documents your birth, these documents all prove you were indeed old enough to compete in the Olympics."

Did I hear him right? Am I deaf from the crowd? I step back to stabilize against the steel grandstand barricade.

"I believe this is yours." He pulls a box from his coat pocket and hands it to me.

Everyone gathered around goes silent. I glance at my family. Dad isn't with them. Mom kisses her finger and makes an x across her heart. Then I look back at the blue velvet box in my hands.

"Go ahead. Open it," Mr. Ruiz says.

My hands shake as I pull open the hinged lid. It's a gold medal.

He nods. "It's yours. You earned it."

I gaze at the five rings on the medal and back up at him. "Thank you. You have no idea what this means." I glance over the crowd, Mom, Lena, and Diego, and slip the heavy medal over my head. "The month since winning–then losing–this medal has been the toughest one of my life."

Diego hands me my phone and takes the velvet box. "There's a new text you'll want to see."

I grip the cold, round disk that fills my hand. My heart pounds as I read. *Please accept my sincere apology. My bambina is sick, so I had to cancel the trip. Please be our guest for a visit on your way home. We are anxious to meet you. Let me know if you can make the trip. Ciao, your papà.*

I stop breathing.

Mom and Lena trade glances, and then Mom smiles and nods at me.

I turn back to Mr. Ruiz. "I have the family that's important to me now, and I wouldn't change a thing."

THE END

ABOUT THE AUTHOR

Addison Brae lives in Dallas, Texas on the edge of downtown. As a child, she was constantly in trouble for hiding under the bed to read when she was supposed to be napping. She has been writing since childhood starting with diaries, letters, and short stories.

When she's not writing new adult and adult speculative and romantic suspense, and young adult contemporary fiction, Addison spends her time traveling the world, collecting interesting recipes, and entertaining. She is still addicted to reading and enjoys jogging in her neighborhood park, binge-watching TV series, vintage clothing, and hanging out with her artistic other half and their neurotic cat Lucy.

Please follow @addisonbraeauthor on Instagram and Facebook and Addison Brae on YouTube.

NOTE FROM ADDISON BRAE

Word-of-mouth is crucial for any author to succeed. If you enjoyed *Off Edge*, please leave a review online—anywhere you are able. Even if it's just a sentence or two. It would make all the difference and would be very much appreciated.

Thanks!
Addison Brae

We hope you enjoyed reading this title from:

www.blackrosewriting.com

Subscribe to our mailing list – *The Rosevine* – and receive **FREE** books, daily deals, and stay current with news about upcoming releases and our hottest authors.
Scan the QR code below to sign up.

Already a subscriber? Please accept a sincere thank you for being a fan of Black Rose Writing authors.

View other Black Rose Writing titles at www.blackrosewriting.com/books and use promo code **PRINT** to receive a **20% discount** when purchasing.

9 781685 134860